Praise for
The Miracle of Mercy Land

"With words spoken like a gentle angel, River Jordan takes her reader deep into the human spirit. *The Miracle of Mercy Land* is a story about the past, the present, and the future all at once, not only altering the hearts of the characters in the novel, but also changing the heart of the reader. A triumph of beauty."

> —PATTI CALLAHAN HENRY, author of *Losing the Moon,*
> *When Light Breaks,* and the *New York Times* bestseller
> *Driftwood Summer*

"A tremendously well-written tale. River Jordan is a truly gifted author. Highly recommended."

> —DAVIS BUNN, best-selling author of *Gold of Kings*
> and coauthor of the Acts of Faith series

"River Jordan takes us on a magical journey to the banks of Bittersweet Creek where the past is revisited and broken hearts are mended. A story told with equal parts Southern charm and supernatural fantasy, this one leaves you dreaming of a world where anything is possible. Jordan has cast her spell again!"

> —SUSAN GREGG GILMORE, author of *The Improper*
> *Life of Bezellia Grove* and *Looking for Salvation at*
> *the Dairy Queen*

"River Jordan's words are so delicious that I read them aloud just so I could taste them. In *The Miracle of Mercy Land,* she explores destiny and will, good and evil, power and powerlessness. If you find it difficult to find a breath of literary fresh air, I assure you, you won't be disappointed in Jordan."

> —KAYA MCLAREN, author of *On the Divinity of Second*
> *Chances* and *Church of the Dog*

The MIRACLE of MERCY LAND

The MIRACLE of MERCY LAND

a novel

RIVER JORDAN

WATERBROOK
PRESS

THE MIRACLE OF MERCY LAND
PUBLISHED BY WATERBROOK PRESS
12265 Oracle Boulevard, Suite 200
Colorado Springs, Colorado 80921

The characters and events in this book are fictional, and any resemblance to actual persons or events is coincidental.

ISBN 978-0-307-45705-9
ISBN 978-0-307-45947-3 (electronic)

Published in association with the literary agency of Daniels Literary Group, Nashville, Tennessee.

Published in the United States by WaterBrook Multnomah, an imprint of the Crown Publishing Group, a division of Random House Inc., New York.

WATERBROOK and its deer colophon are registered trademarks of Random House Inc.

Library of Congress Cataloging-in-Publication Data
Jordan, River.
  The miracle of Mercy Land : a novel / River Jordan. — 1st ed.
     p. cm.
  ISBN 978-0-307-45705-9 — ISBN 978-0-307-45947-3 (electronic)
  I. Title.
PS3610.O6615M57 2010
813'.6—dc22

                                        2010013909

Printed in the United States of America
2010—First Edition

10 9 8 7 6 5 4 3 2 1

For my mother,
who taught me that destiny was a woman's rightful place

ONE

I was born in a bolt of lightning on the banks of Bittersweet Creek. Mama said it was a prophecy, and as she is given to having visions of the biblical kind, no one argues with her. She can match what she sees with ancient words, and truth be told, she is frightening with the speaking of them. Mama can swipe you with her eyes so that you feel like you have either been hushed or resurrected by God's own hand.

On the fateful day of my birth, there had been no signs, natural or otherwise, that foretold what the day would bring. No wild birds roosting in the trees, no funny-yolked eggs, no hints to suggest that a baby was about to show up in a stormy kind of way. The only visible condition at all had been Mama's fat feet. They were so swollen by that time that they were no longer like feet at all. That's what drove her down to the creek bed, searching out an herb known for helping such as this. She had on Daddy's big boots on account of the fact that not a single pair of her own would fit over her feet, and she had just managed to get down to the water's edge when the first thing happened: the storm came up.

The second was I showed up, just as quick and sudden as the wild wind.

Mama tried to call for Ida, but her cries were snuffed by the rolling thunder. So there she was with bolts of lightning crashing all around, hitting the water—she told me she could feel that electricity run through her body, that it was like fire coming from the sky—then she cried out for mercy. That's how me and Mama came to have a private moment suspended in the crook of the bank. By the time Aunt Ida found us, the storm had passed, the clouds had given way, and the blue sky hovered above her like an eagle's eye. Mama said she took one look at me and said the only name that came to mind.

"Mercy," she whispered to me. I answered her with a wailing cry.

Bittersweet is a knotty gathering of simple people who live along the riverbank. The entire place is no more than a boot stomp. It has no official standing as a town at all. It is simply called that by the people who have built their lives along those banks. Had I stayed there, rocking on Aunt Ida's front porch, watching the water rise and fall, fearing the floods and staying on in spite of them, I wouldn't be in the middle of where I am now: Bay City. Well, they call it a city, such as it is. But it is nothing more, really, than a beautiful little town rolled out right around the warm, gulf water bay of southern Alabama. It is a city of refuge, bright with possibilities. Everyone who has ever crossed into this place feels that way right down to their toes. When you visit, it will make you believe that it is a place where you can live in fruitful fullness. All sugar, no spice. Or at least that was what it was like when I arrived.

But that was seven years ago. Everything was more peaceful then, but now, it seemed that the whole world was on the verge of war. President Roosevelt said we were staying out of it, but the dark things that were happening overseas tugged at our ankles like a small, nipping dog. The world would not go away no matter how much we tried to shake it off.

The events that lay before us as a nation were a large, uncharted territory, watery in their shifting possibilities. The only thing certain was that the future would have to reveal itself in due time, and most likely it would be different from anything we had expected. In the meantime we went through our daily routine with a type of laughter we hoped would stave off impending enemies and allow our sacred routines to remain a part of our carefully plotted lives. For the moment the edges of our existence played out sweetly, simply, and untouched by the things we knew were happening beyond the borders of our existence. There was a whole ocean between us and the trouble. It seemed like an ocean should be enough.

Maybe that's why, in the midst of our time of innocence and uncertainty, the very thing that happened to me was the most wildly unexpected: the mysterious wonder of something that I will attempt to understand fully for the rest of my days. I should make a feeble effort at explaining what took place. My words might be nothing more than a ripple across the waters of time, but they are surely better than no record at all.

It began last winter along the Alabama shores.

And it was all because of Doc. That's where the business started.

Doc Philips owned the *Banner,* and owning Bay City's only paper was better than being mayor. It was better than being anybody else in town. People trusted Doc with the most important thing of all—the truth.

The second best thing to owning the paper is what I did. I was Doc's assistant, and that meant I was really the assistant editor. To his credit, Doc tried to give me that title, but it didn't stick because people just called me Doc's girl. That's what they'd say 'cause it made it easy on them. No official title would tarry. They made up their own. Doc's girl. I didn't mind.

The *Banner* was my life, and I loved everything about it. It was a pinch-me-quick-I'm-dreaming kind of situation: the smell of the ink from the printer downstairs. I could probably typeset the whole thing, but that's Herman's job, though I've helped him in a rush, put on an apron, and hit the presses with him showing me the ropes. I know the smell and sound of every corner of the *Banner.* The ticker machines clicking off the news by the minute, going to sleep when nothing in the world is happening but then coming alive all at once when the wires are just burning up with stories. That's my favorite part of the job: getting the skinny on what's happening around the world before most folks have even had their morning coffee.

Sometimes we ran the stories just the way they were, straight off the wire, but other times Doc decided to give them a little local flavor. He'd tie in DiMaggio's home run with what one of the local boys did Saturday down at the park. That's the way he was—"bringing it home," he called it. "Let's just remember, Mercy," he'd tell me. "The news doesn't mean a thing at all unless we're bringing it home."

I always said, "You got it, Doc. Sure thing." But I didn't get a huge chance to bring the big news home. That was Doc's job.

I wrote up the smaller stories that happened around Bay City, like all the events of people's lives that must be made public. Births and deaths, marriages and other procurements. Doc covered the real news—any criminal cases, bank robberies, and kidnappings. Since we hadn't had any of those, he mostly reported on things like the new traffic light going in and the worldwide news from the wire.

But that was before Doc's big secret showed up in town. It's not that I loved the paper less; neither did Doc. How could we? It was the heart of Bay City and the pulse of the world. But then something just appeared—from another world or time or, well, let's just say, it sure wasn't from around here. To say it became a distraction would be a flat-out lie. It became an *obsession*. Doc swore me to complete secrecy so that no one in town knew a thing. But that wasn't the toughest part; he swore me to keep the secret even from everyone in Bittersweet Creek. All of them thought I was going about my regular life, taking care of business and printing the news. They were completely wrong. The greatest story in the entire world had fallen right into my hands, and I couldn't print a word of it.

Two

When Doc called me the morning that it had happened, the morning that gave birth to the secret we were keeping, he couldn't even speak clearly. Miss Perry, my landlady, called me to the telephone, standing there in her bathrobe. She was thinking Doc had suffered some kind of a stroke. I'd been having my dream, the same one I had over and over again, of a man standing in the middle of a deserted street holding something I couldn't quite see, papers blowing at his feet. The dream seemed so important, one where surely I was meant to do something, save someone, but then I always woke up foggy-minded and empty-handed. There were no answers, just images. I was still groggy when I went to the phone. Doc's voice was strained and his message cryptic. "Mercy, my office."

"What is it, Doc? What's happened?" I asked, but the phone line had already gone dead. I must confess my first thoughts were not for Doc's health at all but that news—major, earth-shattering, front-page-headline, stop-the-presses news—had reached Bay City and all hands were needed on deck for a special edition that had to get out fast. Turns out I had everything exactly right and completely wrong all at the same time.

I got dressed in clothes I kept for just this occasion, when we were many hands short in printing the paper: old blue jeans and a work shirt that were made for Bittersweet Creek and could weather any kind of ink storms we might stir up in trying to throw together something fast. I grabbed a sweater and coat and rushed out in the cold morning air. I didn't even bother driving from the boardinghouse; it was easier for me to run, and so that's what I did. I ran right out Miss Perry's front door with her standing there in her housecoat, saying, "Do hurry, Mercy. This could be terrible." She had a tendency to worry some, but I had to agree with her. She was right. It was the kind of terrible that Daddy would talk about from the pulpit, the "great and terrible day of the Lord coming upon us." Of course, that always seemed like something way off in the future or something that had happened in the far-distant past. But I was wrong. I was walking right into a great and terrible trouble that made me think much about Daddy's words, and had I known, I would have trembled.

But there would be time for trembling later.

I pushed opened the door to the *Banner*, and it wasn't what I expected at all. No rushing typesetter to set the headline. No extra hands called in to typeset the special edition. No rattling wire feeds going wild with updates. Matter of fact, it was an unusually quiet early Tuesday morning. The only sound was Herman's morning whistling emanating from the pressroom.

"Doc?" I yelled, throwing off my coat and tossing it on my desk. "Doc?" There was no answer, and I took the stairs to his office two at a time.

When I rounded his door, he looked as wild as I'd ever seen

him. Occasionally, on a day that big news broke, Doc's hair would be sticking out from his running his hands through it over and over. His tie'd be loose, and he'd be wandering around on those legs looking a bit like the scarecrow in Oz, like he could come undone at any moment. This was worse than all those times rolled together. Maybe Miss Perry was right; maybe Doc was having a stroke.

"Look," was all he could manage. He pointed to his desk. "Look," he said, like it was the only word in his vocabulary.

"What, Doc, what is it?" My eyes were still on him, checking for signs of a seizure. He grabbed my shoulders and turned me to face it.

I couldn't have looked away if I'd tried.

My first reaction was to try to shield my face with my hand. At first glance I knew we were in trouble—I hadn't been raised in church all my life for nothing. I backed away from the desk. To me there was no question where this thing came from. Three more steps backward and Doc actually grabbed my arm and pulled me forward.

"Look," he said again, "it's a book." He said this like he was trying to reassure me of something, but it didn't work. I caught my breath and blinked back tears. It was a book, all right. Or at least a type and shadow of *maybe* a book. It was a book if you wanted to call it a book. And I guess to call it anything else, well, where would you begin? It did appear somewhat like a book in the shape of things, but when I looked at it, I knew better. On the cover, the letters—if you could even call them that—moved. That is, the words themselves were formed from gold, and that gold moved like liquid fire.

"Doc, what are you doing with this?" I certainly didn't try to touch it. I didn't have a Daddy preacher for nothing. Touch something like that, and you turned to ash fast.

"It showed up last night when I was working. One minute nothing. I'm at the desk working, with old Harriet here at my feet, and then this wind comes in. I look down at Harry for a second and then back again, and this…" His mouth moved, trying to come up with words, but none could fully describe the piece, so he stopped trying.

I put my hand out to touch it and drew it back again.

"Go ahead. It won't hurt you. I've touched it."

I looked back at Doc in amazement, wondering why he wasn't dead. This kind of thing should kill someone. Just looking at it should blind you.

I counted his fingers. I took a big whiff of the air to see if he smelled like smoke. And I moved my hand toward the book.

"Doc, I can't…" Then I glanced at the book again, and the words moved. That is, they changed so I could read them, lines and curves rearranging themselves, moving from one language to another. It knew my mind; the thing knew what language I could read. "It's alive," I said.

I thought I would touch the cover and then open it, but my fingers at once disappeared into the very pages themselves. I could see words, I could see pages turn, and I could see my fingers at the same time as if looking at them in a clear pool of water. Only this was not water; this was light, a pure energy that moved like nothing I had ever felt or experienced. And I knew the reason for it. There was nothing like it in this world. It wasn't of this world.

At that moment, if I could have, I would have left as fast as I had answered Doc's call. But a name floated, shifted, and settled on that page, and it was too late then. I was watching a life unfold, layer by layer, multiple twists and turns, wrong starts and right endings. The name was Doc Philips. My boss and the man I'd known so well all these years, but here were the things I had never known. He was loving and losing his wife, holding on to Bay City, loving the *Banner*, and even sheltering me. Somehow the layers of Doc's life were before me in all their twists and turns. The dark alleys of his existence and the silent sorrows he carried.

"Mercy," Doc was saying, but his words had little effect on me. I could now no more pull myself out of the portion of Doc's life I was feeling than the sun could change its course. I was lost, wave after wave, years and years. There was Doc as a little boy, as a young man, growing, changing, and making choices; some paths were not taken, some embraced.

Finally I pulled my hand away. I couldn't stand to see those choices. I'd already seen too much. "Doc," I whispered, moving my hands away and clasping them together to keep me from possibly turning a page into someone else's life, "what did you see?"

"What does it mean, Mercy? I've puzzled over it all night."

I shook my head. How would I know what it meant? What did he expect of me? "Doc, we need to…" What was I thinking? "…get somebody. Let's call somebody." That made really good sense to me. And for the very first time in my life, I was thinking Daddy would be a good choice. Mama was good, and Aunt Ida was too, but this seemed like something that needed… I was at a loss for words. Intervention maybe.

"Don't tell anyone about this, you understand? This is something unusual."

"Unusual? I think that's too soft a word, Mr. Editor in Chief."

"You were the only person I could call. You were the only living person I could trust to keep the secret. And to tell me that I hadn't lost my mind. Tell me I haven't lost my mind, Mercy. Tell me this is somehow real."

Doc didn't wait for an answer, which was just as well because I didn't have one to give. He was back to ranting something about how the names change over and over again.

"You've never seen anything like it. I've been with it all night. Never the same name twice. People I know, people I don't know, but now, because of the book, I know them through and through. I know them like…" He didn't finish the sentence, just ran both hands through his hair.

"I don't think you're supposed to do that—look into people's lives that way." I didn't tell him it was his life that I saw. I wasn't going to, either.

"Well, unless it goes away as quick as it came, there will be plenty of time for some discussion about that. Right now we just need to figure out what to do with it and why it's here and where it came from. It's like, like, an assignment of some kind. That's what it is. We need to figure out now what the assignment actually is."

He paced the floor as he spoke. For a while good old Harry tried to pace with him, then she gave up and lay down on the rug in front of the desk. Carefully I walked closer to the book. There were a few things I knew beyond a shadow of a doubt. It was Doc's business if he wanted to approach the book from logic and reason, but I was a Bittersweet Creek girl, and I knew better than that. There was nothing logical about it. My backwoods instincts told me that much. It was a mystery like none of us had ever encountered. I also had a feeling that it was going to bring trouble of some kind but that the book itself was a good thing. Sometimes the world was just that simple. Good or bad, light or dark, yes or no. The book was a yes.

The other thing I felt was that it needed to be protected. You couldn't have something just lying around that could reveal the lives of people like that without it being a danger. Doc was right about one thing: for some unknown reason this mystery had arrived at the *Banner*. It had shown up for a reason, requiring something of Doc. Perhaps me too. Maybe all of Bay City.

"Let's lock it up somewhere, Doc. At least until we figure things out. Let's try to put a lid on this thing before we get lost in it forever." Doc didn't need any more explanation. The draw of that book had kept him up all night so that now he looked bushy haired and wild-eyed crazy. And it called to me in the most peculiar way, like a magnet. I would step away from it, back up toward the wall, and the next thing I knew, I had crossed the floor and was standing right beside it again, my hand outstretched, wanting something I had no words for. Just standing closer to the book made my blood pump harder through my veins. It was as if it possessed life, magnified—

"Absolutely," Doc said.

I glanced up, trying to remember what I had said. The book was disorienting us. It made it difficult to think things through clearly. Doc turned, walked to the window, and looked out at the early-morning light in the streets. A few cars were beginning to pass by below. People were arriving for work. I heard the little bell on the door downstairs ring.

"That'll be Claire," he said. She was the *Banner* first-face person. She did the billing and the bookkeeping and had been at the paper before Doc had taken it over. "Let's try to keep this under our hats awhile. Once Claire gets word of it, we might as well put out that special edition you rushed in for." Doc smiled at me, and I remembered I was wearing my work clothes.

"Well, a girl can hope, can't she?" I grinned at him, a little of my spooked-by-the-book wearing off.

"Don't worry, Mercy. Someday I'm sure you'll put out a special edition that changes the world. In the meantime…" He pulled his journal box from the lower desk drawer and set it squarely in the middle of his desk, lifted the lid, and removed his journal and laid it aside. Then he placed the book gently inside, pulled a tiny key on a chain from his top desk drawer, locked the box, and passed the key to me. "Mercy, keep this key with you, would you? I think it's safer that way."

I nodded to him as I reached for it. He didn't have to say anything more. Doc had already been in that book all night long. He knew more than I did about what power it held for a man to venture into the dreams and desires of another man's life. But just thinking about it made me want to open the book again, to turn page after page to see who it would reveal. To see if I could find myself between those pages. If Doc was there, then surely I was as well. Did it show my past? Would it point out my future? The roads I should take or the ones I should leave alone? I trembled thinking of it, torn between not touching the book and being pulled toward it with a desire to see, to know—both at the same time. Doc watched as I dropped the chain with the key around my neck and tucked it into my shirt.

"Good, Mercy." He looked around the room. "Why don't we place the box in the back of the filing cabinet, just for good measure, and then we can get to work."

I followed his instructions, picked up the box like a holy relic, walked to the filing cabinet, pulled open the drawer, and nestled the box carefully in the very back behind the files. I slowly closed the drawer and turned to face Doc, feeling a little relieved.

"That's done. Now, let's get to work. Go write about the good life in a small place called Bay City, will you?" He turned his attention back to the streets and, I figured, back to the book as well. Then he called out to me as I was leaving, "And, Mercy, don't forget…"

"I know, Doc, I know." So as the book, with all its strange purposes and intentions, slept in Doc's overstuffed file cabinet, I wrote about the good life of Bay City, and I brought the story home.

THREE

Months flew by with a fury. Doc and I spent our days sculling up news. While I attended county commission meetings, school board meetings, and the occasional ribbon cutting, Robbie Jones took the photos to run with the stories. As I wrote the tidbits and meeting reports, Doc paced and mumbled, studying the news from Europe. A man named Hitler was getting a lot of attention, and Doc didn't like it. He watched the ticker machines like a hawk, chewed his unlit cigar, and fell more and more under the call of that book.

Every night when the paper had been put to bed and we knew the morning edition was sure to fly on time, we took the book out of its hiding place and laid it on Doc's desk. Hours would pass as the words drew us deeper and deeper into the lives of the souls of Bay City and beyond. I was always searching for a page that revealed my life, illuminated my choices, and showed me my future so I'd know the way to go, but instead I would swim in the words and the images they revealed until time would find me standing in broad daylight on a sidewalk in Bay City, just like I was there, feeling the sun on my back, watching some unknown child ride by on a bike, and knowing that was his life I was reaching into. Just that one moment in the life of a boy who now might be all lived out and passed on, and I would never know him.

We were transported to hundreds of places. We were living thousands of lives. It was both mesmerizing and addicting. And although I felt guilty about experiencing the lives of others, we were doing it for a good reason. We were trying to get the answers to the questions we asked over and over again. Where did the book come from? Why was it here? What were we supposed to do?

But the answers never came.

One day I asked Doc if we were even looking for the answers anymore or if we were just looking for the sake of seeing. The book made you drunk in a way that wasn't human. Doc said, "I don't know, Mercy. I really don't know. But what else can we do? There must be an answer. There must be a reason." Then both of us got very quiet for a while as we tried so hard to understand.

I was getting close to the end of my patience. I had considered going to see Daddy and Mama on my own and telling them everything. Doc and I had been struggling with this thing so long that winter had given way to spring and then to summer. If anyone would have an answer, it would be those two. They were as solid as the earth, and maybe that was just what we needed right now.

And I'd been having that crazy dream again. Aunt Ida called it a repeater and said it was trying to tell me something. All I knew was I always woke up a little breathless and still, as if I were waiting for the next thing to happen, but it never did. Just a man I didn't know, papers flying loosely around his feet as he stood in the middle of a deserted street. I wanted to call to him, to warn him of something, but then I would wake up. The dream was beginning to haunt me like unfinished business.

I woke from the dream yet again, got up, and stood before the mirror, searching for signs of any strange changes. I reached for the key and draped the chain around my neck. I searched that woman in the looking glass: no gray hairs, no telltale signs of all the places I had been because of that book. Just Mercy Land—the newer version, not the one I'd left behind in Bittersweet Creek. I looked deep into the eyes staring back at me. Maybe the months of getting lost in those pages had affected my brain. Maybe the simple sensibilities of Bittersweet were what Doc and I needed to keep us from losing our own stories.

The days that had led me to Bay City had been full of dreams fueled by Aunt Ida's fancies. In the end it was Ida's typing lessons that had made certain things possible. Now it's not so obvious where I come from, not at first glance anyway; I've mastered lipstick, can manage high heels, and have ironed my hair straight. Catch me walking down the street, you wouldn't guess I had been raised on the muddy ground by Bittersweet Creek.

But it still rises up when least expected. Or when needed.

Bittersweet would find me at the boardinghouse, reading in my room or rocking on the front porch while Miss Perry sat inside, quietly doing her needlepoint by lamplight. All the other tenants would be sitting inside together, talking—sometimes even that old grouch Sam would join in—and I might stroll out onto the porch and sit right there alone, happy to be Mercy Land of Bay City, all grown up and on my own, when Bittersweet Creek

would rise up inside me, and I could swear I smelled huckle-
berries on the vine, wild and woody. I could swear that I could
hear Tommy Taylor whispering a secret in my ear, and the feeling
was so strong that I'd peek over my shoulder to see if he was there.
But there was no Tommy, nor could there be; he'd gone missing
on a hot summer evening when I was fifteen. On the creek one
day, and the next—not a trace. Nothing. No sign foretelling his
leaving, either. Tommy disappeared just as fast from the world as
I had come into it. For a year I wandered the woods, expecting
him to jump down from a tree and say, "C'mon, Mercy, I was just
foolin' around." But now he was only the smoke of memory, and
as I sat right there on that porch, a sad longing would fall across
my heart like a shadow. It didn't last, mind you; it was just enough
to remind me that the creek and my people were not very far away
at all. That I might live in Bay City the rest of my life but Bittersweet was in my bones.

I understood now what Aunt Ida had meant when she wanted
me to make a life for myself. She had lived in a city, had seen the
kinds of life this world had to offer a woman. She told me I had
a good, sharp mind and there were options out there for me to
explore. Said that just because I'd been born on that creek didn't
mean I had to die on it. That's the way she had put it. Said I was
born for something more than making biscuits in Bittersweet.

Ida said St. Louis would be a good place for me. She even
offered to move with me, to help settle me in. I think she was trying to get back to Missouri and to take me with her, but Mama
jumped in and said if I must move to a bigger place, how about
Bay City? She told Daddy we should take a drive to the city for a

look-around. "We have to help Mercy get to the other side," she'd
said, like I was headed for the Promised Land. I knew she just
wanted to keep me closer to home.

"I'm not dying, Mama," I told her, but she just gave me one of
her looks. So I let her and Daddy work it out between themselves.

That's how it came about that Daddy was in his Sunday suit
and Mama in her Sunday dress, riding in the front seat, while
Aunt Ida and me rode in the backseat on a trip they described as
one where we could explore my future possibilities.

"We'll see," said Daddy, who didn't think a girl should be out
in the world unmarried and unprotected. Aunt Ida wore a brown
skirt and a white blouse. Those were her dress-up clothes. She
wore coveralls every day because she said she liked the pockets.
"I'm practical in my old age, girl. Practicality becomes me," she'd
say with a wink.

Daddy asked for the fiftieth time why a girl of my age would
want to leave home when she wasn't even married, and didn't I
know at least one boy around Bittersweet that I liked? I had just
turned twenty, and I started to say something in response, but
Aunt Ida interrupted. "The girl wants to make a life for herself, to
do something in this world. Can't you see that?"

We rode the rest of the way to Bay City in silence. When we
all began to walk the town, Mama squeezed my hand. "I got a
good feeling about this, Mercy," she whispered to me that day.
"Don't be afraid." Her words soothed my soul. Much as I didn't
want to admit it and as brave as I wanted to look to Aunt Ida, I
was as shook up on the inside as a wet cat.

We walked through the town looking at the storefronts on

Main Street. There was a J.C. Penney and a Woolworth's, a Sears, the Bay City Savings and Loan, and a real Italian restaurant named Marie's, where Aunt Ida decided we should have lunch. That's where Aunt Ida asked around about a safe place for a young woman to have a room of her own, and just like that we were steered toward Miss Perry's place.

After we ate, we took a walk toward the boardinghouse, and little by little, Bay City didn't look so scary anymore. The winding sidewalks were sweet, the shady oaks and magnolias lined the streets, the air carried the tang of salt from the gulf, and the people we passed all nodded and smiled. We found Miss Perry's, and every single one of us ventured up to visit what would become my room. It was a tiny space but neat as a pin, with a good bed, a dresser, a night table, and a small desk. Miss Perry had pointed out that the bath was just a few doors away and that she kept a strict curfew. That was seven years ago.

I laugh when I think back at how nervous I was on that first day Daddy drove me in and walked me to the porch of the boardinghouse. My days on the creek had made me a tough girl in some ways, but Bay City was an entirely new world, one where I could see right away that women wore high heels and lipstick as part of their everyday life. My confidence shrank so much that when Daddy put my suitcase down and hugged me bye, I threw my arms about him, crying, "Don't go!"

He was so taken aback that he just said, "There, there," and finally, "You don't have to go through with this."

But I did and I knew it. Aunt Ida had been right all along. I'd have to pull myself up. I wiped the tears from my face and said,

"I'll be all right." Then I added, "Just say a little prayer for me now and then, will you?" We laughed. The idea of Daddy not praying for me was absurd. And I shooed him out the door before my brand-new little grown-up heart crumbled to pieces.

I looked in the mirror again, checked my hair, and dropped the key beneath my sweater. I had other work ahead of me. I was picking up someone at the station for Doc.

"I've decided to retire, Mercy," he had said early one morning. It was a flat-out lie. Why would he retire right in the middle of this?

"What about the book? How can you retire now of all times?"

"I'm not moving away, Mercy. Just preparing to leave my desk behind. Maybe by then… Maybe its purpose here will be finished and us with it."

It wasn't like him to outright lie to me, even though I'd caught him in a fib or two in his time. Normally, I'd call him out on it every time, and he knew it. This time I decided I'd better just let this play its way out; he was keeping something from me for a reason. And I was determined to find out why.

Doc announced his retirement publicly—again. Doc had been declaring that he was retiring every few years since he'd turned sixty-five. That was twelve years ago. No one paid him any mind anymore. But then he added that he was going to hire a man from out of town to take over the paper. This caught everyone's attention but no one's more than mine. A man from out of town? That bit of news spread throughout the city. They couldn't have just anybody reporting on their lives, now could they? It had to be a man of honor, a man who would know what to print on page one and what to bury somewhere on page nine. It would need to be someone who actually cared, just like Doc, about what was going on at night when the citizens were sleeping.

Doc was tough-minded but soft-hearted. He could sneak a confession out of a guilty man even when he was sitting right there with an alibi witness. That's how he got the inside story every time. It was also the side of him that made people feel good about him watching out for them. And that's what they thought of Doc— that day or night he was watching out for the city and their better interests.

He needed to choose someone who was all those things. He couldn't bring just anyone in to do that job. That much was a fact. But instead of choosing someone who was closest to him, someone who possessed all those qualities, someone who loved the paper as much as he did and whom he had trusted with the secret of the book, Doc ended up bringing a total stranger to town by the name of John Quincy.

Then he had the nerve to flip open that pocket watch and say, "Mercy, go get our boy, will you? He should be arriving promptly on the two o'clock train."

Four

The first time I saw John Quincy he was standing in the rain.
The train came to a complete stop, the doors opened, and
a man got off in the middle of what you'd call a tropical downpour.
I knew right away it was the man Doc had sent me for, but he
sure wasn't what I expected. In spite of the rain, or maybe because
of it, I didn't move at all. I just sat there behind the wheel watching him and trying to figure him out. Then the sun broke through
so that the rain was coming down in sheets but everything, including that man, was illuminated by gold. The effect was mesmerizing. A man in a suit, a small suitcase in one hand, a briefcase
in the other. And those shiny black shoes. He was trapped in a
hot, wet light, and I was trapped right there along with him.

Water ran down the windshield and blurred his image. Before
I thought about what I was doing, I reached out to rub the glass
to bring him into focus. But the watery image was on the outside, just like the man. I shook my head and let out a low whistle, realizing I'd been a little too smoked by his appearance and
also that I was letting him stand there getting soaked.

"Pull yourself together, Mercy." I used my best Ida Mae impression when I needed to talk tough to myself; Mama's voice was

better for soothing my soul. I honked the horn and flashed my headlights, all the while reminding myself about the seriousness of the business at hand. Doc was looking for a man to take over as editor in chief whether I liked it or not (he said he might as well leave *publisher* on the masthead for himself until he was boots up).

I would have been a better choice. For being such a great newsman, Doc sure could miss a few things.

John Quincy noticed my headlights flashing and waved with the hand holding the briefcase. He disappeared into the station, and after a moment more he was at the car. I reached over and pulled up the lock, and he got in.

There wasn't a dry stitch on him, and I thought he was the most beautiful thing I'd ever seen. Even from a distance, he was a handsome man. Close up, he looked even better. Like someone in the movies. Who ever thought a Wednesday afternoon could be so pertinent? In only a few months, my orderly life had turned the corner into some kind of complication. First Doc's wild book landed on us, then he passed me over for editor, giving it to a stranger, and now here I was getting suckered into losing my anger just because of his looks.

"John Quincy," he said as he shook off water and put out his hand. "Sorry, but it appears my timing is lacking." He pointed out the window at the downpour.

I started the car and turned the windshield wipers on high before shifting into reverse. I started to mention my name, but it didn't seem a pressing matter at the moment.

"You're going to need a towel and a change of clothes. Where are you staying? The Motor Court, I reckon?"

"Excuse me?"

"Like I said, you need a towel and maybe a change of clothes. I thought maybe you had made arrangements."

"I did not. I did not make arrangements. How completely shortsighted of me."

I glanced over to see if he was fooling around, but he was staring straight ahead and seemed serious about it. "Well, no problem. I'll take you to the motel. There's only one motel in the whole city. There's one farther out of town, but seeing how most folks just walk everywhere they go, you might as well be closer to all the action. Particularly if you really are a newsman, I know you'll want to be in the middle of what's happening." Oh, snide remark number one. I could see Mama shaking her head at me right now, saying, "Mercy, I didn't raise you to act like that." I shooed off my thoughts of Mama.

Of course, the only real action going on in Bay City was the mysterious book business, but I didn't figure that would be a cause for conversation. I wanted to ask him all about what kind of newspaper experience he brought with him since Doc sure had been vague about the man's background. But there would be plenty of time to discuss that later.

The rain stopped as suddenly as it had started. "That was today's thunderstorm," I said. "You can pretty much set your watch by them this time of year. See right over those trees"—I kept my left hand on the wheel, pointed with my right—"past those railroad tracks? Beyond that tree line is the big bay that runs into the gulf. We get storms rising up off that water like you just wouldn't believe." I spent the remainder of the drive from the station keeping myself occupied by telling Mr. Quincy all about some of the storms I had witnessed in the last seven years. I still had plenty of stories left to tell when I pulled up in front of the office of the Bay City Motor Court. Roger looked up through the office window and waved. He lived at the boardinghouse like me. We were a loose family of misfits. People who hadn't found a sweetheart to make a life with or who just preferred a life without one for whatever reason. Mine was a combination of both. What the boardinghouse residents had was a shared table and our standard routines of coming and going. We were all comfortable that way.

I turned slightly in my seat. "Here's the plan. You go ahead and get yourself a room and get changed." I honked the horn and yelled, "Hey, Roger" out the window. "Roger will get you checked in, and then meet me—just ask him where the lunch counter is, he'll know—and come on down. I'll meet you there, and we'll get on to see Doc. He's expecting you, so don't be long."

"You sound like a woman who gets things done." He smiled.

I turned back to face the windshield. "The lunch counter is just around the corner. I'll be waiting for you."

He removed his suitcase and walked into the front office. I watched him walk, then slowly pulled away. So he would take over as editor, and I would have to work with him every day. Maybe there were worse ways to earn a day's pay.

The Woolworth's lunch counter was a staple in the city. It was just as important as the bank, I think, and most days got more business. It had been my first job in Bay City, and it had made it possible for me to move into Miss Perry's boardinghouse. By the end of the first week, my co-worker Mabel had become a friend. We laughed through making a lot of malted shakes. Good friends, yes. Great for movies and dinners at night when I ventured beyond Miss Perry's dining room. I would trust her with any of my greatest heartfelt secrets—but of course I couldn't tell her about the business with Doc. I couldn't tell anyone, and it was hard, almost downright impossible. Aunt Ida would say, "Go throw that thing into the bay and hope it stays there, 'cause it looks like trouble."

"Well, did you get him or not?"

"Who?" I had been lost thinking about that book again. I touched the chain about my neck under my sweater. The book had a way of possessing you even when you weren't with it.

"Who? Who? For goodness' sake, who do you think?" She looked out the big plate-glass window toward the sidewalk. She was so bossy you'd have thought she owned the place instead of just working the soda fountain. The company might own the store, but Mabel owned the world. "Where is he?"

"Motor Court. Stop making a fuss and give me a cold one, would you?"

"Motor Court, huh? So when do I get a good look at him?"

"Oh, you'll get a look," I said. "Don't you worry about that."

"Shot of cherry or no?"

"With," I said. "Mr. Quincy got caught in that rain the minute he stepped off the train. He was a soaking mess. I told him to get dry and get over here with quickness. I expect Doc's pacing his office upstairs, wondering where I've gotten off to, pulling that watch out and then closing it and putting it back. Sent me, of all people, to get him. He could've sent Claire or anybody else."

Mabel put my cola on the counter. "Don't worry, honey. It's not all said and done yet. And no matter what he says or does, you're going to make a great editor one day." She reached out and grabbed my fingers and lifted them up so the ink smudges were visible. "It's in your blood now, kid, no denying it."

"Yeah, well, sometimes a girl might wish she was a little"—I gave her a smile—"different, you know?"

"Really? You? All about the *Banner* through and through. What would make you…" She paused midsentence.

"Oh my," she said under her breath. I knew what that was all about. No need to turn around. "Do you know who he looks like?"

"Yep," I said, "that movie star," and turned on my stool. He stood just inside the door, composed and cool as a cucumber, looking like he had stepped right off the silver screen. I gave him a little wave. He started in our direction, and that was the first time I noticed he had a slight limp. He favored his left foot. I was about to introduce them, but Mabel was one step ahead of me.

"I'm guessing you're Doc's new man. Here to take his place." She said it with a wink. She could be so sassy.

"Oh, no ma'am." His voice was kinder than I'd first realized and had a familiar soft, southern tone. It sounded oddly familiar, but I couldn't quite place it. "Couldn't imagine anyone taking his place."

Something about the way he said it caught my attention. I forgot about his looks and remembered my nose for a story.

"Oh, don't worry," Mabel was saying. "Nobody thinks Doc is really going to retire. See those men over there at the table?" She pointed to the regulars, the retired men who came in every day to fix the world's problems before they went home for a nap. "They've laid money down and taken bets on if he's really going to turn over that desk."

"And what about you?" he asked her. "Where does your money lie?"

Mabel leaned toward him and lowered her voice like they were old conspirators. "My money says Doc'll die with his boots on."

We all laughed at that. Normally, I would have agreed it was most likely that Doc would indeed go out swinging, fingers to the keys of his Royal, typing out one last news story, with that old cigar he never lit stuck between his teeth. That is, I would have thought he would—until everything happened. Something about the book had rattled Doc, and he wasn't telling me what it was. I'd tried to get him to confess, to tell me why now, of all times in this world, he was considering stepping down, but he never answered me directly.

I thought about that for a moment as John Quincy surveyed the room. He was very slow and calculating. A little more intent than he should have been. I'd learned that stories could be lurking everywhere. He was sizing up the place like a man keeping an eye out for the law. *You chose him Doc,* I thought, *and you're gonna have to deal with him now.* What would happen if a man without honor controlled the news?

"We got to get going, Mabel." I paid her for my soda, then John and I walked out into the sunshine.

When Mr. Quincy first stepped off that train, there was a part
of me that wanted him to like me more than just a little. But men
like that didn't go for girls from Bittersweet. And that was just fine
with me; I had work to do. I caught sight of my reflection in the
J.C. Penney storefront. Brown hair and brown eyes, freckles showing through. Just look at me: a brown suit and sensible brown
heels that could track down a story. Just a simple, brown-eyed girl.
I squared my shoulders and concentrated on the things I did possess. I had a backbone full of worthy. That's what Aunt Ida told
me. And something like that didn't come along every day.

Doc's Journal

Mercy may be in danger, possibly all of Bay City. I've kept
my plan from her for so many reasons. At first they
seemed honorable. Now I'm not so sure. The bottom line is,
I don't know what this thing is that I have or where it came
from. More confounding is why it came to me in the first
place. I'm not a great man. The book deserves a man full of
answers who would know exactly what to do with such as
this and perhaps not meddle, as I have. But what man, any
man, even a better man than I, would not try to make
amends with his own past? To repair the loss of things not
done?

To tell you that the book came with the wind would
sound foolish, but that's exactly what happened. An unnatural wind, a mighty wind rushed through the office,
which was impossible, because all the doors were shut up
tight.

It was a late, cold night. Claire had left; even Mercy had
finally gone home. I was still putting the polish on the morning edition of the paper, and Harry lay at my feet by my
desk. When the wind rushed in as it did, Harriet looked up

at me for reassurance of some kind. In the moment it took for me to look back at her and say, "There, there, girl," the book appeared. I turned back, and there it was, front and center on my desk, and I was left with this puzzle. In my old age it may present to me the greatest story of my life.

The only thing I know is that it is critical to something, that it is linked to another happenstance, and that I should play a role in that.

I've covered stories now one way or another for more than fifty years. I've watched the times of man pour through the pages of this paper, and I thought I had seen everything, good and bad, and I tried to write those stories with a passion, with a precision that people would be able to wrap their hearts and minds around.

Now all my words are as worthless as stick people drawn in the mud.

There isn't much hope for them to stand to reason or even to meet the demands of proper description. The beginning of the book possessed lettering that was unfamiliar to me, and while I'm not an authority on languages, I've studied my fair share, have a respectable knowledge of Latin and a smattering of French, and can recognize almost any language at sight. Although I can't read the words, at least I know their origin. These words are beyond that. More like hieroglyphics on a cave wall and yet, letters that seem to speak, letters more like musical notes calling to me so powerfully it is as if the book were saying my name. That was the unction that first propelled me forward.

This work is not made of paper and thread.

It is not something that can be contained, yet for its safety and maybe for the safety of the names held there, I have tried my feeble best. I've given Mercy the key. We've locked it in the silliest of places, that old journal box, and hid it in the filing cabinet—as if that were enough. But I am hoping that something so simple and obvious is the best place of all. I've given Mercy the key more as a symbol than as a guard against myself. I could pop that box with a pocketknife in no time. But my hope has been that Mercy's keeping will set a standard for me to lean to her young but solid wisdom.

Or at least that was my logic. I've already broken the vow I made to myself.

That first night I reached for the cover to open it to the first page, and instead of pages, my fingers encountered *light*. It was as if light itself had become a tangible thing. That light had been layered with more light until the substance could be moved, and when I gathered my courage, I placed my hand on the sheet that faced me. It was at once filled with names. They were in no particular order that I could fathom. The first name started with the letter *M*, but the following one began with a *B*. The names that were held there rose to the surface and receded as I read them so that the entire effect was like looking into a deep lake, watching objects appear at the surface and fall away again. The names continued to rise and recede before my eyes, and as they rose, images and memories, milestones and heart's desires—even destinies—rose with them. I was so overcome with this sense of intimacy that I fell back in my chair and attempted to close the cover and to look away. But the names seemed to rise even farther from the pages, to float before my eyes, and again, all that was attached to the names rose with them. Choices made, bridges crossed, the doors that are open to a man's life—the ones he walks through, the ones he shuts. I sat there weeping, I am not ashamed to say, and if my love, Opal, were alive, she would understand this. To fathom the depth of another soul tried and true. Their convictions kept and lost—how could I bear such news? "No more," I whispered, "please, no more," as the experience consumed me. I felt as if I had lived a man's life, the thin and thick of it, just at the reading of his name. "No more," I whispered for the third time.

But then my name rose before my very eyes. And I was enraptured by my own life. Caught there with the steps, all of them, that I had taken, that had led me here, writing in this journal now as the dark night is casting off its cloak. In those few seconds I relived my life, every second, as if that could be so. But it was the choices I had made that stood out to me—and stood out they did, for better or worse. There had been opportunities lost for good, things I could fill this journal with, of each sacred moment when I busied myself with something and passed up a chance to make a change. Except for *one*. That choice I made, and all the choices linked to it afterward seemed to trigger door after door of other images. Were they real, or meant to be, or only mirages of what might come? I do not know. Another name lifted from that book then and hovered there above what was a page and not a page, written but not written at all, but at once understood. And that name fell on me like a brick, because I saw what could become of that man. Or not become. I saw the emptiness and the anger that fed him. And now I have brought him here.

God, help us all.

FIVE

~

The rain had passed, and the heat was settling back down on us. The sky was clearing outside Woolworth's, patches of blue breaking through, shining on the puddles. I stepped over and around them as we walked, like I was playing an ill-fated game of hopscotch. Just one more thing to make me look foolish in front of this new man for the *Banner*. I stopped in front of a puddle and froze solid. I hadn't asked Doc if he was going to show this John Quincy the book.

Suddenly I was madly possessive of everything all at once. Of Doc, of every nook and cranny of the *Banner*, from the ticker machines to the printing room, and most of all, of that book from another world. It was Doc's book, and it was *my* book. I didn't see any reason that Mr. Hollywood should be brought into our... I was getting seedy in a bad way, I could tell. That's what Mama would call it: sowing bad seeds in my thoughts.

I put my hands on my hips and stared straight at John Quincy.

"So, they call you Doc's girl," he said. He had been trying to make small talk as we walked, but I hadn't been doing anything more than mumbling in return. He was favoring his left leg, and I noticed how the limp had gotten more pronounced as we walked.

"Well, that's how everyone thinks of me, as Doc's girl. Guess that's what seven years can do to a person. It makes it easier on 'em too." I rolled my eyes in spite of myself. " 'Doc's girl.' That rolls right off the tongue."

"I told you my name—well, of course you knew my name—but you never told me yours."

"Mercy Land." I started walking again. We were making our way along the short, curving sidewalks to the *Banner*. Mr. Quincy kept step beside me. A car drove past and splashed water so that we both dodged a little to the right.

"Mercy." He came to a standstill right there, a little smile playing on his lips. "Mercy," he repeated.

I wanted to pinch him and pinch him hard for saying my name as if it meant something special to him. Instead I changed the subject. "Guess you're going to be excited to see the whole place. My favorite part is the noise of the wires coming through. At first it just about drove me crazy, but now, well, I just don't know how I could live without it." I listened to the clip of my heels on the sidewalk and strained for his reply. "Hey, so what's up with you? Doc's been real hush-hush about your history. Just says he thinks you have 'the stuff.' "

"I don't know about that. He just told me he plans to retire soon and was looking for someone who might be interested in taking over as editor."

"Really? And you think you're that someone?" Something about him just wasn't lining up with what Doc had told everybody. And usually Doc was a real straight shooter.

"I could be. At least I'm willing to give it a try." He shaded his eyes from the sun with his hand. It cast a shadow so that they were in the dark and I couldn't read them.

What this Mr. John Quincy needed to discover I figured he'd do in his own time. Besides, it wasn't my responsibility to train him, and run the paper while I was doing it, and follow Doc around town at night trying to figure out what he was doing with that book when he thought I wasn't looking.

Mr. Quincy was supposed to show up with the goods in his pocket. I was expecting him to produce.

We walked along the sidewalk, following the late afternoon shade, passing beneath the old oaks, the moss so low in places it brushed our shoulders. At every cross street the wind picked up from the bay and blew in our direction. When the salt water in the air hit us just so, he stopped right there in the middle of the street and stared hard and long down at the water.

"Haven't you seen the bay before?" A car honked at us to move on. I reached out right away by instinct to take his arm and pull him forward. "Civilized people don't stand in the middle of the street, Mr. Quincy." I let go of his arm, stuck my hand in my pocket.

"I haven't been back this way for a long time," he said. "It's just something to see that new." Doc hadn't mentioned him ever having visited Bay City. "Atlanta is busier every day. Lots of buildings but nothing like that. It's good to see open water."

"So you've been here before, and here I was going on and on about the weather and our summer storms. How long has it been exactly since you were last in town?" I tried to keep my voice casual.

"A very long time." He emphasized the *very*, and I let the matter drop. It didn't appear he had any intentions of elaborating.

Old Man Whistler hollered at us from his yard down the street. We were walking right toward him, but apparently that wasn't good enough. He couldn't wait that long.

Bay City had its people, just ordinary folks doing their jobs—working at the bank, Marie's, the courthouse, the library, and the school—everyone with a job to do and going about the everyday business of doing it. And then it had its characters. Sometimes they were just people who were retired and had more time on their hands for living with a little more color—like Whistler. He had driven the school bus in Bay City for more than twenty years until they finally told him he had to retire because he had been going blind in one eye, and there was nothing the doctors could do to stop it. If they hadn't forced his hand and taken the bus key away from him, he would still have been scaring children into sitting down and behaving.

Whistler'd been watching us for the last block, leaning on his rake and not moving a muscle. There wasn't a leaf to be found in his yard, but he raked it every day. It was a trap to talk to anyone who might walk by, is what it was. He looked at us with his one good eye. His gray hair was long for the style, but he didn't care. I loved the way Whistler looked, and I can't tell you just why, but he was like a deranged mountain man, like a man who had searched for gold all his life and come up empty but wouldn't give up trying for the crazy life of him.

"What you young folks up to?" he asked, and we had to stop to be polite. I didn't mind.

"This here is Mr. John Quincy." I raised my voice so he could hear me. In addition to the eye going out, he'd been going deaf the last few years. "He's here to take Doc's place."

"You say he's Doc's wonder?"

I smiled. "Well, we'll see if he's a wonder at all, but right now he hasn't even met Doc. We're on our way."

"Hasn't met him?" Whistler leaned back on the rake. "Then how'd Doc know he was the one?"

"We communicated by telephone," Mr. Quincy answered.

"What's that?" Whistler yelled, cupping his hand to his ear.

"The telephone," I yelled back at him. "They have spoken by telephone."

John looked at him a little odd, like he wanted to say something, but held back. He seemed a bit perplexed by Whistler and his rake. Or maybe the blind eye gone milky white was a bit unsettling. "Well, we'd better go on and get him settled in," I said.

"Glad to have met...," John said, and then his voice faded away.

"See you later, Whistler," I called back to him. "Your yard is looking mighty nice."

He nodded and gave me a wave, then turned in a slow arc to rake up the leaves that were not there.

"Whistler's all right. You'll get used to him. People in town have tried for years to get him to wear a patch just so he won't scare kids, you know, but Whistler says he's no pirate."

We had arrived at the corner of Main Street and Seventh Avenue. The frosted glass of the front door said in big gold letters "THE BANNER—Your Window to the World." Of all the things in this world that comforted me, that sign was at the top of my list. Hot chocolate was another, a warm fire, Mama's smile, Ida's rooting laugh, Daddy's preaching, and the *Banner* front door. John Quincy started to open the door for me but then put his hand on my arm, stopping me.

"What does he mean, 'the one'? What did Whistler mean by that?"

"Aren't you the one? You know, to take over when he retires? I mean the *one.* The big man who's going to waltz into the little town of Bay City and take over Doc's chair."

His jaw clenched tight, and I could see that he was trying hard not to bark back. My ugly had come through, is what Aunt Ida would say. I had to face facts. I was jealous that he was here and mad that I liked his looks and having him around. It was a hornet's nest right from the start, and I wished he'd turn right around and get back on the next train out of here. My eyes were still locked hard on his.

He stepped closer to me and whispered, "I don't think this is about Doc Philips retiring. I think it's something else entirely."

"Of course it's retirement. What else would Doc want with you?" I motioned to the door, trying to distract him in the process. "Well, that is unless you have some kind of talent we don't know about. You happen to play the trumpet? Doc's got a true penchant for horns." I tried to imitate Doc's voice and swung my fingers to an invisible band. I was actually trying hard to rub off that ugly spot.

John Quincy laughed. "No, no horns. Not gifted in the least musical way."

The air lifted between us, but I hadn't forgotten his words. If he didn't think Doc had called him up on paper business—and I knew Doc was lying about something—then something was up.

My next thoughts were about the book.

I looked at John Quincy so hard I might have seen through him. What was Doc's interest in this man?

Only one way to find out.

"Doc?" I called out. And then again, "Doc?" This time long and loud as I set my purse on my desk.

"Looks like Claire is out to lunch. She's our first-face person," I said. "You know, first face you see when you walk in. But she's missing. Looks like Doc is too."

I tried to remember what to do next, what would be my ordinary kind of a day. To imagine exactly what I'd do if John Quincy were not standing here taking up so much of my tiny space. "Would you like something to drink? Coffee, perhaps?"

"No thank you." He stood with the damp coat draped over his arm.

"Well, I guess you can sit down, and we'll just wait on Doc. He's been expecting you." I knew I was repeating myself, but what else could I say to the man? I didn't even know why he was really here. Unless—my hands moved to my neck for a moment where the tiny key hung from a small chain hidden beneath my sweater—unless all along Doc had figured out something about that book without telling me. Oh, that would really get my goat: telling me all about it, calling me the morning after he got it to show it to me, and us spending months trying to figure out what it meant.

Was it true, perhaps, that the man was here because of the book and not the paper at all?

I walked to the window and opened the blinds so we could see out on the street. There were three old chairs by the door for people who had to wait to pay a bill, place a classified, or give us a story; occasionally the chairs were full, all three of them, and that would be one of our busiest days ever. I loved it when it was like that. Almost like I had gone to St. Louis and gotten a job like Ida Mae had wanted. The rest of the time it tended to be a little quieter—actually, a lot quieter. Behind my desk in the adjoining room were a kitchen and a rest room. Upstairs was Doc's domain. One large office circled wide with windows that looked down on the town in all directions; a big, fine desk that held his typewriter; and two wing chairs on a fine Persian carpet he'd bought fifty years ago from a traveling salesman, or so he said. He said everything just like it was God's truth even when it was a storytelling fib. That was one of the things I loved about him, his gift for unrolling a story. For all his white-haired seriousness, Doc had a sense of humor. Although Bay City was more than a hundred years old, in my mind it hadn't existed until Doc arrived. There was an old photograph of him and one of the first mayors of the town on his office wall, a friend of his now dead and gone. Doc mumbled some days that all the good ones were gone, but then he'd remember I was there and lay a hand on my shoulder and say, "Except for you, Mercy."

When I first came to see Doc about the job, I was so nervous. I wore my reading glasses because I thought they made me look older and smarter, like someone an editor might need. Back then I thought Doc was looking for smart, but he let me know that wasn't it.

"I'm looking for capable, Miss Land. Are you capable of taking care of business?" he had said. "There's a difference between someone simply being smart and someone being capable."

I took off my glasses and told him who I was. I told him about Bittersweet Creek, about how I'd been born right there out in the open on those banks and how both me and Mama had survived. I let him know I could handle the unexpected. He sized me up right then and there and said, "Sounds like you have the gift of grit; now let's see what other gifts you might possess. Have a seat." So I showed him I could indeed type and had a sense about proofing and putting things together. When I was growing up, Ida had bought me an old typewriter and had made me practice, part of what she called homeschooling. It had been some years, but I remembered where my keys were, and it paid off. And I had a natural way of finding a story and telling it true. Those things, coupled with my no-nonsense upbringing, got me the job. I had been here ever since, and I couldn't imagine a life without the paper, without the ritual of Doc pausing every day before he hiked up those stairs, asking, "Mercy, why this misery?"

"Because to suffer is divine," I'd joke, and he'd say, "Smart girl."

I made up different answers every time. It was just something to distract him. Those stairs were steep, I grant you that. When I asked him why he bought the building if he didn't like the stairs,

Doc just said he won the building fifty-two years ago from a Mississippi gambler in a poker game on a steamboat. "The bane of the stairs, Mercy, came with a royal flush." Then he didn't smile at all, and I nodded serious as could be about the bane and misery.

"Reckon it's the price you had to pay for gambling in the first place, Doc."

"Smart girl," he'd said.

It'd gotten to where it was just a fun challenge for me to come up with something new every day, but so far I'd been winning.

I couldn't imagine living without these things that hedged my life neatly into place. But that book of mystery was moving the foundation beneath my feet, and with the appearance of John Quincy, with Doc pretending to retire, it didn't look like normal was anywhere on the horizon.

Even with the blinds open, the office remained dark. As much as daylight surrounded the newspaper, my space was tucked so deep into the building that it stayed dark most days of the year. I turned on the little light on my desk, then went to the back counter and checked the news feeds. It appeared Doc had already ripped them and then stood there reading what he wanted. He'd rip it from the page and let the rest fall to the ground. It wasn't a tidy place.

"Doc?" I called out again, looking up the stairs.

"Excuse me a minute, would you?" I said to Mr. Quincy, and then I suffered those stairs myself. "Doc?" I called again from halfway up.

"I'm here, right here." His old voice was a comfort, just like the front door, and one of these days he'd go on and join his wife, Opal, because that was the order of things. I crossed the floor to stand before Doc's desk. His tall back was toward me, his shoulders leaning forward. He was looking down on the corner where he could see the traffic light and everyone coming and going.

"You were watching, then? You saw us come in?" I walked up and stood beside him, looking out into the street. This was when I loved the town the most, from up here, looking down with Doc like Bay City was a great ship and he was its commander.

"I wasn't expecting him to look like some movie star." He pulled his hands out of his pockets, crossed his arms.

I put my hands in my pockets and sighed. "Me neither." We both stood there contemplating this turn of events. "Well, you didn't ask for a photograph, did you? It was just phone calls." He nodded, and I went on. "He seems nice enough, and if it helps any, he has a limp."

He shoved that cigar in his mouth, turned away from me, and went to his scattered desk. I didn't understand; if he didn't smoke them anymore, how did they keep getting shorter?

"You lighting those, Doc?" Opal had razzed him about smoking for years. Before she died, she passed that job on to me.

I received a grunt instead of an answer. Something that sounded guilty and meant *Don't bother me.* I looked back out the window. Miss Perry's big black Packard was stopped at the red light. Must be her errand day.

"Should I invite him up so the two of you can chat now? You'll have to get started, don't you think? There sure is a lot to do

with teaching somebody about a newspaper. And for your information, he doesn't seem to know a whole lot about the newspaper
business." I was hoping the hint would draw him out, make him
confess what he was up to.

It didn't work.

"Not yet," he said.

"What are you up to, Doc? You told me to always find the
truth and write the truth, and now you are outright lying." There
was still no response. "Tell you what, I'll make some coffee, and
then you can talk to him as you see fit." I went to the door. "You
know, whatever it is you're doing, you can always change your
mind. You can always send him back," I said.

"Smart girl," he said as I was closing the door.

Six

Once Doc had dropped the bomb on me about his retiring, he'd started making phone calls, searching for John Quincy. Doc had tracked him down through a series of phone calls and late-night conversations. That much I did know. He just kept saying that he had to find the right man and that he had heard of this Mr. Quincy once or twice.

I didn't know why this interest of Doc's kept growing with such fervor; I just knew that he was searching and that I was a part of that search. Doc would get on the telephone with an old friend of his, or so he said. Then finally some private detective, a man with a special knack for finding people. It went on like that for months until finally he told the whole town it was just a matter of time. That he had his search narrowed down to one man.

"Mercy?" Doc called down, and there was a pause. That was his way of paging me. I stepped away from my desk and left John Quincy scanning the morning's edition of the *Banner*.

"Doc?" I said, looking up the stairs. He stood there in his pants and shirt, one hand on his red suspenders, that chewed-up cigar butt in the other hand.

"Show him up now, will you?"

"Yes sir." I turned back to Mr. Quincy to make the announcement out of formality, knowing he'd heard every word. He was already standing when I turned around. "Apparently, it's time for you to meet your new employer," I said. "Follow me." I began the steep ascent as the bell chimed on the door and Claire came in, chattering away with her usual stream of gossipy updates. She stopped when she saw Mr. Quincy. I caught her eye. She smiled and said nothing more, and I turned to show Mr. Quincy up. He followed me without a spoken word. I wondered what he was thinking, but I figured he was just trying to decide why he had shown up in the first place. I could tell the stairs didn't come easy to him. That foot of his must have pained him some.

Doc was already behind the desk, his eyeglasses pulled low on his nose so that he looked over them as we entered his office. He had ink on his shirt sleeve. He was always wearing ink. He sized up the man as we walked through the door.

"Mr. Quincy." Doc rose slowly from his desk, leaned forward, and extended his hand over the mountain of shuffled news bits, papers from the wire, and pages he had typed. If Doc had questions about Mr. Quincy, they were not easy to surmise. It was one of the things that made him such a great newsman. His questions came in sneaky and from the side. Drama unfolding right before your eyes. It was better than the movie house, I swear it was, if you ever saw him question somebody who might be guilty of something. Guilty of anything! He was so good at it the police chief borrowed him to get the "story" out of a suspect. Whenever Doc passed on, it would be a loss to the entire city. Maybe they were hoping Doc's man, this man, would step right into those shoes and entertain and inform folks with such grace and certainty.

Doc had a charisma that I wished was born to me. The way he could walk through a room with confidence that displaced the very air. The way he could follow the story from beginning to end, circle around it, and start all over if it required such a thing. Doc had a really, truly great mind. While John Quincy was a younger man, I didn't see him outthinking Doc. That was, if the push ever came to the shove, if there had to be negotiations and my life depended on one man, I'd choose Doc.

"Mr. Philips." They shook hands, and Doc motioned for him to sit.

"Everyone just calls me Doc."

I was making my exit when he stopped me. "Do stay, Mercy." I walked over to the east window, leaned against the ledge, and made myself forgettable. It was a trick I had up my sleeve. Doc often used me this way when working, in case he needed a witness, in case he wanted to make certain he wasn't alone in the office with a woman of a certain variety, or in case he wanted me to give him my two cents regarding the situation about someone's first-person account after the person had left. We'd often sit over afternoon coffee and go through the morning's affairs, and he'd say, "Tell me, Mercy, was he being truthful?" And I'd give him my take on things.

Now Doc was putting up some kind of front to me and to John Quincy. I could see it. It was like a game of cat and mouse. Both of them sizing one another up, but there was something else between them that was different, something I couldn't put my

finger on. I had watched Doc talk to people across that desk for
years, but his manner with John Quincy was unusual, like they
were both following a script they'd been handed only moments
ago. At once highly familiar and extremely circumspect. I watched
them with a discerning eye.

John Quincy glanced at me and then back at Doc. "I believe
we need to speak about the matter you discussed with me on the
phone."

"It's still waiting for investigation and determination."

And then I knew: they were talking about the book! Doc, of
all things, had told the big secret to this stranger! Coming here to
take over the paper, my foot. That wasn't it at all. Doc had brought
him here to try to figure out what continued to perplex us to no
end, which was what to do with this amazing thing. I narrowed
my eyes at Doc, but he wouldn't look at me. John Quincy glanced
at me, then at Doc, then back to me. "Maybe I should, ah, take a
look at the…files you spoke of."

"In due time, Mr. Quincy. So you are aware, Mercy knows
about this, this…" He searched for the word. "She knows about
the present business, you understand? She's known about it from
the very beginning."

"Yes, I know about…the *business*," I reiterated. Maybe Doc
had called him in, but by golly he was right. I had been here from
the beginning.

"But you keep it…where?" He looked about the room as if
the item in question would manifest itself on its own accord. His
eagerness disturbed me. It must have disturbed Doc too, because
he stalled him.

"There'll be an opportunity for that later. At the right time. There really are some things related to the paper I'd like you to see. You do know the news business some, don't you, Mr. Quincy? Some sides to it, anyway?" Doc smiled at him then like they were old friends, but I noticed John didn't smile back. "The townspeople are expecting you to be here for the news business. It might be wise for them to see you out and about for a few days. After all, it's a small city, and a stranger in town for more than a day stirs up the curious. I prefer you draw no unnecessary attention under the circumstances." There it was again, a look exchanged between the two of them. I had learned from the best of them how to read people. Doc had taught me well. But the things that really spoke to me were from Bittersweet. From the mud of the creek, Aunt Ida's sharp wit, and Mama and Daddy's backwoods beautiful truths. Right now those things were telling me a whole lot that these men weren't saying. They didn't know each other, but they weren't strangers, either. My instincts were telling me they had a past to dig up between them.

And somehow I was the one holding the shovel.

SEVEN

ノ

On most weekends I go back to the place that gave me the ability to find the real truth. That was Bittersweet, and it is just like it sounds. It was the good of life mixed with the taste of sorrow. It was unexpected storms that would come out of nowhere—hard, cold rains even in the summertime, thunder that would scare your heart right out of your chest, and lightning like you have never seen. The rains that would last for days on end, turning the banks of Bittersweet into a sopping-wet, muddy mess. Then they would be gone, and the sun would come out so bright you'd think you had imagined it all—except your shoes would be muddy, and the water would be ever rising, higher and higher.

I never wanted to leave those woods. They were made up of things that called to me. Simple folks with simple lives, and I was one of them. But Ida pretty much let me know that to stay would rob me of a different kind of life. "You got a touch of moxie, girl. You need to give it to the world."

I listened to Mama when it came to the things of God. I listened to Ida when it came to life.

Aunt Ida came to us in a biblical way. Having no sisters in this life, Mama said Ida was an answer to her prayer. I have heard her say on more than one occasion that God sure showed his sense of humor in his answer. Aunt Ida chose us when she could've had another life. She was from Missouri, raised on a river like this one. She married my Uncle Crawford, Mama's brother, when he was in the army. She had once been in the army too. "I was a nurse, an army nurse, child," she said proudly. "Three squares and shelter. It was a good life. But then we got married, and I decided not to sign up again." Then he died on her, died from a rotten gut before I was born. His appendix ruptured while he was on maneuvers, and things went bad from there. But Ida decided to stay on with the family in Bittersweet instead of returning to her own people. She had worn a groove of her own belonging into the family. Ida's house was the fourth little house on the high side of the Bittersweet. Mama and Daddy's was the third. You can find more than a hundred little houses scattered through the piny woods up and down the banks.

Bittersweet was my wild place to run loose as a child, but it was mine no more. When times were good and cold, I'd stay close to home, reading whatever Ida had pulled from the library. She had a way of plucking things that would stir my fancy. Summertime was different. It belonged to me and Tommy. He was my best friend in spite of being a year older than me. It was a default situation; we were both only children, so we had no built-in playmates where brothers and sisters would have fit the bill. Tommy lived on the opposite side of me on the river about a mile downstream on the low side of the bank. Sometimes he would try to out-wise me, to act like he knew everything in this whole world on account of his being older, but I knew better. We fished together even though I was no good at it. He wanted someone to keep him company, to listen to the big stories he was telling while he fished. I would just sit there, watching, and mumble something back, mostly thinking about trying to get Daddy to take me to a town large enough to see a movie. Once in a while I got to go. Though money for us was never plentiful, living more by a wing and a prayer, somehow we had enough to share, and Daddy offered to take Tommy along and buy his ticket, but Tommy never came. Daddy said he thought that what we saw of Tommy's life was tough enough and that what we couldn't see was a downright trial. I asked him what he meant, but Daddy just said, "Don't mention it, Mercy. It'll make him think about it, and he lives it hard enough." Daddy knew things I couldn't see.

Daddy was a country preacher and traveled the circuit to every little church that had need of a Sunday-morning man. Most of the time me and Mama traveled with him, but on occasion we stayed behind for a quieter day: Mama on her knees in early morning prayer, me listening to the early birds and thinking as soon as she gave me the go-ahead, I'd go to Ida's for a visit, then find Tommy, and we'd go exploring.

We could walk for miles and miles through those woods, and even if dark was falling, I always felt safe with him around. If a bear or a bobcat had met up with us, I figured Tommy would win the day. He was big on the inside. And in that way, my days were filled with an easy rhythm that played out around Bittersweet Creek.

But my existence is no longer so easily shaped by the curve of that river any more than it is easily threaded by Daddy's faith, Mama's prayers, and Ida's laugh. Or Tommy's crooked grin. My world has changed. Mama and Daddy asked me how my life was in general terms: How was work at the paper? Was Doc being kind to me? Lots of simple little questions like how was the weather, even though I was less than an hour away. But what they really wanted to know and did not ask was if anyone out there was looking promising. If there was a hope of me getting married.

"Living alone is spoiling you, Mercy." Daddy put down his fork and in his most gentle tone said, "It's not natural on and on. You'll get used to living like that, and then it'll be hard for you to accept some of the compromises a person needs to make in marriage."

Mama smiled and said, "In due time, Daddy. In due season. Goodness, let our Mercy be as she is."

"Well, Mama, sometimes due season can turn to dust right before your eyes."

I had a mind to just borrow a man, maybe Roger from the boardinghouse, and ask him to ride out to Bittersweet with me just to ease Daddy's mind from whatever ailed him.

As soon as I could finish dinner, I walked through the nettles halfway up the bank to Ida's little house, where we settled down for a proper lazy rest and talked about all manner of things. Ida rocked and said, "Now tell me, what's Old Doc up to?"

I rolled it all out and told her everything. That was, except for the part about the book. I was so tempted that I put my toe in that water. Just a hint of something going on. I was hoping Aunt Ida might figure it out all on her own to some degree so we could talk about it without me breaking my promise. "He's a little...preoccupied right now," I said. "He has a new project." I was worried that Doc might be going crazy, not a lot, but just a touch, but I didn't tell her why. I also didn't tell her that his crazy was understandable because I might be going down the same road.

It was because of all the nights we spent wandering through the alleys and dreams of other lives. And I so much wanted to spill those stories out right there around my feet on her floor.

"I reckon Doc's found himself a new passion," Aunt Ida surmised.

I set the record straight. "Ain't no woman in Doc's life but the *Banner.*"

"I didn't say anything 'bout a woman, now did I? I said a *passion.*" Ida rocked and leaned way back, her hands folded over the top of her stomach just so. I smiled and put my head back down. "It's common for a man his age to latch on to something new with a fierceness." She was stubborn about the things she knew.

"What's it going to get him?"

"A legacy. Man like that loses a good woman, he's got nothing before him but the end of his days. That is, 'cept he leaves something behind bigger than the whole sky. My guess is Old Doc is out to save the world. Even at the ripe old age of…" She stopped, leaned forward, and looked at me.

"I ain't telling, Ida." I laughed. "Doc's girl keeps Doc's business as secret as I can."

"He's got to be at least seventy-two. Got to be."

"What difference does it make to you?"

"Well, for all you know, Mercy, I might be looking for me a good man." And then we both cracked up at the thought of that.

Doc and Ida. I got the downright belly-laugh giggles and couldn't stop for a while. It felt so good to be in this simple little cabin by the creek. To not be worried for a few minutes about that book or about Doc or about that new man come to town.

Then, because the secret was so much wanting to tell itself, I told Ida about Doc's journals. Telling her one secret was better than telling no secret at all.

EIGHT

ᴗ

Doc Philips loved his wife, Opal, to no small degree. They were smitten with each other for well over fifty years, him all biting and rough edges, smoking those chewed cigars, and his Opal all dark-haired beauty and filled with the special graces that some women have at birth. Being in her presence was like sitting with the queen in a fairy tale. I felt honored just to be there and receive the fancy she took to me, though unearned and unwarranted. But that's the way it was; she took to me in spite of the fact I had no genteel background, no letters behind my name, certainly no acclaim, fame, or social status that would make me seem special. Even in my early days at the lunch counter, she would wait for me to take her order instead of Mabel just so we could visit a bit. Of course by the time I arrived in Bay City, her dark hair had grown into a white halo of an older age, and with every passing year she became Doc's sweetheart more the dearer.

It was his very own Opal who had given me the beauty of her insight, in quiet talks we had in secluded moments, times when I joined her over a cup of coffee, times that I stopped by when Doc thought I was out checking facts on a story. She met me on the street one day—I'm not certain that wasn't something she'd

planned all along, but at the time it seemed purely by accident—
and she invited me back to their home for coffee or a glass of iced
tea. Later when she got to know me better, she'd have hot cocoa
waiting for me. I would stop by while Doc was known to be at the
paper, and we'd sit there on the back porch in view of her flowers
or, if the weather was cold, in their living room by the fireplace,
and she'd tell me things. All our visits took place over the last three
years she was alive, and not once did I tell Doc, and not once did
he come through the door unannounced to find me there. During those visits she shared things about Doc I didn't know. She
seemed intent on sharing things with me I couldn't understand.

Finally one day she told me about his journals. "He writes in
them all the time."

I saw him writing in one of his notebooks, but it never occurred to me what they were. Newspeople were always writing
something somewhere.

"It was at my suggestion when we were first married. He was
always talking, pacing, trying to work things out in his mind, and
you know, he has such a terrific, busy mind. I thought writing
might assist him, help him keep track of all those thoughts. That's
when he began." She walked to Doc's desk at the end of the room
and took out a small key from the center drawer. Then she went
to a box she had built just for Doc. She opened it and took out a
journal and set it before me. "This is just the current one. The
others I keep in here," she said as she pointed to a cabinet with
glass doors. The cabinet was lined with nothing but journals, identical notebooks. There must have been fifty of them.

"That's only a portion. The rest are in a trunk in the attic."

She put the journal back in the box, relocked the box, and put the key back in its place. "Should anything happen to me…or to us… In the event that Doc and I are no longer here, I'd like for you to take them."

I started to protest for numerous reasons. It was too personal a request.

"Mercy,"—she sat on the sofa and motioned for me to join her—"histories change, and sometimes it's good to know what was. To put things into perspective and to be able to hold on to a thread of the past." She was so calm in the telling of it this way. "One day I'll not be here anymore. And someday neither will he, and his journals might be useful in some way."

I sat silently looking at her, the fire warmly glowing beside us, the logs crackling and moving, and Harry let out a great sigh, dropping her head on the floor.

I remember the clock on the mantel ticking, the soft scent of Opal's perfume, and her light blue dress falling gracefully about her. I shifted my gaze to her camellias blooming just beyond the window. It was so peaceful in that moment that it wasn't natural. Bittersweet had quiet mornings and lazy afternoons. This was neither one of those. When I looked back at Opal, she was still sitting, calmly smiling, waiting on my answer.

"Of course I will," I said.

"Yes," she replied in an almost sleepy voice, "of course you will."

When Opal passed a few years ago, Doc was so surprised that it left him breathless. He wandered aimlessly as if searching, as if his desire alone could return her to his side. But the power of resurrection wasn't in Doc, and finally he knew she was gone.

One winter day, two weeks after the funeral, Doc wandered bleary-eyed into the paper. "Mercy," he said, standing and looking at me. I had been working around the clock, nervous about getting the paper out. Taking headlines straight from the wires. Doing everything to keep the daily running even if the paper grew thinner by degrees. Doc took a deep breath and started up those steps without his usual question. Then his feet stopped out of habit, and I waited for him to speak. To ask, "Mercy, why this misery?" But nothing uttered forth from his lips, and for some reason those stooped shoulders, those frozen feet, those wordless lips brought hot tears to my eyes. Finally I whispered, "Because she would want you to, Doc."

After a moment—without ever looking at me—he slowly nodded his head and managed another step. Maybe that was the beginning of what was to happen next. That slight decision to continue. To go on up those stairs and into his different, waiting life.

I made coffee shortly after and buttered up a slice of pound cake and carried it to his desk. He stared out at the gray day, the rainy streets. He spoke with his back to me, his voice hollow and distant. It didn't sound like the Doc I knew but what had been left behind, a carved-out shell of skin and man.

"I went to make her a cup of tea, thinking it would ease her lungs, and she was gone."

I walked around the desk, set the coffee and the plate down, and laid one hand on his shoulder. There were no words I could offer to fix such as this. I thought of Ida then and wondered what she'd say if she were here. Surprisingly, it was Mama's voice that spoke up clear. She said, *Let it be, Mercy. Some things are purposed beyond repair.* And I had no idea what that meant, but I repeated it to him.

"Some things are purposed beyond repair, Doc," I said, and he wiped his face and then patted my hand, and I could still feel the wetness of his palm. We stayed that way for a little while, then he moved his hand, and I slowly backed away without another word, leaving Doc staring out at the cold winter rain.

After that day Doc changed some. At first his steps were a little easier on the stairs, his grief growing at least a little lighter. Each day he paused at the beginning of that banister, and I would offer him the tiniest thing to compel him forward. "Because it's the season," I would say, or, "Gamblers got to pay the price." Anything to keep him moving.

Sometimes you have to force the issue. It's just the way I had to leave and to make myself travel the fifty-two country miles to Bay City. It was a Sunday morning when I made my decision about leaving. I don't know what came over me exactly. But it came just the same. I knew I had to leave Bittersweet Creek or I would die just the way I'd come: peaceful down by the creek, contented with woods and water. Ida said I was cut from a cloth for a different purpose. I was nineteen years old.

"I'll come home often as I can."

Ida didn't say much more. She was going to miss me in the mornings. That had been our habit, but now our habits had changed. She would have to fit in around the off days of my existence. Before Daddy drove me for the final time over that big bay bridge, Ida said, "See you later," at her door. The next morning I went to work at the job I'd found, taking orders at the lunch counter of a five-and-dime. One of those first regular mornings, I was still learning the ropes when Doc and Opal came in together. They mesmerized me. They were married in a way that made them mysterious. Occasionally I could hear one whisper and the other laugh. Immediately I knew they were something special.

"Who's that?" I had whispered to Mabel, who was trying to show me the proper way to make a malt.

"Over there? That's the king and queen of Bay City."

"The what?"

"Just fooling you, but really, I guess if we were going to have such, they would be the ones. Don't they just look the part?"

"They do."

"That's Doc Philips, publisher and editor in chief of the *Banner*. Who would we be without the news? And that's his wife, Opal. She takes care of special causes. You know, worthy people, places, old historic sites. I would say she's a do-gooder, but that's not true. She's just somebody who does good. But those manners of hers! They make me a little nervous."

Months later news got out that Doc was searching for a replacement at the paper. His right-hand gal had been Judy Roberts, who had gotten married and given up the wonder of working.

On Sunday I traveled to Bittersweet where I sat on the porch with Ida, explaining about this news and what it might mean.

"I think I'll talk to him about it," I said.

"But what does the job do exactly?"

"I don't know. I'd been hoping you could tell me." We both got a kick out of that.

"You'll find out. You went to Bay City for a reason. This might be the beginning of it."

It was Mabel who told me the way it was. "Judy does whatever Doc needs to help him get the paper out every day. Now that I think about it, no wonder she's getting married. She needs a break." She'd laughed at her own joke, but I wasn't laughing. I was trying my best to figure it all out. "She types fast, takes notes, files things, reads the rough print, writes some of the pieces, and runs errands. I reckon she does everything." Mabel had leaned over and whispered in my ear so the manager, Mr. Coats, wouldn't hear, "You thinking about applying for that job?"

I nodded yes. "I can type pretty fast."

"You're young. You can do it." Mabel said it like she was an old woman, when she was only in her twenties herself.

"You're young too, Mabel."

Mabel smiled at me. "You're as young as you feel, girl." She gave me a wink, and she was off refilling a coffee and talking about the weather.

I went that day as soon as I got off from work. I was still wearing my waitress uniform. What a poor sight I must have been. Poor and pitiful or not, seven years later I was still ushering those feet up the stairs.

"Why this misery, Mercy?"

"To help mankind receive its dream."

Doc would nod, put his left foot on the next stair, and, with his hand on the banister, ascend that staircase one more time.

Then he'd go home to Opal in the early evening, and I'd go home to Miss Perry's to my room with the flowered wallpaper and a boardinghouse dinner that suited me just fine. Later there would be a good book waiting in the evening, and I'd lose myself in some story about people with magnificent lives in faraway places. This was my routine for the last many years. After Opal passed almost four years ago, little by little Doc's routine was busted up, and with it so was mine. We worked later and later into the evenings. Sometimes I'd pick up sandwiches from the diner and eat hovered over my desk at the *Banner* or in Doc's office upstairs and be too tired to even turn a page of a book when I went home.

I told Aunt Ida all of this.

"An inheritance of journals, huh?" she said. "Well, I'll be a contrary canary." And she pushed the rocker hard, raring back. "I guess when Old Doc goes, you'll see what's all the fuss with so many words to write."

What I didn't tell her were the details of Doc's new quest, this thing that had invaded his life, had now invaded our time. And I didn't tell her how the book was starting to have an echo effect, images from the pages rising in the middle of the day and hanging like a mist around my mind or before my eyes. No, the mystery of the book I kept to myself. As well as the mystery of John Quincy. I had a feeling things were going to get a little strange.

NINE

John Quincy had moved into Miss Perry's boardinghouse. It didn't occur to me that this might happen. The *Banner* was enough, knowing about the book was too much—and moving into Miss Perry's was over the edge. But the town only has two choices for lodging: short term is the Motor Court; long term is Miss Perry's. When I first moved out of the woods, I thought the town was a bustling, big city. It's not. Choices are good but limited, and gossip only has to make one circle before it is right back where it started.

There I was one morning, walking out from the bath down the hall in nothing but my robe and house slippers when I heard a man's voice drifting up from downstairs. A different man's voice. Everyone knows Old Sam Ivy's voice; it's a low growl on his best days. He's the grouch that keeps the room in the downstairs corner. And it wasn't Roger's voice. His is higher and much softer. This was different in a familiar way. This was the honeyed-up voice of John Quincy, and I knew it. I went to the top of the stairs and stood there still damp from the bath and growing warmer in the natural air. I made sure I stayed just out of sight so I couldn't see anyone below and they couldn't see me, but the voices were rising clear and clean. They were coming from the dining room, and there was no mistaking it. It was John Quincy talking with Miss Perry.

I rushed back to my room, dropped my robe, and moved as fast as I could to find out what this business was all about. Was he telling her about the book? Was he selling me and Doc out already? The morning light was catching the water glass on the desk, casting blue light across the old wood. I stared into my tiny closet at the lack of color. Brown dresses, brown skirt, brown suit. One blue dress stood out, and I grabbed it and threw it over my head. My blue shoes were still a little sensible, but at least they had a heel.

I threw the key around my neck, tucked it into my blouse, and then put on my nicest jewelry, a white beaded necklace and earring set that Doc had given me of Opal's. A quick brush of my hair and I stopped cold by the mirror. "What are you doing, Mercy? Get a grip right this second!" But my stomach still fluttered as I grabbed my handbag and walked out my door. I wanted to breathe naturally, to look calm and unmoved by John Quincy's presence. I paused at the top of the stairs to collect myself. Then I slowly tiptoed down the stairs, listening. John Quincy was saying something, and Miss Perry was laughing.

When I walked in, they both looked up from the table, all smiles.

"Good morning," he said, talking to me, sitting right there at my morning table where I had eaten for the last seven years, like I had invited him in. Oh, he was just so comfortable in all my personal spaces; my nervous meter moved over to mad.

"Well, what a surprise." I put on my Ida voice. Serious and

not easily moved. "Miss Perry, looks like you have met our new stranger in town," and then I winked at him and moved to the buffet to pour myself a cup of coffee. I am not a winker. I don't even know where that came from.

"Yes, yes." Miss Perry's voice was full of spark. "Mr. Quincy has moved in with us while he takes care of Doc's business."

Thank goodness my back was turned when I heard this news. I slowly poured the milk, stirred in two teaspoons of sugar. When I raised my eyes to the mirror over the sideboard, John Quincy was studying my reflection. Miss Perry was studying Mr. Quincy.

I forced a smile and a steady hand. When I turned and reached to pull out a chair, John Quincy stood up, ever the gentleman, and assisted me. Miss Perry looked from one to the other of us. Then she rose to bring me a plate of eggs and grits and biscuits, but I told her just toast if she didn't mind. I didn't think I could chew. I had Mr. Quincy sitting right there across the table from me, making small talk with Miss Perry like he had been living there since day one—and making me spitting mad.

"What's the matter, Mercy? Have you lost your appetite?" Miss Perry passed me a plate of fried potatoes. "A little something to go with that toast?" They were my very favorite and the one thing she could cook well. It was hard to mess up a potato.

"No ma'am, just things on my mind is all." I took my cup toward the kitchen. "More coffee, anyone?" But I could tell they were engrossed again in their conversation. Miss Perry was asking questions, and John Quincy was answering them politely and patiently.

No, he was just here to help Doc, he told her.

Yes ma'am, he had visited our lovely city before, but it was a very long time ago.

He was just a boy at the time, he said.

I put down my coffee cup and leaned against the kitchen counter. The hydrangeas were blooming outside the kitchen window. Big, full bushes. Miss Perry sure did know how to grow things. "You were here as a boy?" I heard the amazement in her voice. I thought to mention this to Doc—that John Quincy had indeed been to Bay City before. Just in case it mattered. Then I could hear Miss Perry laugh at something he had said, and I peeked my head around the corner. They were both smiling, and he was eating those potatoes, a big forkful headed for those perfect teeth. I'd have to talk to Doc about this. Surely there was someplace else he could go until this business was over, and so I purposed to make things go faster, tell Doc that time was of the essence. He liked that kind of talk. That's what I'd say: "Time is of the essence, Doc." Maybe that would speed things up. Get Doc to tell the whole truth and get whatever real purpose he had for John Quincy out of the way.

"Perhaps you'd like me to walk you to the office, considering we're both going the same way." That's the way he said it. Like it was just natural for him.

I considered the possibilities. "That's quite all right. You go ahead of me, and when you see Doc, tell him I went to check on those papers at the courthouse like he asked me to." I picked up my purse and put on an old sweater that was hanging on the coat tree. Then I studied my reflection for a moment in the hall mirror. "Miss Perry, that was a lovely dinner," I called out.

"Breakfast, dear. That was breakfast." She smiled at me from the table.

"Well, I'm off." I stepped outside, closed the door behind me, and caught my breath. I don't like being perplexed or getting a surprise that unwinds me. This man did both those things.

I walked toward the courthouse for good measure just in case anyone was watching, but I wasn't about to file anything this time of morning. I just needed to walk and think. I figured I'd just meander, give John Quincy time not to shadow me, and then I'd go in.

It was a pretty time of morning along the streets of Bay City. But then, I couldn't think of a time—not a single, solitary time—it wasn't pretty here. It didn't matter the weather or season. Everyone agreed that Bay City was something special not only to look at but also to feel. People who traveled through would stop for a bite at the lunch counter, and right away they'd start asking questions like "How does one get along around here?" And "Do you love living here?" Or "Just how much does a house cost in the city these days?" Come to think of it, I imagine many of the folks who were now fine, upstanding citizens had at one time just been passing through. Bay City took hold of you in that way.

I took a left by Daisy Parker's house. She was up there on the porch like she always was. She didn't get out much because of her condition, so she waited on her porch for news to come to her. And come to her it did on such a regular basis that she was able to deliver the society column every week.

"Hey, Miss Daisy," I called out, and she waved. She'd have liked for me to come up and visit, to sit and chat with her like I used to before this book business had distracted us to no small degree, but today I picked up my feet a little faster and walked as serious as I could down to the bay where the channel poured out to the gulf's warm waters. I wanted to look at the wide-open space, to be able to clear my mind and just be alone. Maybe the answers to my concerns were waiting out there on the horizon.

I breathed in the warm, salty air as I drew nearer. A tugboat was chugging out there, and I searched for it along the waterway. I'd never been on a boat in my life, not like that, not out in the deep salt water, but I loved to sit and watch them for hours on end.

I turned and looked up the street. Miss Daisy had carried her walker to the porch and was trying to navigate the ramp, so I started back her way. She was determined to have her say even if I didn't intend to porch-sit with her. She had made it halfway across her yard when I reached her white picket fence.

"What day is it?" she called out to me. She had a big voice for such a little woman. She was spring fancy in a yellow dress with a white belt, like she was going somewhere special.

"It's Thursday, Miss Daisy."

"And what time is it?" She was slowly inching her way closer to me.

I looked at my watch. "It's half past nine, Miss Daisy." I left the sidewalk and went up to her gate, picked up the morning copy of the Bay City *Banner,* and held it, waiting for her.

"Gerald is supposed to throw the paper all the way up close to the porch."

"Yes ma'am, he must have been running behind. I'll have a

word with him about it." The paper carriers were not my area. I
knew them, but they picked up from Herman and reported to
him. There was no point in telling her that. But I loved those
kids picking up bundles and riding their bikes all over Bay City
to deliver the news before the sun was well up. I really loved them.

"Speaking of behind, if it's half past nine already, shouldn't
you be over at the paper by now with Old Doc? Seems to me you
got business, you two, or there won't be a paper tomorrow."

It's hard to keep the truest secret in Bay City. Even the ones
that should be kept most dear. "It's true; we do." I passed her the
paper. She took it and eyed me, much like Whistler, but her eyes
were clear blue and sharp. "And I heard about that man come to
town. The one that got off the train."

"John Quincy."

"That's the one. I heard about him." She began to pull the
rubber band off the paper, to unroll it and glance at the front page.
"My, my, looks like we are in for some warm weather. I don't think
you'll be needing that sweater."

"What did you hear about John Quincy?" I tried to read the
back of the page she was holding, searching for my name on the
story about the county trying to enlarge the fairgrounds. That was
major news, so I got a front-page byline.

"I heard he wasn't married. That he might be a prospect for a
girl or two around here of proper age." She turned a page and held
her gaze now on something on the other side, something I couldn't
see. "You suppose there's a girl of proper age around here who
might be looking for a husband?"

"Not that I know of."

"Really? Why, I heard he was at least six foot in his flat feet. That he had shoulders like a bull and a voice like marmalade."

"Why, Miss Daisy, do you mind me asking your sources, because they seem a little smitten?"

"Mercy Land, tell me this, is he marital material or not?"

I thought about that for a minute. How was I supposed to answer the way I wanted to and be honest at the same time? "For somebody, sometime, someday, maybe."

"Hmm. Well, maybe you'll think of somebody who might get married sometime one of these days." She closed the front of the paper, folded it down, and held it with both hands back on the walker. "Guess you'll be headed over to the paper now, a little late but not worse for it."

I looked up at the blue sky. A few puffy clouds about but nothing of portent. "Not so certain." Miss Daisy and her yellow dress were not going to chase me off to the paper just yet. "I might just call Doc and take the day off. Take a train ride over to Mobile for the day."

Miss Daisy smiled at me, but she held her peace. She turned and began to get herself back to the porch. Then she spoke up clear as a bell while she was on the move. "You'll do the right thing, Mercy. You're a good girl."

I shoved my hands into my pockets and walked toward Main Street, head slung down. Why did everyone always expect the best of me?

Doc's Journal

Mercy's been gone all morning. I've been watching out the window, looking up and down the street for her. I tried to work on a piece about the expansion project for city water lines, but before I knew it, I'd be watching for her again. I'm counting on her more than she knows. She's kept my secrets, and I'd keep hers if she had any. That's what friends do for one another, odd friends though we may have become. I'm her employer, and she's Doc's girl, but it's more than that. She's been to me for years a kind of glue that money can't buy. Mercy can be trusted with small keys and big problems.

But now Mercy is upset by John Quincy. Afraid and trying to hide it. I know what troubles her. No one can take Mercy's place. Not in my life, and not at the *Banner.* Then of course there are other matters. I may be an old man, but I'm not without my memories. My guess is she took one look at him and lost a little bit of her heart. And that's a part of her she reserved for those ticker machines. I've seen her eyes light up at the sound of them going off all at once the way most women would look at their wedding dress. Mercy is in love with the news business. But she underestimates herself. She thinks having one thing means giving up the other. And now here's this John Quincy person messing all that up and me the cause of it. What am I to do? If I can change one thing, just one thing, shouldn't I do that? Opal would see it differently. My Opal adored that Land girl. I don't think she ever let on just how much. And that's a shame.

The truth of it is I'm sorry I got Mercy into all of this, but what choice did I have? It's a strange thing for a book to show up unannounced on a man's doorstep, even stranger for the pages to manifest themselves as these did on my desk in an evening when I was alone. And the strangest of all for them to glow, to shudder like they did in a breeze of their own making. "Harry! The impossible is before us!" I exclaimed to her, but Harriet laid herself down full force and sighed. She seemed not the least bit interested in the phenomenon before me. The ink, a golden color like none I had ever seen. An angel's pen, perhaps? No such gold exists, I'm sure of it, and yet this is what formed the words that were rising and shaping themselves in repetition. I stood before them, pulled off my glasses and wiped them on my sweater, then placed them back again. Nothing changed. I put out my hand so carefully, touched the first sheet, and lifted the page before my eyes. It looked legal in nature, actually contractual, and the name on top, in curved and elaborate writing, was that of one young Miss Mercy Land. That's when I had to sit down.

The first loose page was all about Mercy. My Mercy, who stayed ink stained from the Royal ribbons, kept a pencil stuck behind one ear, brought me coffee, fought with me over stories, and in her funny way helped me to climb those stairs each day. Mercy Land, it said. Followed by her date of birth. The word *Bittersweet* was visible, then it was gone, falling into the remnants of something else, and the words kept changing so that I saw what I held in that one simple page, and this is when I began to weep as an old man freely can, because I held the entire life of Mercy Land. One sheet had more layers below its surface so that looking at it was like looking into a deep well of words. Below the surface were the other layers of the past, and then a layer of the future, and then the truth. My weeping was profound. You would have wept too. Surely you would. To hold a life in your hands, as it were, from birth forward. To see the balance of days on end. And coming up from that page of Mercy's life, there was a strange sweetness, part of me already forgetting what I had seen and part of me knowing that Mercy Land was to be trusted and that the book itself was safe in her keeping, along with other things. I sat for many hours considering what I'd seen, and as much as I didn't want to bring her into this business of discovering what the book was about, I knew Mercy was at the center of its purpose here.

That night I never slept at all and carefully, ever so carefully, began to immerse myself in those pages. What I found there was mesmerizing, shocking, revealing. I knew

most of the names before me. Familiar townspeople. Faces
I had grown as accustomed to as my own reflection in the
mirror. Faces I had watched age right along with mine.

I wish so much I could sit with Opal at our usual time in
the evening. I wish I could have come home to her, laid the
book before her, and told her all my perplexing questions
about its meaning and appearance. Opal would have known
what to do. She would have. Her calm and steady answers
would have flowed like new wine. I would like Opal's blessing
somehow, some way, before I move forward in showing this
amazement to that man John Quincy. I'd like to ask her
why I have this sensation that the book itself is in peril,
that perhaps in some strange way it's actually here for our
safekeeping, but how could that be true? How could any
mortal guard such as this?

And where is Mercy?

TEN

I felt better. Salt air, a few bay breezes, thinking about all the things that were going on in other parts of the world helped me settle myself down. The fact was, I loved my city. I loved my work. And I was privileged to have this wonder of a thing fall into my hands. I knew the book was passing through us. That it belonged elsewhere and was only here for a short while. That it was here for a reason, but as soon as that good reason was found, it would leave us as suddenly as it had appeared. And I still wasn't certain that we were approaching discovering its purpose, but Doc was right about one thing—it had to be protected. It was the kind of thing that could stir up madness. A hunger for people to try to keep it or own it. Or worse than anything, to try to profit from its prophetic powers.

Doc was waiting for me when I walked through the door. He must have been watching me stroll up the sidewalk. He stood at the top of the stairs with those glasses on his nose, his hands on his suspenders, and the tiniest piece of a cigar stump between his teeth. He looked like a wild story of a man and needed a haircut.

"Mercy." It was not a question but a call.

"Yes, Doc?"

"Upstairs, please."

I placed my purse on my desk, glanced at the wire sheets rolling to the floor. My strongest urge was to grab the news, to see what had happened all through the night, but I turned and placed one hand on the banister, one foot on the first stair. I looked up. He was still standing there watching me. I asked, "Why this misery, Doc?" He just smiled, turned, and walked into the office.

I scanned the room for John Quincy, but there wasn't any sign of him.

"He's not here. I sent him out on the streets." Doc waved a hand slightly in the air. "Busy work, you know. Told him to go find me a story." He paused a moment before he continued. "I think he has been a bit confused by the turn of events." He moved to the window and motioned for me to come stand beside him.

"What do you see, Mercy?"

I looked out into the sky above and down into the streets below. The traffic light was turning green, and a car cleared the intersection. The neon sign of the restaurant was silent now, but when dusk fell, it said Marie's in blinking red. Now it was just a washed-out color in the sun. A woman held her Sears shopping bag with one hand and her little girl's hand with the other. Doc's car was parked directly below and beside the door. In my mind's eye, I saw all the folks down at the Woolworth's lunch counter eating BLTs with those thick-cut fries and drinking fountain Cokes. I saw the Usher twins sharing a malted and Old Lady Grey in the back of the store, near 'bout blind and trying to find her way through the aisles. I saw Joyce Manning down at the Bay City Savings and Loan, counting a stack of ones. I saw the tugboat going farther out toward the deep waters and the bridge that went over the bay and connected the city to the inland. I saw the train trestle running next to it and beyond, past the next three stops inland, all the way to the stop twelve miles outside of Bittersweet. There I could see Mama, Daddy, and Aunt Ida and all the people like them, born of sweat and misery and love. Full of more laughter than they had reason for. I saw the bitterroot herb down by the creek, growing green beneath that wide blue sky where the trees fell back and gave way to water, air, and space. I saw my history rising up from there and traveling across that railroad to where I stood now, to what had brought me to where my feet were planted.

"I see it all, Doc."

He looked at me. "I know you do. That's what makes you so special. Now"—he turned back to the desk, pulled out his chair, and sat down—"we have work to do. You are aware of that, aren't you?"

"That man has moved into the boardinghouse."

Doc sighed, placed those black-spotted elbows on the desk, and looked at me, chin in hand. Then he motioned to the chair before him, and I sat down. "It's not forever, now. Where did you expect him to go, Mercy? What were his choices?"

I looked past Doc and out into the blue sky. "What are my choices, Doc?"

"Mercy, you and me, we've made a promise to the people, haven't we?" He pulled out a fresh cigar and bit the tip off. The old one he threw in the trash can across the room. I knew this maneuver: it was his thinking, stalling, winning tactic. "And the reason we made a promise is because we believed in what was out there." He pointed to the window with the unlit cigar. "And we believe what's in there is a strange but real phenomenon." He nodded to the tiny cabinet that stood in the corner.

Then I thought about Bittersweet Creek, about Mama and Ida, about me offering up my capable to Doc all those years ago. So I got up my gumption and said, "You told him about the book, and you didn't even talk to me about it first." I leaned forward. "And you are not fooling anyone with that retirement business."

He looked hurt. "Oh, I'm not kidding about that replacement or about retiring. I think the biggest story of my life is behind those doors, waiting for us to figure out why it's here or how to use it. Why, Mercy, don't you think I could have already made headlines with that thing? I could have charged people admission to see it and be making a fortune in my old age."

"I got a feeling if you did that, you'd catch on fire and burn to ash on the spot."

"Yeah, well, to tell you the truth, I think you're right, or I would be tempted something terrible." He was rubbing his chin like the temptation might still be there. "At least for the story part. Not for the money. But look, even I know that something like that isn't for making headlines. Which makes it pretty ironic that it falls into my lap, of all people, don't you think?"

I reached for the chain, pulled the key from around my neck, and held it out to him. "Look, Doc, it's yours. You know it's yours." But he shook his head no. "Why do you want me to be some sort of keeper for the thing?"

"I didn't choose you for that job, Mercy. The book chose you."

"Then why didn't it show up in my room instead of your office?"

The bell rang downstairs. "Where's Claire?"

"Gone to help her niece with a new baby. Back in a few weeks, she says."

Then that honeyed voice called up the stairs, "Hello?"

"He's back," Doc whispered.

"I don't like his looks, Doc."

"Well then, concentrate on his limp."

"Anyone up there?" John Quincy called again.

I ventured to the top of the stairs. "I'll be right down," I called, and I could hear him pausing and then settling himself. I turned back to Doc, and he was sitting, face in hands, eyebrows knitted smartly together. "That limp doesn't bother me none. I think I'm the only one who notices. And it's not even exactly the looks." Doc narrowed his eyes at me and pinned me to the truth. "Okay, okay, they bother me some." I looked at the thread on the hem of my dress. "But it's this sense that I've met him before that unsettles me some. There's something about him that…" What else could I tell Doc about this inkling of mine? "You know, having him so close, having to work with him was enough already, but now…" I stood and raised my hands. "Now with him moving into Miss Perry's, well, I'll have to be on my toes at all times. I'll have to be on guard every minute he's around."

"Yes, I agree. You certainly will. We'll have to be careful, Mercy," he said with a lowered voice.

"Then why did you bring him here in the first place?"

"I expected him to be…different. He's got an air about him that, well, I hate to say it, but… Okay, Mercy, look here. He's not exactly who I said he was, okay? He's not a newspaperman, but he does have some experience, and I do think he will be of assistance with this mystery, but again…" He stood up and began to pace as if he were before a jury. "We need to rope him in little by little…"

"But," I interrupted, "you called him for a reason. You went out of your way to track that man down and lied to me about why."

"Now, I wouldn't call that lying, Mercy, and it wasn't to lie to you. I was just, um"—he waved the cigar in the air—"painting a picture for the town. I didn't want you to be part of that kind of paint job, you understand?"

Seven years I'd dedicated to the paper and to the man—and I did understand. That was his logic. He was protecting me from dirty work by keeping me in the dark.

"Yes, I called him about the book. And for good reason. And I'll tell you all about it. I meant to all the time. I wanted to. I just didn't want to put you on the spot. And who says this John Quincy couldn't develop into a fine newspaperman?" He caught my skeptical eye. "It could happen; it really could. It would be the best thing for him. He does have some background in the ink business, I'm telling you. And he needs…" He stopped midsentence, seemingly a little overtaken by whatever had occurred to him. "Take him for a walk, will you? Take him around the town, down by the water, to the park. Maybe up to the church to see Opal. Let him settle in a little."

"I think he's settled in just fine, moving into my house like he did." My feathers ruffled, I slammed one fist into my palm. "Besides, I have news for you: he's been to Bay City before. Long time ago, he says. Maybe he knows more about"—I nodded to the file cabinet—"*everything* than he's saying."

"I want him to see the town through your eyes. From the better side of history. Let him look at things"—he paused and ran his fingers through his hair as if he were wrestling something I couldn't see—"show him things as they should be."

"Then you'll tell him whatever you think you need to about the book? Please, let's get on with this book business because, Doc, it's starting to affect me some."

"How's that?" He looked concerned.

"You know what it's like walking through that book. Well, now sometimes in the daylight hours, I'm caught up just like I had the book out, just like I had turned the page into someone's life."

"Go on, Mercy," he urged me. "He's waiting on you. We'll talk more when we're alone." And with that I had to put my contemplation of current circumstances to rest, walk down those long stairs, and plaster on a smile for a man I didn't trust but who, so far, had never done me wrong.

ELEVEN

John Quincy and I casually strolled down the sidewalk. The shade covered us along the way, blanketing out the sun every few steps. That salty air I loved so much encircled us. The magnolia flowers were beginning to open along the way, and the overall awareness of the day awakening in front of us overtook me. I stopped completely and looked around me. I had kept my face so much in that book, and my mind in it when I wasn't there, that I had almost missed the fact that summer, in all its Bay City glory, had arrived. John Quincy stopped as well, but he was watching me. I resumed our walk and began to try to mimic the words of Mrs. Hidreth Brown, president of the historical society of Bay City, which provided the only guided tour of the city.

"The trees are a particular pride to Bay City," I said, pointing to them up and down the street just like Mrs. Brown. "You can tell that many of them are well over a hundred years old, and if you notice how the streets and sidewalks don't run exactly parallel, it's all because of the trees. The town was built around them instead of cutting them down."

John Quincy looked at me again with that peculiar smile. "I

think it's quite commendable. A town that went out of its way to save something. Now that's something to be admired."

I looked at him out of the corner of my eye, trying to see if he was being sarcastic. I couldn't tell, so I added another item to the list of things I didn't think I liked about John Quincy. I should've been able to tell full well; I could read people like one of my books. Maybe it came from years with all those news stories and sitting in on Doc's tidbit-gathering sessions. But this one? No open book at all. He had all his cards hidden up his sleeve. "So tell me, Mr. Quincy. Where exactly do you come from?" I resumed walking and turned left, this time to wander up the hill to the church to visit Opal's grave like Doc had told me. "Where are your people?"

"John," he says. "It's just John. No formalities necessary." He walked along beside me, not answering the question at all, as if I'd never asked, until he finally offered up, "Gone. The people I came from are gone, and better the world for it."

I didn't comment at all on that. We walked on silently side by side, up the walk that meandered far and wide through Bay City. It was one of the things that I first found so charming about the place. Bay City always seemed like a city on a hill to me, like something God would write about in the Bible. A place of refuge in times of trouble, people called together by a silent power that would gather them.

"And you, Mercy? Where are your people?"

"Bittersweet." Then I realize one word might not be answer enough for a man from out of town. "Bittersweet Creek. It's not even on the map really, not even a town. It's just a place back up in the woods, but that's what we called it, and everyone knows. It's just up the road, but it might as well be a thousand bus stops away. A thousand, I tell you." I started to laugh. "You should have seen me those first days I was here. Coming out of those woods, why, I felt like I was going to Paris. I didn't want to stay here at all, almost turned around and went back home, but Aunt Ida had told me ahead of time it was for my own good." I hushed. "I've been rattling on like a freight train."

"You can rattle on like that anytime. You can tell me anything, Mercy. I'll always be willing to listen." He looked straight into my eyes and was so sincere that I halfway to the blue sky believed him.

Then I caught myself. I had to remember where I was from and that I wasn't going to be fooled by anyone. There were many things I could credit Bittersweet Creek for, and one was it produced a tried-and-true people. I decided that the straight-up historical tour guide was better than me personally revealing too much about myself. I didn't even know this man. Besides all that, I had a job to do. I was just following Doc's orders.

"On top of this hill is where Bay City built the first church, and it is still the only church. Apparently, the town charter council back in the beginning of Bay City decided that one church should be enough for people, so they erected one big old church. They chose this bluff because it is the highest point in Bay City, and they wanted the church to be visible everywhere. History says the church is on an old Indian burial ground, but I don't know that that's true. 'Course I don't know that it isn't, either."

"Guess it was all Indian ground at one time," he said. He

removed his jacket and loosened his tie. He moved easy and smooth, making me think once again of someone in the movies, of how well he could have lit up the silver screen.

We resumed our walk uphill, slowly meandering under the old, mossy oaks. I could tell that hills and stairs were not where he was strongest, and I didn't know if the limp was from a recent hurt or an old injury, maybe something he'd had since birth. I thought it would be rude to ask so I kept my silence and was satisfied to meander at a slow pace. The shade cut the sun a little, but it couldn't whip through the humidity. It was summertime and it was hot.

"Of course, human nature being what it is, there was eventually a split or two. Folks decided God was one flavor or another, so now services are broken into different denominations all week, different times."

"Still one church?" He smiled and seemed to really enjoy this news.

"Still. I think all in all it is a favorable solution. The church bells were added later. See that tower right there adjoining? That's not as old."

"And which service do you attend?"

"The truth is, Mr. Quincy—"

"John," he corrected.

"Truth is, I don't attend any service in Bay City. On Sundays I visit my mama and daddy." I figured there was no point in revealing that on a lot of Sundays, Daddy was the preacher. Or on other Sundays we'd be in the community church, me up front, on the first pew. I knew, come Sunday, Mama would have on her best dress and be ready to go. There was no denying Mama's passion. She had one just like Doc's: all-consuming. Daddy did too, but his was quieter, more "love your brother." Mama's was Old Testament melt-you-to-the-ground fire. Oh, but don't misunderstand. She was also as kind and sweet as Sunday mornings. You could just never predict when Mama's passion would rise up.

"Your Sundays are reserved for Bittersweet."

"Yes, they are."

"I'll make a note of that," he said. I started to say, *No need,* but I restrained myself.

We arrived at the top of the hill, both of us ready to rest a bit, to let the wind from the water catch us and cool us down some. The church was magnificent. Simple but solid. The church bells rang on the hour, and you could hear them all over the city. Sometimes I thought I heard them in my sleep, but really they stopped ringing at eight. Started again bright and early at seven in the morning.

"So this is it." The solid oak doors were cut in an arch, the windows all stained glass, the front of the church facing out over the bay. "This is the church."

"And the graveyard," John Quincy said.

My eyes wandered to the right of the church and up beyond it, behind it, to the graveyard. "Yes, obviously. Everyone on this side of the bay, no matter which service they attended, or not, seems to be buried here."

"No favoritism on placement?" John Quincy's voice dropped to a respectable low tone reserved for libraries, churches, and graveyards.

"None that I can see." We wandered through the white tombstones, some of them as old as the town itself, angels carved into the faces of them. "I'll show you Opal's grave. This way." I led him to two plots laid down side by side. The headstone had both their names, with Opal's dates from beginning to end and Doc's just when he started.

"So Doc comes here, sits, and talks to her?"

"Did I tell you that?" I shaded my eyes and looked closer at the twitch of his jaw, looked for any changes around his eyes. If I hadn't told him, how would he know that?

"I don't think so." He crouched down and shifted the jacket to his other shoulder. "He just seems like the kind of man who would make it a habit to visit her. Or, you know what I mean, her grave."

"I know what you mean." I didn't know why I kept looking for something just under his skin, just out of sight, that would reveal the true history of John Quincy. But I felt something was hidden, so I kept on. "You're right about that. He is that kind of man."

John studied the headstones for another moment. "And this is it? Just the two of them? They never did have children of their own then?"

I shook my head. "Guess it wasn't meant to be." Something about the way he phrased it stuck out to me. Another note I filed away for later, something maybe Doc should hear.

"What's meant to be or not meant to be—now that really is a mystery." He stood and faced out over the bay. The breeze found us on the high place, the smell of salt and brine mixing with all the green. Way off in the distance a lone sailboat made its way across the bay.

"Beautiful, isn't it?" We looked out at the wide-open water and, just on the horizon, the inlet island that sheltered us from the gulf.

"It is." He raised his arm and pointed before us. "Have you ever been over there?"

"The island? Well, it's not really an island, but it looks like one from here, doesn't it? There's a finger of land that connects it way out to the east end. More marsh than land, so you do have to have a boat. Unless the water is low like nobody's business." I laughed at the thought of it. "Then you might be able to get across, wading in above your knees. That might last for about an hour, but then it'll start coming up again, and you'd be stranded on that strip of sand. It's not much more than a glorified sand bar with trees. Good enough to act as a barrier for hurricanes though. They still hit, but it slows 'em down some." It was obvious that he was contemplating something fierce.

"Mercy?"

There was something familiar in the way he said it, something personal. He said my name like he was getting ready to confess the whole world. "Yes?" I said, wondering what might be revealed.

"I do believe I have worked up an appetite." He smiled, and his true words, whatever they had been, were sealed closed.

With that we turned and walked out of the graveyard, past the doors of the big church, and meandered our way back downtown along the wildly winding sidewalks.

Later we had lunch at Woolworth's, and in spite of myself I had a good time. It's hard for a girl to keep her guard up forever. I think it's even harder when that girl is getting treated to a lunch that includes a cherry Coke and french fries.

"This is where I started," I said, looking around as Mabel caught my eye from behind the counter and winked at me. She was still just as happy as she'd always been and every ounce as sassy.

When he smiled with no comment, I ventured a little into other waters, the ones about his past. "When Doc was searching for someone to maybe...work at the *Banner,* there didn't seem to be very serious newspaper history in your background."

He lost his easy smile, but then it surfaced like a quick shot of the sun breaking through those clouds. "I had enough drama at a young age to last a lifetime. I assure you that is the truth. Besides"—he tapped his left leg—"I had some trouble with my leg."

Trouble with a leg had nothing to do with his newspaper background or a lack of it. From what I had gathered, the man had moved as frequently as the seasons came. Just notes of history here and there and odd scraps of paper—a tiny, confusing trail. And where a past should have been, a childhood, a family—absolutely nothing. I picked up the salt shaker and sprinkled the fries once more and lifted one to my lips. "Stories are not discovered or written by limps, Mr. Quincy." I took a bite, then another. "Matter of fact, I would think a slight limp such as yours could even have been used to your advantage. Furthermore..." I had to toss in a

word that Doc would use when questioning an eyewitness, and I
proceeded with just that language. "Furthermore, had I been in
your position, I would have leaned heavily on that left leg"—I
said this with just a little more feeling—"to elicit the sympathy of
people at exactly the right time, of course, in order to get them to
tell the true story I wanted to hear to start with."

"Seems like you have been paying very close attention to Doc
Philips in your days with him. Why, I do declare, Miss Mercy…"
He was fooling with me now, acting up to distract me, I knew. But
I enjoyed that wink he gave me. "I think you might have a future
before you that involves the newspaper business. And questioning
all kinds of witnesses."

"Oh, you might just be right, John, but let's hope it's not one
where I have been called as a criminal witness myself." I toyed
with my hamburger while he ate his like a man with a healthy
appetite. "If you don't mind me asking, how did you get that limp?"

"You mean the one I'm not using to its fullest advantage?"

"The same."

"Auto accident."

"You driving?"

He took a bite, shook his head while he chewed. His jacket
was off, his shirt sleeves rolled up, his forearms tensing slightly
with every move. I didn't keep the company of men much. There
was Doc, Roger, and Sam Ivy at the boardinghouse, who barely
said anything, and then different townspeople who greeted me
cordially, but as far as a sit-down lunch, a movie, a date, my calendar was wide open. When I thought about it, it was too wide
open for days and months on end. But I was serious about my

future. Aunt Ida had instilled it in me. A girl had to make tough choices sometimes.

But then again, maybe Miss Perry had been right. Maybe I should have made the right moves to be certain I had been introduced properly to that new science teacher who had moved to town. Or was he a math teacher? I made a decision while watching John Quincy eat that I would make my social calendar a little bit more of a priority. Maybe my choices didn't need to be so limited and lonely.

As if reading my mind, he asked, "And what do you do, Mercy Land, in your spare time? That is, when you're not visiting Bittersweet and not dissecting the man in front of you? Is there someone special in your life?"

I felt the red creeping up my neck until I thought flames had lit my skin. I searched the lunch counter to see if anyone had noticed, but they all seemed engrossed in their own lives, lunches, and conversations. Then I caught Mabel's eye, and she saw. Bless her! She rescued me. Before I could catch my breath or answer, she was standing at my side, picking up John's empty plate.

"Everything okay here, Mr. Quincy? Get you another Coca-Cola?"

"John," he said, "and one more Coke would suit me fine. Mercy?"

And then he noticed that I was watching him in a certain way. I distracted myself with a french fry and nodded my head. I wasn't going to tell him about the few brief boyfriends I'd had in Bay City. No point in that, because it didn't amount to much, just a sort of courting that ran its course. One boy moved away, and the other, well, I finally had to tell him that he was wasting his time with me. It got to where spending time with him was more of a chore than anything else. I realized that his coming around the boardinghouse or waiting on me downstairs was really just an interruption to my reading, and that didn't seem fair to him or to me.

I had to get back to the business at hand: Doc and that book and what it might mean for me and everyone else. My personal life would have to wait until another time. Of course I didn't know if that other time would ever develop, but I had to remember I was only being a tour guide today—not out on a date.

"Why don't I take you to see the school now and the library? Between that and a tour through the Ladies' Garden Club, I think you will have seen more of Bay City than you ever hoped for."

The look on his face was again unreadable. I did my best; I tried to mentally put on Doc's spectacles and to fathom how he would read that expression. When that didn't work, I tried Aunt Ida's great sense of human nature. But it was Mama's look that passed through my eyes and caused a vulnerability to suddenly surface, a softening that was so strong and so quick I almost reached my hand across the table to console him. Instead I placed my hands in my lap and looked out the big window. I told you Mama's looks could stir men's souls to repentance. I just had never known it was something I had inherited.

TWELVE

I was almost asleep when the sound of the porch swing drifted up and tugged at me. In a little while, it pulled me fully awake. I moved from the bed and leaned out of the window. It was true: someone was out there swinging.

I had a hunch it was Doc.

Miss Perry didn't like me taking my screen off, but sitting on my windowsill and staring out into that big old magnolia was one of my favorite things to do in the evening. I almost called out to Doc, but it was late, and there was no need to disturb Miss Perry or Roger or old Sam. Most of all, no need to alert the newcomer down the hall, John Quincy, to Doc's presence. I put on my robe and slippers, quietly opened the door, and tiptoed down the creaky stairs. In my seven years of living in the boardinghouse, not once had Doc made an unexpected appearance. He had come to dinner just once last year at my insistence, but other than that, not a sign of him.

I opened the door and stepped out into the cool night air. In spite of being summertime, a north wind had caught us by surprise, and the air had dropped a good twenty degrees by nightfall, something we were all much grateful for. When I stepped out the front door, Doc was sitting in the porch swing, chewing on that cigar calm as you please, like it was something he had done every night for a thousand years. I have told you he had that way of making himself fit the occasion, and this was no less one of those times.

"Doc?"

"Mercy,"—he stopped the swing—"come join me."

I did as I was told, which was part of my job, all in all. Doc stuck his legs out again, heels flat on the wooden porch, and pushed us off just a little. I waited for him to say something, but he seemed content with the silence. This was one of his reporter tricks. I knew his moves. Doc was out to get me to confess something. First things first. Throw the people being questioned off kilter; catch them at a time when they least expect it. And then—pow! The rest was front-page history.

Eventually his voice came out real soft and low. "What do you think about him now?" He knew that only a few windows away the man in question was potentially listening in on our conversation. I thought things over for a moment, looked up at the shadow of Doc's profile. He stared forward and didn't look my way.

"Do you know how late it is? After ten o'clock, in case you weren't paying attention. What are you doing out at this hour?"

"Who says I'm not always out at this hour?"

I couldn't argue that. He had been sighted on more than one occasion. Maybe Doc wandered through the town scaring everyone who saw him moving along those winding sidewalks. People had mentioned it to me lately out of concern. Of course, my question to most of them was, what were they doing up past their bedtimes? That hushed 'em.

"You don't normally come up to swing on my porch during the day, much less this late in the evening. What's gotten into you?"

Doc chuckled, pulled that nasty-looking cigar from his mouth, looked at the tip of it like it was glowing. "What are you not telling me about him that you'd like to?"

There was a creak from the house, and we both immediately paused the swing, our feet hitting the porch at odd angles so we lost our glide and the swing jerked sideways to and fro. Then we listened for a minute while the swing came to a stop, but there was no other sound.

"What's to tell? He moved in here; I told you right away. You asked me to walk him around; I walked him. The last two days you have asked me to introduce him to everyone from the butcher to the mayor, like that has anything to do with what's really going on, which of course I know it doesn't…" He motioned for me to lower my voice, which had been on the rise, so I continued in an agitated whisper. "Well, it doesn't, and you know it doesn't. Anyway, I've done all that. What is it you want me to tell you?"

"I made a promise, Mercy," he said. Then he pulled those specs down on his nose. "And a promise never dies." Doc and his ever-loving logic, and I didn't even know what he was talking about.

"What promise? You promised what to who?"

"You've been holding back on me. I know it by the way you

watch him when he isn't looking." He put the cigar back to his mouth. "Let's have it."

Oh, there was no getting around him. When he said, "Let's have it," at his office, the jailhouse, or the coffee counter, it was all over. My days of biding my time were up.

I looked up at the windows. My window was the first at the top of the stairway and now had a soft glow where I'd turned on my bedside lamp. Two windows down was what was now the temporary home of one John Quincy. It was dark as could be, not a light on in there. In spite of that I could have sworn I saw something move.

"Shh." My finger went to my lips, motioning for quiet. "Doc, let's walk a bit, shall we?" I stood and pulled my robe tighter around me. Doc got smoothly to his feet and followed me across the porch and out to the path that led to the flower garden in the back of the house where we would be out of the way of open windows and listening ears. When we reached the far back corner of the yard where the azalea bushes had grown almost as tall as I was, we stood in the light of the half-moon and discussed matters at hand.

"He's hiding something. That's all I can tell you. I kept trying to decipher what it was, figured you'd come across it yourself in due time, Doc. You're the kind of man to figure it out. Catch things that are flying right over my head." We still kept our voices low.

"That's true, Mercy, but all men can get tired." He looked up at the moon and then off into the trees surrounding the house. "Old and tired," he said again, like he was talking to himself.

"Snap out of it, Doc." I didn't mean any disrespect, but he let me be myself, and because of it, I had a habit of speaking my mind. That meant doing what needed to be done. Right now, Doc needed to be his best self. "We've got no time for you to be talking nonsense about old and tired." Sometimes Doc slid into what I'd call a depressed state of being. Concentrating on his age, spending more time by Opal's grave, preparing himself for going on. He would even tell me, "There's a business to dying, and I've got to be about that too." But right now we had the book and its ever-loving questions, and there was no way Doc could go be with Opal and leave that to me. I would have none of that. "We've got business to attend to. You can't be weary of welldoing. Not yet. And if you can't read him, can't see the man for what he really is, we'd better quit right now, 'cause we won't make it round the next corner."

Doc stared down at me with a most serious face. Then he smiled full and broad. "That's my girl. Just wanted to be sure you were still in this for the long haul, Mercy. Come what may, you know, in spite of me calling him back."

I gave him my best eagle eye.

"I mean in spite of John Quincy showing up."

"What have you done, Doc? Where'd that man come from?"

"You're falling for him, aren't you, girl?"

"You old romantic. Who am I spending my moonlight spring night walking though the garden with, hmm?"

"Mercy, I haven't been truthful with you, and I want to be." He put his hands in his pockets and looked down. "I really do."

I stood there waiting in the light of that night sky, Miss Perry's night jasmine blooming and giving off that intoxicating smell. I waited so long for Doc to go on that I could swear I could hear those gulf waves crashing on the other side of the bay.

"What is it?"

Then, just like that, Doc turned and was moving through the rose bushes and the heady night jasmine.

I ran after him, which wasn't easy in the slippers. I grabbed his elbow. "You can't keep secrets from me at a time like this." And then so many things came to mind at once about Doc's mission, the book, the gold ink and letters, the strange echoes surfacing from other lives. About John Quincy being who he said he was or wasn't, about Doc keeping things from me. All I could say was, "No secrets, Doc."

"Mercy, get some rest," he said. And then he was on the sidewalk before the house. He turned once and motioned to me as I still stood there in the middle of the dark yard. "Go on with you." And he motioned again to the door.

I stepped inside and climbed the stairs, wondering about everything.

Doc's Journal

I was out walking as has become my late-night custom, wandering the crooked sidewalks, evaluating the criteria of the plan stacking up in my mind. And like so many nights these months, I found myself there on Mercy's street, looking up at her window, watchful, seeing if things were all right. As if my being there would protect her from this unknown thing that tugs at me. This didn't concern me before the book appeared. But now, I know there is an unrest in my soul. I do believe that the choices of man are being tested, none more than mine. I find myself saying that over and over as I walk, telling Harry as she plods along with me most nights, "The choices of man are being tested, Harry. We need to look alive." My choice had been made when I found him, brought him out of that cesspool he called his life, but a flimflam man is what he is—or what he has become. It never occurred to me that he would stir those strings in Mercy's heart that have been silent now oh so long. No, I never expected him to look like he was a feature in *Movie Mirror* magazine. The book's purpose here being fulfilled was dependent on Mercy. I knew this in spite of my private plans. In spite of the fact that my plans were already causing confusion in her life. Opal, dear Opal, why aren't you here to set me on the straight path?

I went up on the porch, sat in the swing, and thought I'd rest my feet awhile. I was tired. No, beyond tired. I was weary, and this habit of walking when I should be asleep was taxing me. Maybe I should realize that I'm approaching eighty. I'm not a young man of fifty anymore. At my age less walking and more rest might be good. At my age retiring certainly is the right thing to do. But until this business with the book is settled, rest would be a wonder in itself. As I said, Miss Perry's swing and a rest appealed to me in the late-night hour. I thought nothing more than to quietly do just that and then move on toward Harry waiting by the door at home. The lights were out in the house. It appeared everyone was sleeping.

Then, a few moments after I sat down and was enjoying the night air, the front door opened, and there she was. A specter in a white robe, her hair wild, and her eyes looking like a schoolgirl's. She renews me sometimes, that girl does. I wish Opal were here to witness her and to hear me telling the latest funny thing that Mercy said. She can come up with doozies.

When she stepped through the door, I decided it was time to put my cards on the table, but not all at once. As much as I trust her, and I do, with everything, we have moved into places where her heart might make choices out of her character. Our Mr. Quincy appeared, and he was not what I had expected. Not just his good looks, but a cold edge like steel has found its way into his heart. His anger rages beneath the surface. Oh, he hides it well, particularly well. Too well. And Mercy doesn't know this about him. What she does know is a handsome man is at her right hand throughout the day.

What might become of that? How has it affected her so far?

No doubt Mr. Quincy was listening from his window. I didn't need to see him in the dark to know that he had been standing there trying to hear every word we said. Mercy suspected it as well, and we moved off into the big backyard, away from listening ears. The thing is, right now her heart is still only slightly fluttered, but when she finds out the truth about him, everything will change. No matter how many hours I've spent covering the news, writing stories, sometimes the only thing we can do is live moment to moment and let life play out just the way it has a tendency to do. Whoever expects love to show up when it's least anticipated? Whoever expects the essence of light and living stories to appear on their desk top?

I told her I wasn't being truthful with her, but I told her no more. Maybe my mind can rest a little easier tonight, but I'm feeling guilty for what I've done. Nervous about the outcome. I've dug in my heels now by not showing John Quincy the book. There's something about him—that frozen anger, that hard look in his eye—that has frightened this old man.

When Mercy closed the front door, I stood by the magnolia tree for a while, quietly watching and waiting. In a little bit her room went dark, so I knew she had gone to bed. I searched the other windows for a sign of him stirring—he didn't strike me as the kind of man who retired early or who slept easily. Nothing but experience would tell me such. Mercy has her ways, and I have mine. Years of dealing with the innocent and the guilty, the average and everyday, the phenomenal tragedies and small-town miracles have given me my own thermometer for truth. In my seventy-seven years I have learned this simple thing: time will unfold most plans and purposes of its own accord and bring most things to light.

The night air was getting even cooler, and I breathed it in with relief. The humidity had lifted, and for a moment I thought of making a small fire when I got home. But that seemed absurd for this time of year.

I turned along my street, taking my time and not in the least bit of a hurry, regardless of the late hour. This was the time I liked most, when people have had their simple suppers and, after a little news or gossip, made their way to bed; children have said their prayers and gone to sleep. It left me walking peacefully in a quiet world, save an occasional dog that would bark at my passing. I'd say, "It's only me." And at the sound of my familiar voice on the night air, they'd recognize me as just Old Doc, no threat at all, and go back to bed.

I put my hands in my pockets and wandered through

the streets at a slow stroll. The streetlamps were casting just the right amount of light for some well-worn thinking. No sound of cars, no friendly, chatting neighbors, nothing but my own footsteps…and then I noticed it, a slight echo that sounded behind me. I slowed to admire the roses blooming in Mrs. Sheffield's lawn. The footsteps slowed with me, and when I stopped suddenly to turn and admire one up close, there was a soft flash, then nothing. I was being followed.

For fifty yards or so I meandered on, trying to appear as nonchalant and unaware as possible. Then I did an abrupt about-face, ready to confront my stalker, but no one was there. I considered doubling back, checking on Mercy to make certain she was safe and secure, but I'd watched her go into her room and turn out the light. Surely all was well. I turned and resumed my walking.

Soon I was securely at my own front gate. As I let myself in, I heard them again. Only this time they were not the least bit hushed, no attempt at stealth. Whoever it was retreated casually out of sight but not out of earshot. "That's right," I said aloud. "You go on your way, and I'll go mine." Then I opened the gate and wandered into the yard with Harry as she meandered under the bushes. I looked up to the heavens and watched the summer stars flickering on this unusually cold night, wondering what would become of us now that this had begun. The answers, I felt, were just like I had told our Mercy. They would appear in due time and not a moment sooner.

Thirteen

John Quincy

She suspected I was watching them from the dark corner of my room. I could see her glance up at my window. I knew that a visit this late at night was out of place for Doc Philips. Their voices had started out low, then they dropped to a whisper, almost to nothing. Still, I'd catch her looking up, searching. Miss Perry had put me in the room down the hall from Mercy, one empty bedroom between us. She didn't know me in the least bit, but then why would she? Why remember a little tattered kid, anyway? Not much fuss there. But a part of Mercy suspected something all along. I could feel her eyes on me when my back was turned, when she thought I wasn't aware. I was always aware. She sensed something; she did. I would expect no less from her. She had always been good at that. Even as a kid. Barefoot. Flowered dress. Wild hair tossed to the side of her face. Feet in the creek water and all smiles. *Don't you know me, Mercy Land?* I've wanted to ask. A few times I've almost said those words. A few times I'd come close, and it's only been a matter of days since I stepped off the train. But I wasn't expecting to see her. It never would have occurred to me in a million years around the sun that she'd still be tethered this close to Bittersweet. But there you have it. Sometimes it doesn't matter how far you run, you're right back home again. Truth is, I didn't recognize her at first. Things happen. People change. She grew up. She's not that country creek-water little kid anymore. And of all the funny things in this world, she's become Doc's girl. The surprises have been never ending.

He was the one who had found me in that seedy hotel in Atlanta. A man knocks on my door one day, and I pull myself up to find a stranger, some private detective asking to come inside. Doc's been searching for me for months. *Well, well,* I think. The man passes me a number and says Doc Philips will be waiting for my call. I wait a few days for good measure before I ring him.

It'd been twelve years since I'd last laid eyes on him. What was the hurry now?

But when I eventually called, apparently there was a rush. At least to Doc and his hurried, whispered voice. He told me he had something, some kind of book. How it had just appeared suddenly but that it might make it possible for a man's past to be changed. That perhaps we could fix what had happened to both of us. I couldn't imagine what needed to be fixed in Doc's world, but it was obvious a whole lot needed to be fixed in mine. After all, around Bay City he was the man who brought the entire world to their doorsteps, who reported on their lives as if their events were breaking news.

When Doc and Mercy disappeared into the yard, I opened my bedroom door and slipped into the hallway. I leaned over the stairway, searched for signs of people moving about, but everything was dark. I tiptoed downstairs, wanting to know what Doc and Mercy were up to.

The kitchen, I decided, would offer me a better advantage. I walked quietly through the dining room, pushed opened the kitchen door. The window over the kitchen sink offered a direct view of the back of the house, and there, looking through the edge of the curtains, I could see Doc and Mercy standing in the pale moonlight at the corner of the yard. Miss Perry's shady spot was a quiet place where she liked to sit on her bench and have lemonade in the shade of the afternoon. Mercy was a bright contrast to Doc's dark shape. His hands were on his suspenders, and he was leaning down, telling Mercy something. For a moment I thought of stepping outside, walking through that rose garden to the back, and confronting them both. It would have given me the upper hand in that moment to come as clean as a whistle, to tell them my own secrets and why I was eager to finally see what Doc had called me down here for. *Change a man's past? Sure, that would help a little bit, but why not make up for lost time while we're at it, huh, Doc?* That's what I wanted to say to him. But to Mercy? What would I speak to this woman who smelled of gardenias so that I wanted to bury my face in her hair and breathe her in? To that image of the freckle-faced Mercy standing there in Bittersweet Creek on a sunny day? No, there were still too many questions unanswered. I hadn't even seen this book of theirs yet, and I needed to get my hands on it for more reasons than one. But, to my surprise, not telling Mercy the truth of who I was hurt me. I thought I was finally beyond much hurt in this world. Throughout our days I've wanted to take her hand and say, "Remember me."

For me, being raised on Bittersweet Creek meant learning to
do without things. Other people, people in Bay City, for instance,
might have things that were a little more uptown, but not where
I came from. Not for Mercy, either. I was the boy who wandered
away from the woods, followed the train tracks, and crossed the
trestle. I wandered into Bay City like a shadow beneath the sun.
The city had called to me, pulled me over those tracks. That's
when Doc Philips first caught my attention, or more precisely he
had captured my imagination. When I first saw him, in that suit,
and watched the way he walked, the way people nodded and
stepped out of his path, I thought he was some kind of law mar-
shal or maybe even a gunslinger. Considering we weren't out West
and didn't have marshals or gunslingers, neither one of these
prospects was likely. But a boy can wish and wonder.

And he was somebody that had a kind of power. I could tell
at a very young age that whatever he had, it sure didn't come from
the likes of what I had back in Bittersweet. That old soggy-bottom
place didn't produce anything like him. That life was all dark,
poor, and broken.

Bay City felt like a refuge. At that time it might as well have
been the largest city on earth. It allowed me to see greater possibilities than what I had known. Made me able to see bigger, to
think larger, and to hope for a future that had never belonged to
me. At that age I thought that in Bay City a person could be something other than what he was at birth. And at a very early age, I
figured that out. I learned how to sidle up to people and offer to
rake a yard for a quarter, to carry someone's groceries home for a

dime, to chop wood, to scrub, grub, or grabble with any tool they had for a job they didn't want to do themselves. It made no difference to me how dirty or tough. Surviving made a difference. Scrambling out of where I came from made a difference. By and by they gave me a new name. They called me the Bittersweet boy.

"Look here," they'd say. "You don't need to pull those weeds. The Bittersweet boy will do it for a quarter, I tell you. Just a quarter." And so I did. I pulled weeds for Miss Perry, helped her spread mulch in her yard, raked in the fall. I made myself handy at the grocery, waiting around the front door for people to need a young boy to carry a bag home for them. Year after year the Bittersweet boy ran the streets, picking up change for odd jobs he could do. Doc got so used to me hanging around the paper, looking for an extra nickel, that he finally hired me near 'bout full time. And suddenly those dimes and quarters and meager offerings started to double and add up. I buried them soundly in an old coffee can beneath the big old loblolly pine that got struck by lightning but lived on there on the high side of the creek bank. That old coffee can became my saving grace and my due-season dream.

But my due season never came. And now the city of my deliverance has delivered me back unto itself.

Cilla was waiting for a special word from me. She knew why I was here better than I did. She always knew things I didn't tell her, things that I left unsaid. What should have been hidden from her never was. I hadn't made a phone call since I'd arrived, and she would be looking for me. And no matter how far I traveled, she would find me. There was no point in my trying to hide.

I stared out the window at the darkness. It seemed that Bay City had called to me this time just a little too late to make things right.

FOURTEEN

Blessings and curses. It all came down to a matter of choice, Pastor said, but I was less than spellbound. I sat as still as I could without tapping a toe or bouncing a knee, afraid that Mama would notice and give me a look with her Old Testament eyes. What I wanted to do was turn around and make funny faces at Aunt Ida, sitting in the back. Daddy put his arm around me and patted me, as if to say, "Calm down, Mercy. It's just a matter of time."

I'd had that dream again last night, right on time. And I can't lie; I was nervous. This time I had been standing alone with the book, turning those pages, searching for John Quincy's name over and over. Then all I saw was me standing in that dream with the man in the street, papers blowing around his feet and me trying to call to him to come back or turn around or stop. I don't really know what I was supposed to say, but it was something. I woke myself up mumbling. Then I lay there for a while and fought the urge to rush to the office and get out the book instead of getting dressed for church and driving to Bittersweet.

After the service we went back to the house for Sunday dinner. Mama had cooked early in the morning before church, so we had cold fried chicken, potato salad, and a berry pie. I sat at the table, thinking about the dream and the book and John Quincy and Old Doc and the paper and wanting so much to spill the beans about all of it and get some serious opinions. Instead, I slowly spooned the pie and listened to the small talk about what had been happening in Bittersweet Creek. Then as soon as it was viable, I said I would walk Aunt Ida home.

We left the porch and walked through the yard out to the high grass. I had boots on that I kept here just for the likes of working hard in the yard with Mama. It wasn't the kind of place to be wandering with open-toed shoes. It was a different world here. Me learning to wear high heels wasn't going to change the nature of the snakes moving through the grasses of Bittersweet.

Ida linked her arm in mine. We wandered the path like we had these many years together, falling into rhythm as we made our way through the trees.

"Why've you been so antsy today?"

We made it into the little clearing. I could see Ida's house in the distance, and it was always refreshing to me; just the sight of it made me breathe a little easier. I knew that beyond her door, judgment rested its case and peace came easy. I reached down and pulled up a long stem of Indian grass and put it between my teeth. I didn't feel so antsy now. It just felt good to be out walking, to smell the grass, and to feel the sun beaming down on me.

"Ah, it'll wait," I told her.

Later, when we had rested our feet a spell and sat drinking a pot of Ida's strong coffee, I tried to tell her something without revealing too much. I started in telling her about Doc coming around to the boardinghouse so late. About him there on the porch, swinging.

"Why would he do such a thing, Ida? It's been almost seven good years now me being his girl, taking care of business, keeping his secrets even."

"Mercy, Doc's getting old. He probably couldn't sleep, went out walking, and then needed to rest a spell. He's just old-timey is all. He knows there's a new man in your life. Maybe he's checking up on you."

"I didn't say anything about a new man." Ida looked at me with one eye closed. "All I said was that a man had come to town."

"And?" She still had just one eye bearing down on me.

"And that he had moved into the boardinghouse."

"And?" Ida waited for my answer.

"And it is just about driving me crazy. Crazy, I tell you. I'm not sleeping good 'cause I know he is just two breaths down the hall. And if that wasn't bad enough, he'll be right down there at breakfast, beating me down there every morning, already at the table and charming Miss Perry up one side and down the other. It has been like that every morning. Then Doc will send me off with him all day like I'm some tour guide or like I'm supposed to introduce him to everybody in the city when I should be writing up stories or finding something better to report on than what movie is playing down at the theater this week."

Ida opened both eyes and crossed her arms over her wide chest. "What movie is playing?"

"What's-his-name in *Dangerous to Know*. That's not the point. The point is, that man is a distraction to me."

"It's that distraction what makes the world go around." She leaned back in her rocker and looked at me squarely. "But that's not all that's going on with you." Ida put both feet on the floor and leaned in toward me so far she almost touched her nose to mine. "Got me a strong unction that you're up to something else. Want to talk about that some?"

I put my fingers to my chest and ran them over the outline of the key even as it lay hidden beneath my dress. I knew it troubled Ida that I was holding something back from her. We didn't keep secrets, and now I seemed to be full of them. What I wanted to tell her was everything. What I said instead was, "My secrets all belong to someone else. They aren't mine for the telling, Ida."

"I know," she said. She leaned her head back in her chair again and closed her eyes. That was Ida's way of saying it was hush time. I went over to the little bed that Aunt Ida had called mine since I was a kid, the one that stayed right there in the corner of the main room. I lay down and pulled the blanket over me for comfort more than warmth. I could relax now in Ida's presence, knowing that even with my secrets and dreams, I'd rest easy. At least for a little while until night came.

FIFTEEN

Ida was right. I was troubled by that man in the house more than I wanted to say. My simple routine, my lovely life, had been vexed by him. It had only been a few days, and I was tired of it—the big worry about what to wear, to do, or to say next. I was tired of suddenly caring more about how I looked than what news I could stir up to tell in a sleepy little city.

I left my room, locking the door behind me. From the hallway I could already hear John Quincy eliciting a laugh from Miss Perry. There she was, tidy as a church mouse, smiling silly across the table from him. He was polished, looking like he was ready for Monday. Roger had already left for the motel, and Sam sat at the end of the table, grumpy as usual. I decided right then and there to have coffee at the *Banner* and skip the table chatter this morning.

John Quincy lifted his cup in salute and said, "Good morning." His smile was almost enough to melt my resolve, to have me linger. Almost. But what would any of that result in, really?

"Not eating, are you?" Sam asked me with a mean face.

"Good morning," I said, and without another word,

pocketbook in the crook of my arm, I opened the front door and was gone. I stepped into the morning sunshine.

One more second and I would have been sucked into a piece of Miss Perry's pie for breakfast and her remarking on things that were none of her business except she made them so. Things like, "Mercy has never once been engaged, even at her age. And you, Mr. Quincy, are you committed to a woman? Do you believe in the sanctity of matrimony?" I could hear her now, and I picked up my feet and tried to make faster time to the sacred space of my desk, that waiting coffeepot in the kitchen, and a quiet I could trust.

I was more thankful for the *Banner* than I ever had been. The dusty old building, the high ceiling, the order of my little desk. My typewriter and the smell of ink. I closed the door, put my purse on the desk, and made my way to the tiny kitchen. "Doc?" I called at the top of my lungs. "Doc? Are you here yet?" There was no answer.

Coffee and pound cake would make an excellent breakfast blocks away from the boardinghouse, Mr. Quincy, grouchy Sam, and those prying observations of the well-meaning, nosy Miss Perry. On one occasion I had even commented to her that it was nobody's business but mine whether I ever got married and that I could very well just become an old maid if I so chose. We had been sitting on the sofa on a Sunday evening, listening to *The Jack Benny Program,* and it had been very peaceful. Then Miss Perry had questioned me about the teacher who had recently moved to Bay City and if I had a notion to see to it I was properly introduced. That was when I made my comment and when she went about her needlepoint as if she had not heard me, pulling the threads tighter and tighter. I could hear the thread entering the cloth and exiting a few times before she remarked, "Mercy, the natural way of things is for a woman to have a husband. There is no denying that."

I wanted to point out to Miss Perry that she was old now and had never married, but then my comment about becoming an old maid took on a new significance. I had been mouthy and blind. "I'm sorry, Miss Perry. I didn't mean…"

"I know what you meant, Mercy." She had laid her needlepoint in her lap. "Perhaps I don't want my lot in life to become yours too. Perhaps I know exactly what that feels like in the long run, and I hope for something different for you."

In six-some-odd years, that was the deepest and most personal that Miss Perry and I had ventured. Maybe she had been right. Maybe my future held something different, but right now it was just the traffic outside the office, the sound of the coffeepot percolating, and—

A crash came from upstairs. Automatically, my fingers flew to the key held there on the chain.

I held the knife for the pound cake in my hand and approached the stairs. Again there was the sound of a crash, a falling of sorts that came from Doc's office. I started to call out, to yell, *Who goes there?* but decided against it. Was someone after the book? Could that be? After all these months had we grown lazy in our thinking? Thinking a locked box in a filing cabinet in Doc's office was just the greatest of fortresses? It might not be any kind of help at all. Who were we fooling? Someone had found us out.

Someone surely had snuck around and discovered there was more going on with Doc than just this business of him retiring. All that late-night wandering, his muttering, his musing—he had obviously let on something to someone and led them straight to here, to everything. Surprise might be my best advantage. I could call the police, but by the time they arrived…what? The book could be gone. I tiptoed up the stairway and whispered, "Why this misery?" before I caught myself.

At the top of the stairs on the landing, I slowly peeked around the corner of Doc's doorway only to discover—Doc. It was Doc, out of sorts. His hair stood on end, and he was as rumpled as I'd ever seen him. I stepped into his office.

"Doc?" It was all I could manage. He didn't seem to notice me, so intent he was on discovering something. All his desk drawers were pulled out full tilt, and there were papers scattered over the desk top. Some were spilling onto the floor so that the desk looked like it had exploded.

"Doc?" I said again and approached the desk.

Finally he looked up. "There you are, Mercy. I've been looking for you all morning."

"What do you mean? It's still early, and I just arrived."

"Well, I mean I have been looking for you since I arrived." He stood up his straightest, tried to lace his fingers through his suspenders as was his habit, but they were off his shoulders and had fallen to his side. He looked down and then up at me with a wry smile, slowly pulled the suspenders up over his shirt, hooked his fingers appropriately, and said, "We've overlooked something of major importance."

I surveyed the office, wondering what the overlooking might have included. The desk chair had been turned to the floor; one of the two chairs in front of the desk was overturned as well. I reached for the one next to me and set it right side up. "Rushing around the desk a little this morning, were you?"

"When we were reading the names…" He ran his hands through his hair and made it look wilder. "No, no, would you even call it reading, Mercy?"

I tried to answer, but Doc was off on a rant of some kind. My concern about him mentally slipping a little was back, only now it was multiplied.

"You know exactly what I mean. It isn't reading at all. It's something like reading but…" He stopped, laced his fingers into the suspenders, stood calmly, and considered me. This brief act of normalcy made me exhale, and I hadn't realized I had been holding my breath.

"Maybe we should just tidy up a bit before that John Quincy gets here."

He nodded in agreement.

"This is…" I searched for the words for what lay before us.

"A ramshackle mess." Doc sat down in his chair, placed his elbows on his desk and his head in his hands. "I thought all of this would somehow be a neater process. I had forgotten about that boy, and then I remembered something when I was going through the names in my mind."

"All of them, Doc?"

"Just playing over what we've seen, the way that the words, the lives, rise and fall to the page, and then I was wondering—

Mercy, do you and I see the same names? Do we see the same lives?"

We had never discussed this. The experience every time had been so powerful and to a large degree left us speechless. Was it possible that we were looking at the same pages and reading different words? And Doc was right; it wasn't reading. It was more... experiencing. Living.

"I don't know, Doc. What names have you seen?" My stomach growled loud enough for Doc to hear.

"Is Miss Perry no longer providing you breakfast?"

"I skipped out this morning. Thought I'd just make coffee downstairs." Doc made a noise like an old clucking hen. "What? I just thought I'd get an early start." He was no fool still, but no doubt about it, he was getting strange. "What's up with the names? What are you trying to find out? What difference does it make to you if you see a name or you don't?"

He stood suddenly and started to pace the floor back and forth in front of the window. For a little while he didn't answer me. "I started making a list of every name I could remember. I thought it would be good to have a list handy. To carry it with me, put it in my briefcase, to keep it by the bed in the evenings just in case."

"In case of what?"

"In case I thought of something. In case someone's face suddenly came to mind in such a way that I needed to make a note— jot down a reference." Then he looked at me and disclosed, "Those echoes that you spoke of. I have them too. I didn't want to scare you. I didn't want you to take that book and toss it in Bittersweet Creek, and don't think I don't know you've considered it. I keep stepping back into those lives with my eyes wide open too. But when I do, I try to remember and to write a note down next to the name or the face that I saw."

"It's a frightening thing, living other people's lives."

There went the hands to the hair again. "We're trapped in a riddle, Mercy. A riddle that feels like it's driving me mad."

"All riddles have an answer."

"I should have said, 'Come quick, Mercy. I have a riddle from another world.'" His eyes were wild, he looked bona fide crazy, and I wanted the Old Doc back.

The bell chimed downstairs, announcing that someone had arrived.

"That would be our Mr. Quincy, I presume." Then after a moment we heard his voice say, "Hello?" But neither of us answered. We looked around the office, at the scattered papers and file folders. "You go on down and busy him, will you? Give me a little time to make some order out of this chaos."

I walked to the top of the stairs and called out, "Be right there." Then I turned back to Doc. "Most of my time these days seems to be spent escorting him around and distracting him from you. Tonight you and me, we really need to talk. And not stumbling around in someone's flower bushes. Because it's never going to get done this way, and if it never gets done, who knows what might happen? We'll both be crazy in the end, and that book will fall into the wrong hands. The wrong hands, mind you, and that kind of power wasn't meant to be played with." I stepped back toward him. "It came to you—to us—for a reason, surely. Surely it did."

"When a new story presents itself, you have to be able to see the whole picture in order to tell it all and tell it true. I'm just trying to see the whole picture. That's all."

I walked back to his desk and lowered my voice. "This is not an ordinary story. You know that. This isn't one of your headlines for the paper." He studied me hard. "No disrespect, sir." I softened my tone, and his face softened with it.

"I was chosen for a reason. Now what would that be? There's only one thing I've thought of Mercy—only one."

"There's no one to defend in this case." I continued whispering just in case Mr. Quincy had started to climb the stairs of his own accord. "At least I don't think there is. Right? It's just their names and those wild words in there showing us people's lives." I pointed to the filing cabinet. "We've got to figure this out and get back to the business of our own lives and the *Banner.* I mean, have you noticed lately that we're just putting in stories from the wire? Besides Miss Daisy's "Sunday Society" and a few easy things on meetings here and there, what news have we reported on? I don't think we have even covered the school board meeting. Wasn't that Tuesday? But I wasn't there. It's small-town news, Doc. They're simple little stories, but they're our stories. That's what makes them so important. We've got to keep bringing it home. Right?" I waited for the answer I wanted to hear. A tone of leveled calm in his voice.

"Well, that's all true." Doc took a step back from his desk, with hands to suspenders; he moved his stump of a cigar to the other side of his mouth. "Mercy, you should know: you will replace me when I retire."

I could see that he wasn't joking. My stomach did a deep dive from the high board without John Quincy being anywhere near me. Then a new fear set in. There was no way I could fill Doc's shoes. No way. "I'm just Doc's girl. The go-to girl. I do what needs to be done."

"The go-to girl. I like it. We can use it in a headline. I can see it now." He raised his hand to an imaginary masthead. "Go-To Girl Takes Over the *Banner*." Then he smiled his old, worn smile.

"Sure, Doc, like that's going to happen."

"Of course, a new equation has been thrown into the mix. One Mr. John Quincy, handsome and charming, and if I'm not mistaken, he has a soft spot for you. You might want to settle down and give up being a news hound."

"Soft spot? Ha!"

"Should I come up?" The voice was nearer, on the first steps.

"Go on now. Meet me here tonight—later, after dinner," Doc whispered. "And we'll go through the book one more time before we show it to him. That is, if we show it to him at all."

He turned his back to me then, and I knew he wasn't being rude. He was just looking out the windows, as was his way. Trying to think things through. I quietly closed his door to give him a chance to clean up that huge mess, wondering what in the world Doc had gotten me into and sure wishing I could tell Aunt Ida everything.

"Good morning again." John Quincy stood by my desk, watching me walk down the stairs. "I seem stuck in a holding pattern here."

"It's tough knowing what the next move is sometimes, isn't

it? In just an instant, it can all change." I walked into the kitchen determined to get the coffee started and not in the mood for small talk. "More coffee, or have you had your limit?" I sliced a piece of pound cake and stood eating it with my fingers. He followed me into the little kitchen and leaned now on the doorframe, his arms crossed over his chest, lips forming a smile. "Cake? It's nice to see a woman not afraid to eat."

"Oh, you mean without the good sense of manners, I suppose." I took another bite of the cake. "Guess my Bittersweet is showing through." I took the last bite and brushed my hands off in the sink, ran them beneath the water, then reached for my coffee cup and saucer.

"I don't mind."

"Neither do I, on occasion." I opened the fridge, took out the cream. "I just try not to make a habit of it." It was my turn to smile. "Particularly in Bay City." I sat at the tiny table. John Quincy pulled out a chair and joined me. We sat there with me having coffee and him having nothing. Occasionally he smiled at me; other times he looked out the tiny kitchen window, but we didn't speak. Then he surprised me.

"I don't think he trusts me," he said, rolling his eyes to the ceiling. "I was wondering if you happened to know what the real reason is for my being here. He has you carting me around town for people to see me, but the reason he called me was because of something strange; it had nothing to do with a job. He said a man could change his past with a book and— Look, I don't know why he hasn't opened the thing, that is, if it really exists at all. Why's he dragging his feet?"

I wasn't going to be moved by his slick behavior, his sudden honesty. Like I would fall for that, and I let him know so.

"I'm not fully certain why you're here, and of course he doesn't trust you." I wanted to add, *Neither do I,* but I kept that part to myself. "He has to make sure you're on the up and up, I guess. Maybe that you're not a thief. Maybe that you won't try to steal something that doesn't belong to you."

"And exactly what would I be stealing? Could you describe it for me?" Our knees were almost touching, but he leaned in even closer toward me. "Because I know it has nothing to do with his retiring the way he has tried to make the whole city think."

"You're wrong about that, I bet. I'm sure in some way it has everything to do with his retiring." I got up from the table, placed my empty cup in the sink, and turned to face Mr. Quincy from a distance. "You have no idea what you've stepped into, but if things go according to developing plans, you'll know this time tomorrow."

"You were always so tough, Mercy." This was said so low that it felt more like a vibration through my body than actual words.

"What did you say?" I took the tiniest of steps forward.

"After all these days you still don't recognize me?" He leaned forward on his seat, elbows on his knees, chin resting on his propped-up hands.

"What?" I could barely believe what I had understood him to say. "Recognize you?" I couldn't imagine not recognizing a man the likes of John Quincy. How could anyone forget that face? Yet there had been moments when his voice—no, no, the cadence of his voice had been familiar. "Trust me on one thing. We've got

enough secrets floating around here. You want to tell me something, go ahead. Come right out with it. No beating around the
bush—who are you?" That was Ida coming out in me again, I
thought. But then I realized maybe it was just me. That raw-grit
girl from Bittersweet who wasn't afraid to call a spade a spade.
Somewhere along the way, working for Doc and being part of the
newspaper, I had gotten over a bit of my shyness. Guess it was the
part that felt like I didn't belong or might not be good enough.
Doc had given me a chance, and not just him but all of Bay City,
to test myself and find myself worthy. Now our wonder boy was
throwing me loops and surprises like a wildcat. Only smoother.
Foxier.

"I wouldn't want to spoil all the fun now of you figuring that
out. Doc Philips has to figure out if he wants to keep me, if he
chooses to let me in on his little secret like he said he would. But
you, my Mercy Land, just need to remember me. Just like I remembered you."

And with that he got up and walked right out that front door.

Sixteen

I expected John had just gone for a short walk. Something to clear the air or at least his mind. But after an hour he still wasn't back. I climbed the stairs to Doc's office and gingerly peeked my head in the door. He had for the most part put the desk back together; the files weren't in their proper places, but at least they had been put into stacks that resembled a kind of order.

"Um, Doc?"

"I know. I heard the bell. Watched him walk down the street."

"Do you know what he just told me? You won't believe it. Says that I know him. That I should have recognized him by now."

Doc sat down in his chair with a heaviness. "Somebody followed me home last night."

"Followed you?"

"Yes, yes."

"From Miss Perry's?"

"I couldn't tell you where from, just that they were there— following. They could have been following me all night, but I didn't notice anything until later. Now, that makes no nevermind. It could have been him, or anyone for that matter. There's plenty of reason with what's in there"—he pointed toward the cabinet—"for someone to follow."

"You know, I've been thinking, this little key and that box in the filing cabinet—we need to remember how that thing showed up in the first place, right? It could just disappear without us ever knowing it."

"It hasn't. It won't."

"But how do you know?"

"Because you're wearing the key, and that means more than you imagine. I don't know why the book came to me in the first place. It should have just fallen straight into your lap, but, regardless, I've been trying to decide if our John Quincy had a chance to start over, would it change his life? Then when he arrived, I knew he was lying about something. That doesn't seem like a good way to start off, considering what we have in our hands. I mean, I know about his twisted past. I know about his coming and going from city to city. I know he's a bit of a flim-flam…"

"A what?"

"He's a hustler. A con man. Still, that didn't bother me because I thought it would be a big part of the fix. But something else is eating him. Something he brought with him that I didn't know was there until I laid eyes on him. And you said so yourself." He pointed at me as if this tangled mess was my fault. "You said yourself that you didn't trust him and that he was hiding something."

"The fix? What fix? Doc, you may have gone over the deep

end. I just want you to know that. You need a haircut too, in the worst way." I figured if I was telling him he was crazy, I might as well work in a few extra details.

"I've been concerned that you'd get seriously smitten with the man and that it might affect your good judgment."

"I'd have thought you knew me better than that. I've walked the dog and helped you stay up all night to set the paper. We've waited on the big news so the headlines could go out right. We've been through too many stories together, including the one you have locked up in there, for you to think some man's gonna smooth talk his way right over me."

"I understand, and all of that is true, but what I know from years of reporting the news is that the emotions of the human heart are a powerful grace. And that they can also get a person into a whole heap of trouble."

"You know the people and the place I come from. They have taught me right from wrong. That doesn't change ever."

"It may not change, but, trust me, those lines can become extremely blurry when passion ignites the fire."

Doc had more experience with the human condition. Just like Ida said, he was testing me, and she understood it. I guess I needed to step back and accept it. Even a heart like mine, someone determined to be true, apparently could make a swift turn. I made a note not to overestimate myself.

"The point right now," I said, "is that apparently I know our Mr. Quincy. Only I don't have a single recollection of him. Not a one."

Doc smiled then. "Oh, I bet you do. You're just blinded by what's right in front of you. For one thing, his limp threw you off."

For the first time since I'd come into the office, I sat down. Apparently Doc knew everything in this whole world. "Doc, you knew that he knew who I was, that maybe I knew him, and you didn't tell me about it?"

"I couldn't sleep at all last night, Mercy. So I walked and pondered."

"That's a three-dollar word you don't find in the paper." He was always telling me that newspapers were for people to read and get the story the first time.

"Okay, I was thinking—hard. I thought about the first night the book came to me, the way it arrived, and the amazing thing that it is. Isn't it a wonder, Mercy? Truly, isn't it a miracle of some kind we don't even realize?"

"I realize it, and, yes, it's an amazing wonder. What were you saying about who he is?" I sat on the edge of my chair, waiting for him to go on.

"Well, something kept tugging at me yesterday. So I went home, walked old Harriet one more time, and then started thinking of the names I had seen. Since it was so unseasonably chilly last night, I even built the smallest fire so I could sit there by it, re-creating a little of the mood of that night the papers first came, thinking it might spark a detail perhaps I had overlooked. I sat by the fire in my old reading chair and started writing down the names as they came to me. There I was, of course—easy to spot my name and yours. There was Miss Daisy and Miss Perry and

Old Man Whistler. And then many, many names of people I recognized from the news but don't know personally. I just know of them. But one thing kept bothering me. It was like an itch I couldn't scratch, and had it been a decent hour, I would have come over to get you and said, 'Let's use the key. Let's see again what this page, this name holds.'"

"Who is he, Doc?" I asked him straight-out. I had been sitting there going over every Bay City man I'd met or even passed on the street in the last seven years. There was no sign of him there. Not on the sidewalks, not around the corners, not at the lunch counter, or even for a flash at the movie house as the light dimmed. Not even the profile of his face. "Just tell me."

He leaned over his desk toward me. "You won't believe it, Mercy. It's…" Then Doc stopped; his eyes grew wide. He started again. "He's the…" He chomped down hard on his cigar butt and leaned back in his chair. "Well, I'll be. It's the darndest thing. I was going to tell you, but it's as if the cat's got my tongue. I can't say it."

I was tired of all this foolishness. I stood up and grabbed his fountain pen from his desk and a sheet of paper. "Write it down." My voice came out more commanding than I meant, but I had been on edge all morning, and things weren't getting any easier.

Doc nodded in agreement, took the pen, scribbled something down, and pushed it across the desk to me. I picked it up and stared closely at the paper.

"Very funny, Doc." I put the paper back on the desk. "You know very well that I don't read Latin."

Doc snatched the paper back and peered at it closely. Then he looked at me and back at the paper. "I don't write in Latin either, and I don't think that's exactly what it is. That's not what I wrote down." He looked back up at me. "It appears to me that whatever is attached to the book in there is attached to our Mr. Quincy as well. Maybe I was meant to call him. Maybe he really is supposed to be here. And apparently you recognizing him for who he truly is, is just all part of the puzzle. I can't tell you that information. If I could, I would."

We had reached a new point in our trying to decipher why the book had arrived, exactly what it was, and what the two of us were supposed to do about it. "I miss things being the way they used to." I stood and walked to his window, watched the cars go east and west along Main, thinking of what life used to be like. Now when I looked at the desk and at Doc, I could clearly see how we were so off kilter from where we used to be. "I want everything to go back to the way it was."

Without me even being aware of his movement, he had come to stand beside me, laced his fingers behind his suspenders and stood there, looking out over the city. Then he laid his hand on my shoulder.

"Maybe it will. When this business is finished, maybe things will quietly go back to the way they were. Maybe the arms buildup will settle, and peace will come quickly to Europe, and Superman really will save the world."

"What should we do?" There was a hush then that fell in the room. How can I explain this to you? It was an unnatural silence of the kind you can feel move like a wave through the room. Doc and I were talking, and a deep, deep hush came in that door so heavy our very words seem muffled. It was something downright tangible, something that raised the hair on the back of my arms. Something had entered the office with such fierceness that Doc and I both turned together, looking to the door, searching for where it was or could have originated. The tough root of that Bittersweet girl was shaking in her shoes. I reached out and grabbed Doc just above the elbow and none too gently. "What is it?"

Doc said nothing. He continued to survey the room. Then without any hesitation in his voice, he said, "The file cabinet. Check the box." And although he was speaking normally, the words I heard seemed to come from far away. I let go of his arm and moved quickly. I pulled the small chain from around my neck and lifted the tiny key from it. I looked over at Doc one more time to be certain before I opened the file cabinet. He nodded yes, and I continued. I pulled out the drawer, moved the files from the back, lifted the locked box out, and closed the cabinet.

It was at once mesmerizing and impossible to believe that a space such as this—an ordinary, everyday, regular file cabinet in a small town newspaper editor's office—could hold something like this. I carefully unlocked the box and reached for the book to lift it out. My fingers touched those pages made of light, and immediately my breath quickened, and my eyes filled with tears. Somewhere Doc was calling me. That is, I could hear him, but his voice sounded thousands of miles away. A barely there voice, and all I could hear was my name. Nothing more. No indication of what the calling might mean or entail. It was a mere distraction, my name, like a mosquito hovering on a summer night. The words, if you could call them words, began to lift and move, as if they were music being played. I reached out to place my hand on them, to touch that first page, to even try to lift the word from the page, because that's the way they moved. It was as if the words were living and breathing things. I heard my name called from faraway again, but it made no difference to me. Then a hand was on my shoulder, and it was Doc, standing next to me by the cabinet. "Put it back, Mercy."

It was as if he had stepped into my life from another world. It took me a minute to focus on him, longer to focus on the words themselves. Slowly I closed the book, placed it in the box, locked it, and took it dreamily back to its place, then shut the cabinet. I think there had been music from somewhere, because now my footsteps sounded dull and empty. Neither of us spoke for a while.

I sat heavily in the chair and looked out the window. It seemed that it was late afternoon. "Where did the day go?"

"I don't know," he said. "It appears those words are from another time. It affects us in that way, Mercy. Five minutes becomes five hours."

I could hear Mama's voice in my own mind, saying, *"A day is as thousand years, Mercy, a thousand years as a day—just imagine that."* I had always nodded my head and smiled just to make her happy. *That's beyond my imagining,* is what I wanted to say to her. But now I understood just a touch of what she was talking about. And that touch was enough to make a shiver run up my spine.

Doc said, "I do believe you could use a little fortifying. How about, after we get the paper laid out and put to bed, I take you to dinner?"

We stood side by side, ripping stories from the wire, passing pieces back and forth to each other. Doc would shake his head yes, meaning run it, or no, meaning drop it. I put the runs in a stack and let the rejects fall on the floor. When he was satisfied that we had the stories we needed to make at least a meager *Banner* morning edition, we made our way out into the street. It was early evening by the time we locked up and walked down the street, both of us still silent, no doubt still thinking of the most recent paths we'd taken in the book upstairs. I tried to concentrate on the sound of our steps along the sidewalk, the sound of real footsteps happening in the present moment walking down the sidewalk in the early summer evening.

Seventeen

Doc and I passed Marie's without even thinking about it, in spite of the fact that it was one of our favorites and right across the street. I think both of us were in the mood to keep moving. To keep putting one foot in front of the other and breathing in the air. We walked like that for almost a mile. Passing folks we knew but just nodding in the process. We didn't stop and make conversation.

I wondered where our John Quincy person had gone off to, if he had simply taken himself back to Miss Perry's and was holed up now in his room. I thought about asking Doc, but before I could mention a word, he chimed in.

"He'll show up on his own accord, Mercy. He's wrestling with something."

"Am I that obvious? I hadn't said a word."

"Really? That's strange. I thought you'd asked about John Quincy."

We turned the corner and started walking toward the bay. Both of us knew where we were going, and there really wasn't a need to discuss it. We were headed for Mozell's café and the best fried chicken, greens, and iced tea in all of south Alabama. And I decided right then that if she had made a pie that day, I was getting a big slice. A slice of buttermilk or peanut butter pie felt like it would go a long way toward making up for a day full of nonsense and wonder.

Once inside the door, Doc and I said our how dos and went on through the café out back where the little tables were set up near the pine trees. We looked at evening light filtering through those pine needles and commented on occasion or nodded at another customer who would stop by to chat with us a spell. Everybody was used to seeing both of us out and about. And that was what made it a good life: the fact that a face could be recognized around the corner and down the street was a good thing. The fact that Doc was always in such good standing, that the news was something everybody needed, and that I was the go-to girl at the paper meant we got a little extra special treatment from time to time. I didn't mind that, either.

We ate until we couldn't have taken another bite. Then we waited until the plates were cleared before we spoke much about anything.

"Strange air today," I said when we had finished our dinner.

Doc looked over his shoulder and said quietly, "Let's take a walk, Mercy."

When we left Mozell's café, we wandered down by the bay, toward the dock. Doc had his head down and his hands in his pockets. When he spoke, he almost whispered so that I had to lean toward him to hear what he said.

"I wish Opal were here."

"You're always gonna wish that."

"I could rant and rave about anything, and she'd calmly tell me the best course of action. I don't know how many times I went home and talked about something, and she'd be the one who would tell me ever so easy how to take the next turn. Where a story should go or what was the most important headline." He smiled. "Did I ever tell you that she was the one who told me to hire you?"

"Thought you hired me on the spot, Doc. That's the way I remember it anyway."

"Opal told me to hire you the minute we knew Judy was leaving. She told me one day after you had waited on us at the lunch counter. 'There's your girl. That one. You can trust her in the thick of things. Trust her with anything,' she said. Isn't that something?"

If there was a mystery for us to solve, and there was, we somehow lost track of it that night walking by the water, looking at the shrimp boats tied up for the night. Maybe it was just what Doc and I needed. Time to put all that other business out of mind, to talk some about Opal. Then we just stood there, loving how the water met the sky. After a while Doc walked me to Miss Perry's on his way home. We stood at the gate and looked at the house.

"What if he's in there wanting me to remember him? I don't know him, Doc. Believe me, I'd remember that face."

"You're just looking at the wrong side of him." He pointed to his chest. "Look on the inside, Mercy. That's where you'll find him."

"That crazy book has you talking in riddles too."

I left him at the gate and walked up onto the porch. I opened the door as quietly as I could; I wasn't in the mood to make conversation with anyone. Miss Perry had her back to me, doing her needlepoint and listening to the radio, but as soon as I put one foot on the stairs, Miss Perry called out, "You missed your dinner."

I took a backward step and turned in her direction. "Sorry, Doc and I had a working dinner."

"Is that so?"

"Yes ma'am.'

"You tell Doc I'd love to have him over for dinner sometime soon, would you?"

"Yes ma'am." I turned to go, determined to make it up the stairs, but before I knew it, she was calling out for me again.

"Strangest thing. I haven't seen hide nor hair of our Mr. Quincy today. Seems he missed his dinner too." She dropped her needlepoint to her lap. "Was he with you at dinner?"

"No, Miss Perry. He was at the office earlier. I haven't seen him since then."

"Strangest thing," she said again and picked her needlepoint back up.

"Well, good night," I said and then practically ran up those stairs to my room. I immediately went to the window—Miss Perry had obviously had someone replace the screen—but I tugged on it till it loosened, and I gently laid it outside the window. Then I sat on my ledge inside the magnolia. Times like this it was just like a tree house, and I needed that moment right now. Some night air and the safety of my own room. A sense of belonging.

I waited until I was absolutely certain Miss Perry had turned off the radio and gone to bed. The house was quiet. I put on my robe and made my way quietly to the kitchen. It didn't matter the weather—my penchant for hot chocolate was strong. Strong enough to have me tiptoeing in the dark of the night. I had opened the refrigerator to take out the milk when the light fell across the room and highlighted a man sitting quietly at the kitchen dinette. I did the only thing possible. I clutched the jug tighter and prepared to throw it at him with all my might. I had my arm reared back to pitch when he started laughing.

"What's so funny?" I asked.

"No doubt about it, you are a Bittersweet girl."

"What makes you say such a thing?"

"Any other girl would have screamed and dropped that jug, not prepared to pitch it at me."

He took a bite of what looked like Miss Perry's leftover chicken casserole. He was still wearing his suit from earlier in the day and had a cold plate before him. It looked like he had come in late and Miss Perry had obliged him with a dinner. That was her habit and a kind one. If she knew I was working late, she'd make my plate for dinner and leave it covered on the little table.

"You make a habit of eating in the dark and scaring women without warning?"

"For one thing"—he pointed out to the backyard—"I love to look at her yard in the moonlight."

I nodded. It was like me sitting on my windowsill. "Care for some hot chocolate?"

"No thanks," he said, "but I would love a glass of that milk you're holding."

I silently poured the milk for him, got down the cocoa, and started stirring in the powder and the sugar. "I make the best hot chocolate in town. You just ask anyone." I stirred the milk and rattled my brain, searching for his face in every back street of Bay City. I stood right there and closed my eyes and hoped for a flash of recognition, anything at all, a face in a crowd at a ball game, someone passing me on the streets, any little old thing.

"I'm so glad she didn't cut down these old magnolia trees," he said. "I know they grow close to the house, but it wouldn't be the same without them."

And then of all things, a face came to mind. A face from a long, long time ago. A dirty, scratched-up, scrawny face. I dropped the spoon and turned around. There, sitting at that table, caught in nothing but the light of the little lamp, why, it wasn't John Quincy at all! I rushed to him and knelt down by his side before I'd thought of myself. He grinned at me hard, and when he did, I knew beyond a shadow of doubt. "John Thomas Taylor," I said, "you have come home."

"What took you so long to see me?"

"That's a crazy question." My milk was boiling over on the stove, and I ran to it. "Look here, you have me in such a fuss I am making a mess of everything." I turned to him with a hand on my hip. "Tommy, why didn't you tell me? From the minute I picked you up, right there and then. And before—why didn't you say something before on those phone calls with Doc, just letting him go on and on like that?" But the fact of the matter was, I was happier in that very moment than I had been maybe in all my life. "Tommy Taylor has come home!" I shouted it loud enough to wake Miss Perry, and I didn't care. "Do you hear me? He's come home!" He jumped up from the table and grabbed my arms softly so that I hushed and looked straight at him.

"Shh, you don't want to wake up everybody in this house." He dropped my arms, a quick and easy scolding. "Besides all that, I'm not sure I want everyone to know about, well, about everything. Not about me being here and not about that book. I did want you to know though. That part is true. And to be fair to you, Mercy, I didn't recognize you right off, either. Not really until you said your name and I looked again. You're all grown up."

"When I said my name! Why didn't you just say something plain like, 'Hiya, kid. It's me, back from the dead.' Do you know that all of Bittersweet was crazy worried about you? Search parties were sent out everywhere for you. You were just completely gone." I took my hot chocolate to the table, sat down, and took a sip. It was scalded. I didn't care. "Tommy,"—I reached across the table and touched the back of his hand—"your poor mother."

"She knew I was alive. She knew the truth from the beginning."

"She knew? Well, if you say she knew, she knew. I mean for goodness' sake, Tommy, she was at your funeral service, which of course didn't include you 'cause you were missing, and she cried like you were gone to be with Jesus in every sense of the word. I got to hand it to her—she really put on a good show."

"I imagine since I was gone for good in a way, it gave her license to cry."

I looked down at my cup. I thought the whole day had been strange up till now. But this took the cake. Tommy Taylor sitting in Miss Perry's kitchen. I studied his face, wondering if there was anything at all I could find of that poor Bittersweet boy. Anything I'd missed that I should have recognized right off the top.

"I saw my mother once in a while, but it was always on the sly from him—Daddy was no good for no one. I tried to get her to move away with me, but she'd have no part of leaving. I don't guess she'd have felt comfortable somewhere else. She promised never to tell a soul where I was."

"Well, she sure kept that promise, I'll tell you." There was so much I wanted to ask him. "Where did you go? Why did you not let us know you were alive?" I thought about what this meant and what kind of news it would be when it leaked out. Oh, it would travel from house to house as the crow flies. Nothing would slow it down. Everybody in Bittersweet Creek would know by sundown once it got started. "I don't think I can keep your secret. Now, I am really, really good at keeping secrets, but this one, it will be the test of all high tests. And from Aunt Ida, oh, I don't think so. Mama will be suspicious. But Aunt Ida, oh you know her, she's gonna get me. She will take one look and needle me till I turn blue."

"Listen to you talking like you are a good bus ride away from here. You have reverted to your native tongue."

"And what might that be, sir?" I could joke with him now. I could just be myself. Why, this was my very own Tommy Taylor of Bittersweet Creek. They could never keep us apart as kids. He'd even swim halfway across the creek and me the other half. When the drought hit us, we could walk across no deeper than our knees, the big sand bars of the creek bed rising to the top, and that amazed us so much we hoped it would never rain again. "When you went like you did,"—tears welled up in my eyes—"Tommy, I thought you were gone. Thought you were dead. Like the coyotes had eaten you up or some old swamp monster had taken you away. Every man in Bittersweet searched for you." I covered my trembling mouth. "Why didn't you tell me?"

He looked away from me, stared out into the moonlit magnolias. "Mercy, I'm not sure you would understand. It was as bad for me where we come from as it was good for you in other ways. I had a hard time of it growing up."

I took this news in quietly. I tried to let it settle along my heart, around the broken edges he'd left when I was fifteen. And I tried to think of a reason that he would resort to such a drastic lie. We had been the best of buddies. But then I had a sudden image of him and his daddy riding through those woods and his face as sullen as I'd ever seen it, and when his daddy looked out the window at me as they passed on the road, his eyes were so angry, they were pure black. Somewhere in that blackness was the answer, but I didn't need to push Tommy too fast.

This was enough amazing truth for one night.

"And now, here you are, alive and sitting in Miss Perry's kitchen, eating leftovers and scaring me in the dark."

"And almost getting my head busted open with the milk jug in the process, I might add."

"And, Tommy…"

"It might be better if you called me John. It'll make it easier for you eventually. I had never planned on coming back here at all. I wasn't prepared to see anybody. Doc found me and told me about this, this… I don't know, Mercy. What is it? You tell me what that thing is, and I'll be done with this game and get on with whatever kind of life I was having."

The thought of him leaving hurt. It actually hurt physically. My whole body tensed at the thought of him turning around and leaving. At the thought of me losing him again.

"Where were you when he found you?"

"Atlanta. Had been there six months."

And then, because he had been honest with me on two tiny things, I told him.

"We have a book in our possession that can reveal the maps of a man's life. Where he's been and maybe where he ought to go. I'm not sure about that part. I can tell you this much: it shows you more than you should know. It will show you a man's whole soul faster than you can blink an eye."

John, as I had to think of him now, sat adjusting to what I had told him. But me, well, just thinking about the book could put me in a place unlike anything I had ever experienced. Once you held it, once you touched it, even thinking of it would affect you. John Thomas Taylor, this new John Quincy, slowly rose from the table, put his empty plate into the sink, and then of all things, kissed me on the top of my head and said, "Good night, Mercy." Before I could say another word or a "wait a minute," he had left the kitchen, and I could hear his footsteps on the creaky floorboards of the stairway.

I was left sitting at the kitchen table, alone in the dark, staring out into the vast backyard with some of the greatest news I'd ever received in my life. And there wasn't a single person other than Doc I could tell it to.

EIGHTEEN

Morning came early the next day to Bay City. I hadn't fallen asleep until the sky was turning a smoky gray, the sun somewhere just below the horizon. But even then, when I did finally drift off, the dream would not let me sleep a few hours without showing up. The man in the dream had his back to me, and now I could see that he was in Bay City. A breeze was blowing, and he held something I couldn't see in his hands. Pages were dropping to his feet and being picked up in the breeze, blown away, and tumbling down the empty street. There was no other sign of life at all; nothing moved—not a car, not a person, not a leaf. Somewhere in that dream I was calling the man's name, but it eluded me every time.

I clasped the clock in my hand and tried my best to open my eyes, barely aware of why I was so sleepy until all of last night, the late-night kitchen part of it, came back to me in detail. I brushed the dream and the bedcovers off and rushed to get dressed. First, I needed to see John Quincy's face in the daylight hours and see if he was really who he said he was. What if he really was a trickster? Doc had said he was a con. What if he knew all about me and it had been some elaborate hoax to—what? What good would it serve him or anyone else? Well, never mind. I wasn't going to be played for a backwoods fool. Matter of fact, I should march downstairs in my bathrobe and confront him right in front of God and Miss Perry and anybody else within shouting distance. Why, it was a dirty, rotten game that he had known who I was for even a minute before telling me. To go on like that for days. There was no reason for it, was there? I sat down in the small chair by the desk, trying to wake up and think clearly. Or was there? Could he have a reason I didn't know about? Something he wasn't telling me? I softened a little just at the thought that the rightful John Thomas Taylor of Bittersweet might very well be alive and well and…and sitting downstairs at the breakfast table! Quicker than most mornings I managed to put on a simple white dress and rush into the dining room, fully expecting him to be there putting on his usual show.

The dining room was empty, but I could hear Miss Perry in the kitchen. I followed the sound and was a bit shocked at the sight of her. She was still in her bathrobe at this late hour. Not like her in the least bit. In seven years I had never seen her in such a state.

"I'm sorry." She glanced up at me, her face pale and waxen. "I'm a little under the weather this morning." She was stirring a pot on the stove. "Would oatmeal suit you?"

"Of course it would." I poked my head back around the corner of the dining room. There was no sign of our newcomer. "Would you like me to watch that for you?"

"You know,"—she stepped away from the stove—"I don't mind if you do. I think I'll just sit a moment."

She sat in the same chair as I had the night before. I moved to the stove and stirred the oats.

"Mercy, you should tie my apron on. You're going to get that white dress spotted before you know it, and you're looking so pretty for work today. Of course if you go near that printer, you'll have ink all over that." I did as she suggested. Pulled her apron down from the hook by the stove and tied it about my waist. I put two bowls down on the counter, got the cream out, and smiled at Miss Perry. She looked a little better sitting down, but having her in such a shape was a little worrisome.

"We have aprons at the paper. But I'll be careful. I'm not the printer, you know. Maybe if you just rest today. Is it a touch of the flu? Mama says those summertime flu bugs are the worst kind."

She waved her hand in the air and said, "It'll pass. Good chance it's just my age finally catching up with me."

I couldn't argue with her too much on that point. Miss Perry was forever old. She had been gently getting older, staying busy in her garden, growing her roses, azaleas, and jasmine, but time was time any way you looked at it. The years did stack up. I set her bowl down in front of her and offered her the sugar and cream. Then I took my oatmeal and sat beside her to keep her company.

"Seems to me someone might have had some company last night," she said while she spooned sugar in her bowl.

"What makes you think so?" I asked. She might be puny, but she wasn't dead.

"I know how to read the signs, young lady." She took a bite of oatmeal and gave me a wink. "Particularly when they are in my own kitchen sink."

I smiled at her. I wanted to rush out the door so fast to find that Tommy Taylor known as John Quincy and look him in the eye! But it would have to wait for just a few more minutes. One look at Miss Perry's pale face made me slow down my pace.

"It appears that your new guest has quite a love for your magnolia trees."

"Sounds like someone else I know. I also know you lifted that screen out of that window again. Mercy, one of these days you will fall right out and onto your head if you're not careful."

Oh, brother, did she have ears to hear! And it seemed the oatmeal was doing her enough good for me to ease up on worry. "Okay, now." I stood up and untied the apron, moved to the sink, and rinsed my bowl. "Doc is waiting on me, but you call me if you need anything."

"Might be someone else there waiting on you too, dear." She smiled, working her way into her matchmaking shoes.

"Why, Miss Perry, whoever do you mean?"

That got a little laugh out of her. She was still chuckling as I walked out the door.

"Doc?" I rushed into the paper, calling to him. "Doc?" I was laughing as I ran up the stairs, still calling. I had the news story of the day. I opened the door to his closed office. No one was there. The front door had been unlocked when I arrived. I had thought nothing of it. But now, Doc's office didn't look as though he had been in yet. Without hesitation, I walked to the file cabinet and reached for my key. I didn't want to wade into the mystery of those pages alone, but I wanted to know they were safe in their keep-ing. I pulled open the drawer, reached in the back...nothing! I searched again, running my hands under the file folders and then moving them completely. Empty.

Immediately I thought of our mysterious John Quincy. His story about being the missing Tommy Taylor. Surely it had been a lie. Surely the fact of the matter was that—oh, I should have seen this coming. I started down the stairs. I was halfway to the bottom when John Quincy walked through the door. I froze there, watching him. He looked up at me, standing there in the door. The downstairs was still dark, but the morning sun had been at his back when he walked in. And I knew when his face was caught in that shadow and light, the way that he looked up at me, there was the same expression of a boy from a lifetime ago, standing below an old magnolia, saying, "C'mon, Mercy, let's go fishing. You can't sit in a tree and read all blasted day." It was the slight tilt of the head that did it. Then I sat down on the stairs, and against all my better inclinations, as tough as I was, I started to cry.

"Tommy Taylor,"—I wiped my cheek with the back of my hand—"did you steal the book? Because it's gone missing, and if you did, I swear I'm gonna whip you solid."

He laughed and shook his head and closed the door. Then he slowly came to where I was on the steps and sat down next to me. He put his arm around my shoulders and said, "Little Mercy Land, I have never even had the privilege of seeing this so-called book, much less stealing it, but if I have to be whipped, I'd rather it came from you than anyone else."

Then I laughed. Apparently, he really was my Tommy Taylor,

the up-and-gone-missing-all-these-years John Thomas Taylor, who now for reasons I wasn't certain of yet had become the new John Quincy of parts unknown. And I would have to learn to meld the two of them together, to somehow recognize the boy in him that used to be and the man that he had become. I'd have to practice his name and keep it on the tip of my tongue so I didn't mess up and give him away. And I'd have to do it on the sly without help from Aunt Ida or Mama if I was supposed to be keeping yet another secret.

"Doc's secret book"—I thumbed over my shoulder—"is missing."

John lifted his arm from my shoulder and turned around, glancing upstairs. "And it was up there?"

I put my elbows on my knees, my chin in my hands. "This is really bad news. Very, very bad news."

He rested his elbows on his knees the same as me and said, "I see." We sat there until he shifted his gaze to me.

I wiped my face again, and I smoothed my dress out around me. "I'm sorry, but you should know—I didn't trust you. I didn't trust you from the moment you got here. I knew you were hiding something." I punched him on the shoulder. "I just didn't know what you were hiding was you!"

"And what about now? Do you trust me now?" Both of us looked like we were sitting back on the Bittersweet, whiling away a summer day, getting ready to vote between going fishing or looking for arrowheads.

I searched his eyes, and then I thought about my mama,

about how she said a lie was a lie, even if it was told to make the truth seem sweeter.

"Let me ask you this. Where were you this morning?"

"What does that have to do with trusting me?"

"You were missing. The book is missing. Just answer the question."

"Eating breakfast at Mozell's. There was no sign of Miss Perry in the kitchen this morning, no sign of you, so I thought I should make do on my own. Sausage biscuits and gravy. Did I pass?"

"No, not completely. I trusted that boy I used to know with everything in this whole world. But what's happened to you since then, what's become of you, I don't know." I shrugged my shoulders. "I want to trust you, that's for sure, because it would be so nice to be able to tell you…"

Then the door opened, and Doc walked in. He wasn't wearing his suit or his suspenders and looked more haggard than I'd seen him before. In unison we both stood to our feet.

"Good, I'm glad you're both here," he said, like we had been the ones missing.

"Doc!" I rushed down the stairs to his side, touched his arm. "Doc, the book is gone."

"It's safe, Mercy. Don't worry. Let me catch my breath a minute, will you? I'm feeling my age this morning."

I looked at his face, and for goodness' sake, he looked pale and pasty, like Miss Perry had. Maybe something was going around.

"Doc?"

"I'll be fine, fine. And the two of you, have you…officially met?" He looked from one of us to the other. I nodded my head.

"It's John Thomas Taylor, risen from the dead," I told him.

"Yes, it appears the Bittersweet boy is back." He looked at the stairs and sighed. "Why don't you get us some coffee and a bit of cake if there's any left, and we'll begin our story right there in the kitchen, where all good stories should start, don't you think?"

We followed him into the kitchen, where I made coffee, and we crowded around the little table as Doc sat down like an old man, caught his breath, and prepared to tell his story.

NINETEEN

I had planned a quiet evening of taking Harry out for her walk, then reading for a while. The business of the book, of trying to tell you about the book, John, has taken a toll on me. All of it being more of the things that a logical man cannot put into order. But I have been trying."

I poured coffee into three cups and for the second time that morning set the sugar and the creamer on the table. He kept talking as I sliced Miss Perry's pound cake she kept baking for us and put a small plate in the center of the table. There was no room for formalities. We would just have to share. Then I took my seat. We were crowded, the three of us, but it made no nevermind. John and I were seated close together, and Doc had put his long legs out in front of him, leaning back in the little chair as best he could. He stirred cream into his coffee, took a sip, and continued.

"Just as Harriet and I were turning the corner last night, making our nightly circle around the block, I heard footsteps. I was being followed again. Then as rational a man as I may be—not given, I believe, to misplaced fears and wild imaginings—I was overcome with a foreboding that a lot more was in danger. It was a feeling that crawled up my spine like nothing I ever remember and one I do not wish to repeat. I walked along a little further and paused, and with the pause the footsteps behind me would stop altogether. I began to hurry Harriet along. Only instead of hurrying her home, I hurried her toward the office. Had I thought about it more clearly, I would have taken her home and gotten the car. Harriet has those short, stubby little legs and those long ears, and neither one makes for quick travel. She tried her best to keep up with me, but I was so caught up, so suddenly desperate, that I picked her up and began to walk faster and faster to the corner."

"You didn't!" I knew that running was okay for Doc, but carrying Harry? I had pulled her along on her leash before, and she was solid dog. Harry was well fed. Harry was a bit paunchy.

"More than that, the closer I was to the office, it seemed the more compelled I was to run. Before long I was running with her as hard as I could. When I arrived, I was so winded that I almost dropped poor Harry, but I managed to fumble for the keys, open the door, and at least get us inside, where we both collapsed." He picked up a slice of the pound cake and took a bite. "She is no worse, but I have to say I feel a little shaken by the evening still. Although Miss Perry's pound cake does help the recovery process."

"Please, Doc—last night!"

"Yes, yes, I'm moving on." In another bite the cake was gone. "So there I was, collapsed on the floor, when I thought I heard a noise from upstairs. *Thought,* mind you, but I couldn't be certain. What I was certain of, however, were the footsteps I had heard on the sidewalk, and then they stopped just outside the office door. Then I thought—mind you, again I said *thought*—I heard the noise upstairs again. A slight clicking it was. I was trapped between the shadow on the street and that sound, but I knew I had to manage to get to the book to see if it was safe. It had been my first and foremost concern. Instead of walking to the stairs and going up them the natural way, I crawled like a child to the first step, making certain that I kept my head low. I don't understand why this morning, but last night, in that moment, I felt so vulnerable. Marie's was lit up in neon across the street, and the red glow fell against the window shades, and all of it—the footsteps and the noise and the light—combined with the sound of my own exhausted heart to make me even more fearful. The thing is, I am in no way a fearful man. I have seen firsthand the results of fear of every kind and what it has made of itself from the stories I've covered these many years. Fear has a nasty way of working man's nature raw to the bone, but it has been my blessing over all these years not to know that kind of fear. That is, until last night. Perhaps an unwarranted fear. I have nothing to show for it. I must say, I have protected the book. Maybe my efforts were worth something after all.

"Never mind. The point is, I crawled up the first few steps, crouching low like a baby. Then I finally stood and grasped the banister with all my might. The first thing I did upon reaching the top of the stairway was to quickly reach for the light switch. I flipped it and was at once so startled by the light that I jumped. The file cabinet had been opened and the drawer pulled slightly out. I pulled it open wide, and there in the back, in its usual place, was the book, just as it has been for these many months. It was as if a panic of strange dimension had ensnared me. I grabbed the box.

"I closed the file cabinet and carefully made my way down the stairs where Harry had decided of her own accord to wait for me. Like me"—he looked at John pointedly now, as I knew Harry's habits well—"she has suffered the stairs, and she's no more fond of them than I am."

"Go on, Doc, with your story."

"Where was I? Oh—Harry was waiting for me there at the foot of the stairs. I knelt and grabbed her leash with one hand as I carefully peered out the blinds, searching up and down the street. When I saw no one, I rushed out the door, barely stopping to close it. Harry had to practically fly, with her little paws barely touching the pavement as I rushed her home, where I sat up then with the book the rest of the night, holding it there in my lap in the living room."

"Were you followed then? On the way back?" This was the first time John had spoken, but he had a point. "Most likely someone was still waiting and watching for you to leave the building. Even if he stayed hidden."

"I didn't hear or see anyone on my way home, but with the sound of my heavy breathing and Harry's paws trying to keep up, I doubt I would have heard an entire marching band, much less someone at least attempting stealth."

It occurred to me that all of this must have been taking place while John and I sat at the kitchen table late last night, talking and watching the magnolias. That gave me a little comfort. He couldn't have been the one following Doc, because he was with me. I glanced over at him, however, and thought of the fact that someone had been in the office. But if someone had been here, wouldn't he have taken the book? Who but the three of us knew of the book's existence? Doc was still talking, and I turned my attention back to him and the story. I touched the key beneath my dress, thinking what little good it had been.

"Occasionally I would doze, sitting straight up in my chair, but then I'd wake with a start and grasp the book tighter until I finally fell asleep again. In the long run I believe that Harriet seems to have survived the ordeal much better than I have."

"Poor, sweet Harry." Miss Perry wouldn't allow me to have a pet because she said if I had one, then anyone could have one and she would be overrun with furry beasts. I couldn't argue the point, but it had endeared Harry to me even more. "But the book, Doc? Where is the book now?" As soon as I asked, I was sorry I had. For some reason I still didn't want this John Quincy to know about its location yet. But all that was about to change. He was obviously here, alive and well and in Bay City, living in Miss Perry's just like I was, and the days of his life were tied to the book just like mine. That reason was still murky water to me.

"Yes, exactly where is this book?" With the way that John Quincy asked, with the tone of his voice, an odd cold ran through me. I looked at him then, and he caught my expression, knowing full well what it meant. His blue eyes looked cold then as well. Not at all like the warm smile of my backwoods buddy. Not at all like the man who had kissed my hair and left me sitting last night in the kitchen. I glanced at Doc, wondering if he saw the same thing I did.

"In due time, due time." Doc stood up, put his hands to his waist, and leaned back. "What's most important is to take care of the immediate business at hand. And that is for this old man to carry himself home for a nap. This confounded, convoluted situation will have to wait until I have slept for twenty years, or until two o'clock—whichever comes first." He had left the kitchen and was already at my desk as I shrugged my shoulders, both perplexed at his nonchalant attitude and relieved that he hadn't brought out the book right then and there. Doc reappeared in the doorway as I was putting our cups in the sink. "Why don't the two of you take a ride through the countryside? The fresh air might do you some good." And then the front door opened and closed behind him.

I didn't know what to say. For a moment my feelings were so confused—from the elation I had felt all night to the feeling I had right now. John still sat at the table, and I felt his eyes on me.

"You're right not to trust me." He toyed with his coffee cup in front of him, turning the cup in slow circles on the table. "I've got nine lives, you know."

Was it a true confession or a method to throw me off guard?

"I don't know about nine, but I can certainly count two. But why can't I trust you, John Thomas Taylor? You of all people? I used to trust you with my eyes closed. I'd jump right out of those magnolia trees without even telling you, and you'd catch me. I don't know why I trusted you so hard and true then, but I did. So why in the world would I not trust you now?"

Either the question or the comment had caught him off guard. And maybe because of it, he answered honestly.

"Because there are complications."

We looked at each other across that small kitchen, and it could have been some old gunfight showdown at the movies. I could tell now, just like I could this morning when he walked in, the moment I saw him with that light spilling over his shoulder, that at one time he was the boy I knew. But I also had no doubt that what he was telling me now held a large portion of the truth, whether I liked it or not.

"Go on," I said. "That's no way to leave a girl hanging."

This time he looked away for a moment over my shoulder, to the kitchen window. "I'm not the man that Doc thinks I am. I'm not the man you wish I was, Mercy."

Suddenly I missed Aunt Ida terribly. I missed her no-nonsense and the certainty that she was the same and would never change, unlike this ghost from a past that had washed away when I was just a girl. I missed Mama's soft voice and that gentle touch of hers and Daddy's sitting like a rock in his chair in that little house. I was overcome with homesickness that didn't have any place in Bay City. It was my home. I loved it for good and forever. But I missed my yesterdays and what that felt like all wrapped around me. The constant, same old comfort of those woods and my people. This Bay City business, this confounded situation, as Doc called it, had worn me out as well.

"I'm going home, John Thomas Taylor Quincy, stranger and liar, man with nine lives. I guess if you are willing, you can come along to Bittersweet Creek, but don't expect a lot of conversation out of me, because I am not in the mood."

He smiled then like I had just offered him a ride to the moon.

TWENTY

Aunt Ida poured iced tea into three glasses, and we took them out to the porch. I was already regretting having invited John Quincy along. I couldn't tell her who he was, only that he was Doc's new man, and then I couldn't even think of the word for that, so I just said, "the man that Doc brought in on the train." She seemed to accept this without much comment, just a good glance and a nod of her head. I was having a harder time than I expected. The secrets I kept were getting thick on my tongue, desiring to be told. I wanted to throw myself at Ida's feet, to hug her knotty knees, to tell her everything I knew, what I suspected, and what I didn't know about at all. But it wasn't the time, so I put on a fake smile that made me feel mean.

Besides that, I wanted her to myself. I wanted to come throw myself on the little bed that belonged to me. I wanted to lament to Aunt Ida even if I couldn't see which way was up or tell her a word about any of it. At least I could let out the misery part, and she could soothe me or tell me to straighten up. Right now either one would have been good medicine; we were having iced tea with John, who was rightly Tommy Taylor from the low side of

Bittersweet Creek, sitting on her little porch, making small talk so nice. It made me so mad I wanted to spit.

The new John Quincy of Bay City talked about how his life had been in Atlanta, what big city living was all about, and Ida just sat there taking it in, nice as you please. He talked about it like he had lived there ten years. Oh, what a dog and pony show he put on. The more he talked, the madder I got. I could see now what Doc meant by a flimflam man. A con indeed he was. I looked real close at Aunt Ida to see if she had recognized a single bone in him, if she saw the ghost of the boy he used to be, but if she did, she didn't let on. It wasn't noticeable the least bit with the looks of him and that starched shirt. He had rolled the cuffs up and sat like a gentleman. He had actually pinched his trousers to not wrinkle them as he sat down. He still had on those shiny black shoes he always wore. I wanted back that boy who had been my buddy; but it looked like those days were good and gone.

I had to content myself with listening as Ida tested John Quincy on other affairs of the world. She was deeply interested in what was going on outside our little community, but that he would know about it all as well, even though he had been living in Atlanta, surprised me. They covered the president's latest fireside chat, and both of them agreed that what was taking place overseas looked like trouble. Ida asked him if he saw politics in his future, and he said he didn't believe so. I had to say he was patient with her, kind even, and then it occurred to me for truly the first time that he had also known Ida all of his life. Maybe that part of him really was contented to be here and enjoying his visit with an old, familiar face in spite of the fact that she didn't know him from any other stranger on the street. Aunt Ida seemed to be smoothly taken with everything John Quincy said. She stood smiling and waving as I drove away.

Daddy was another story.

I had driven straight to Aunt Ida's, but there wasn't a single chance today of me getting out of Bittersweet Creek without stopping by to see Mama and Daddy. Chances were, they had been watching at the window as I drove by. The sound of a car on the creek road brought folks to their windows and porches to see who might be going somewhere or getting a visit. It was the sound of life out there in the world, and no one wanted to miss a single little piece of it passing by their door.

It was dinnertime when we arrived, and Mama had chicken and dumplings on the stove, one of my favorites. She added plates at the table and invited us to sit down. Daddy bowed his head and asked the grace, and when I looked up, he was staring straight at John Quincy like he had been watching him the whole time. He wasn't even closing his eyes like he had taught me to do. Then he looked at me, but I couldn't read his eyes. Maybe it was just because I had brought a man home to visit. Maybe it was because he was a certain kind of man with his turned-up cuffs and his shiny shoes. Or maybe Daddy saw something else right away. Something even I had not seen.

Mama was another story. She was so happy to have us in the house and at the table it could have been Christmas morning. She was offering one more spoon of dumplings, one more piece of pie, a little more of this and that until her face was flushed from all her up and down, up and down. She had her girl with this handsome man at her table, which gave her a crazy hope that a wedding might be just around the corner. That was enough for her.

On the drive home we were both quiet until we reached the bridge that crossed the creek, and John said, "Stop the car, would you?" I started to say no to him, to say the middle of the bridge wasn't the best place for stopping, but the fact was, traffic was slim. I put it in park and left it running. He leaned way out his window, looking at the water. "You know how many hours we spent down there?"

"All our lives," I answered. I was looking at the water on the opposite side. The cypress trees along the edge, the thick bay magnolias and pine trees. "I have to say I've never seen a place with so many wonders. Not really. Not even Bay City. It's a different kind of a wonder but not like this."

He pulled his head back in, leaned it against the seat as he looked at me. "You're a wonder, Mercy."

I looked at him for a minute and had an overpowering urge to kiss him. To just lean across the seat and kiss him like nobody's business. Not the boy I had run the creek with but the man-sized version of him that sat in my car. The one who had managed a lively conversation with Ida and a gracious dinner with Mama and Daddy in spite of Daddy's attitude. The one who was oh so collected and seemed to be laying it on thick. Instead of acting on that impulse, I looked in the rearview mirror, put on my sunglasses, and said, "That I am."

TWENTY-ONE

It was late afternoon by the time we left Bittersweet. We had the windows rolled down, and the air started getting cooler. You could tell evening was coming on. Doc was nowhere to be found when we returned. He wasn't at the office, and when we drove past his house, his car wasn't there. Maybe he was just out to eat, but I found it a bit disconcerting not knowing. It occurred to me that I had known where Doc was most minutes of the day as long as I'd worked for him. We drove the perimeters of Bay City, down to the water, along the pier, by Mozell's in case he'd driven over for dinner. We passed up and down Third Street a few times and by the office again. There was still no sign of him anywhere. That meant there was no sign of the book.

The only thing left for the time being was to go back to the boardinghouse and wait for word from Doc or morning, whichever came first. The idea of going an entire night without knowing that Doc was okay, considering how he had been early that morning, considering that I hadn't seen the book since he'd moved it, was even more disturbing.

The house was dark when we arrived, and there was no sign of anyone. Not grumpy Sam or Roger or Miss Perry. And there was no indication that dinner was in the making. We stood in the dark foyer, taking in the quiet, and then wandered through the kitchen. All the lights were off. I walked down the hallway on the first floor and knocked on the first bedroom door. "Miss Perry? Are you in there? Are you all right?" There was no sound from behind the door. I tried the doorknob. It was locked, but that was an old habit from having boarders; she locked the bedroom door with her key when she left.

I ventured two doors down and knocked on Sam Ivy's door. "Sam? Sam? Are you in there? Sam?" The door jerked open, and there he stood, wild-eyed, bushy haired, and meaner than a rattlesnake.

"Looking for somebody, are you?"

"Sorry, Sam. I was worried about Miss Perry. She was sick this morning, and she's not in her room."

Sam glanced over my shoulder at John, who stood silently behind me. "What you looking at, mister?"

"Oh, Sam, you know this is John Quincy, the new man." He looked at John Quincy, still not satisfied. "Doc's new man," I stressed. "You've met him at breakfast."

"Oh, that's the one, is he? Well"—he eyed him up and down—"he still don't look like much to me, but I reckon he'll do. He sure don't look like no Doc Philips, I can tell you that much."

"About Miss Perry—do you know how she is? Where she is?"

"Haven't seen her all day, and the kitchen's dark. Had cold oatmeal for breakfast and not a bite all day. Went in for dinner a little while ago and not even the smell of smoke. Looks like I'll have to eat a cold sandwich for dinner if I'm able to make it."

He was fishing for me to make him something, but I wasn't biting. Sam was more than able to do anything for himself. He was just contrary about doing it.

"Well, all right then, Sam. If you hear Miss Perry come in, tell her I asked about her, will you?"

"By the way, I didn't like today's news. Not none of it. Worst newspaper you ever printed." He closed the door.

I stood there looking down at my shoes. Sam was a grouch rain or shine and every day of the week, but he was right. I wasn't even sure what Doc and I had managed to put together for the paper. We might be a small paper in a small city, but we'd always taken such pride in the *Banner*. I didn't want that marvelous, magnetic book to pull us so far into other lives that we kept losing pieces of our own.

"Looks like it's just the two of us." John's voice was all honey, or maybe I imagined it that way. "Why don't we take a walk, and I'll buy you dinner? My treat."

"I'll tell you why." I walked down the hall, into the living room, and turned on the lamp next to the sofa. "Because you, sir, are a big fat liar. You've been one all day long. I don't know how you can just sit there with Aunt Ida and with Mama and Daddy and not let on to them who you are. I couldn't do it. I just couldn't do it." I almost threw myself onto the sofa. "But you know what? I did do it. I lied all day for you, and that's not who I am."

"I know it's not." He said it so sincerely I almost believed him. Almost.

"And Doc's missing, the book's missing, and I need to be in the company of someone I can trust."

He came and sat down next to me, reached for my hand, and held it in both of his. Part of me wanted to jerk it away, to shove it in my dress pocket out of reach. Another part of me had wanted to touch him all day. That was the part that won out.

"The book, Mercy." His hand tightened a little on mine. "Tell me again about the book."

Oh, there it was again, the sudden feeling that something wasn't right with him, that he knew more than he was telling or that his intentions were not honorable. Not worthy of—what? Doc's good faith in bringing him here, maybe. I pulled my hand away then and shoved both of them into my pockets for safekeeping.

"It's not for me to tell you about it. I've told you enough already." I stood up and walked to the window, looking up and down the street in hopes of seeing a familiar car pulling into the driveway. "That's Doc's business. And he'll take care of it when he comes back."

Even as I said it, something rose up in me that made me think Doc was in trouble. I didn't know what kind, but I knew it was up to me to find him, to make it possible for him to finish what he had started.

I looked at John Quincy and wondered about him in the worst way. Then I made a decision. It fell as firmly into my heart as anything I've ever known, and I knew it was the right one. I wasn't going to lie for him anymore. John Quincy needed to come clean about who he was. With the folks of Bittersweet and maybe with himself. But how he did it and when he did it was up to him. Until he did, I wasn't going to trust him farther than I could see him. Because the truth and my trust were wrapped together now like a single coin. And until I could trust him, I was going to keep him right where I knew what he was up to.

"Dinner sounds lovely, Mr. Quincy. Just let me freshen up, and then maybe you can tell me all about what you've been up to for the past twelve years." The look in his eyes was not exactly warm.

DOC'S JOURNAL

Someone has been following me again. I keep the book hidden, and I keep moving it. I'm becoming a different kind of man in the process. For one thing, the fear creeps back in. My confidence has always been such a strength. And there Mercy is, the key about her neck for safekeeping, but how can she protect anything such as this? Why did I ever believe her keeping the key would be the answer? Something about her being from Bittersweet Creek compelled me. Something about the way she had said she was Bittersweet through and through, and I thought, *Aha, a girl to be trusted.* Opal, bless her soul, said the same. "That one you can trust," she told me, and I told Mercy that. I believed her. And when I saw Mercy's story in that book, I could see why. It was full of light, full of miracles—and then that's all I could remember when I turned a page.

I found him and called him, this John Quincy, into our midst. I will have to look him in the eye and level. He thinks I don't see through him, but I do. I see through him because I know who he is and what he's capable of. Something has gotten hold of him. Oh yes, I can feel it. To think his showing up was on my account. I might as well have given him a free pass to take the book, to do with it as he saw fit. That's where the problem arises. My concern is that his doing as he sees fit might be the end of all of us. Or that he will devise a way to bend time and circumstance to suit his need. Which really isn't very different from what I intend.

I worry about it being taken by a force that would somehow use it against the entire city. And that in the process innocent lives would be altered into...nothing. Perhaps I can still fix this. Even now, I know what's stirring in his blood—something hateful, something criminal. Too many late nights in jailhouses, too many back-of-the-room courtroom dramas. I know the spirit that has taken him. The darkness that comes out of those corners of his soul and then recedes again. It may be hidden from much of the world, but it's not hidden from me. And it's not hidden in the book. I've seen him there. His name, his face, rising and falling before me. The roads he might have taken, the ones washed out forever. Maybe there's still a way; maybe there's still time for him to change. Or if not to change, then to begin again.

TWENTY-TWO

We walked out the front gate and turned left. The evening was warm, but a breeze coming from across the bay felt so good we decided to walk. John—and it made it easier on me to call him that, to let Tommy slip back to being a memory— John suggested Italian, so we walked toward the only place in town that served Italian food: Marie's. The fact that it was right across the street from the paper, that we would be able to see if Doc pulled up or if suddenly a light came on upstairs in his office, was probably no small reason for the suggestion. John was as eager as I was to know Doc's whereabouts—but I felt like it was for other reasons.

Inside, the restaurant was beautiful. The atmosphere changed from midday, when Marie's hurried through lunches, and the tables were bare Formica that could be wiped down in a moment. Now it had white tablecloths and flickering candles. Under other circumstances I would have said it was romantic. Okay, it was romantic. From the moment we entered, they gave us the star treatment. After all, I was Doc's girl.

After John's initial reaction to my question of where he'd been, I didn't expect to get much out of him. But now he seemed to have warmed to the idea of sharing stories of his life in the big city of Atlanta, even if it had only been a few months. He told me that his apartment was within walking distance of Peachtree Street and that Bay City seemed in some ways almost as small as Bittersweet by comparison.

"I find that hard to believe," I said while taking a bite of the eggplant parmesan. "We have big-city food and cars, and, look, we even wear shoes." I wasn't going to be outdone by him. He was putting on a bit of show, entertaining me, trying to fit the part of who I thought he was now, but I knew he had practiced for whatever quick trick he was pulling. And I did know he was performing for me. I excused myself for a moment to go to the powder room, but it was the kitchen door that I entered.

Mama Marie was in the kitchen and so were her son, her two daughters, and a young boy I didn't recognize.

"Mercy!" She was always happy to see me in the kitchen or outside the door. "Is everything all right?" She wiped her hands on her apron and left the stove to give me a hug. "Where is Doc tonight? He no come with you?"

"That's what I was wondering. Have you seen him around today?"

"Not today. Not since the last time." She turned and spoke rapidly in Italian to her family. I heard her say Doc's name in the middle of a stream of other words I didn't recognize. Then a chorus of "Yes, Mama's" rippled across the kitchen. "I'm sorry, Mercy. Nobody has seen him."

I thanked her as she said, "You have to eat the tiramisu. I

make a special one for you." Then she winked at me. "And your friend? He is special? Maybe new sweetheart for you?"

"No, Marie, no sweetheart." I shook my head. "He's here to work for Doc. To help him." Which, even as I said it, seemed to be absurd. He was a hindrance and a distraction in every way, is what he was.

"Maybe he is a sweetheart later. After work is finished."

I smiled at her and made my way out of the kitchen and back to the table. And there he was, sitting and waiting on me, checkered tablecloth, candles flickering, watching me with an interest that seemed to be more than a little friendly, more than professional. I hated the way my heart jumped when I saw him. He stood up as I approached the table, pulled my chair out for me, and we resumed eating.

Later we had the tiramisu while we talked about music. Anyone watching or listening from a nearby table would have thought we were just two ordinary people out on a date. But nothing could have been further from the truth.

Then John did something that wasn't the least bit fair by asking me if I remembered the day we found the arrowheads.

Should I have clamped down on him? Refused to answer at all? Forced him to be one person or the other?

The question made me remember him as he used to be. Searching for anything along the creek was one of our favorite pastimes, but that day was our bonanza. We sometimes found an arrowhead or two, and we'd even discovered some broken clay pieces that might have been a pot. On rare occasions we found a

bone but nothing we could swear had been from an ancient burial ground. But this day we had found two perfectly shaped, preserved arrowheads. Not in separate places, one here and one
scattered over there. We found them side by side, as if someone
had arranged them there long ago. We sat down and considered
them. We made up stories about how they had been preserved
in such a fashion and why. Then we did the only fair thing—we
divided them. One apiece. That had been our last big discovery
before he had gone missing. Now this John Quincy was rolling
out Tommy Taylor stories. But why?

It reminded me of Doc's old philosophy of surprising people in the interview. Asking a question of them that they weren't
expecting.

"I still have mine," I said. "Where's yours?"

He looked away. "Lost, unfortunately." Then he looked back
at me with what appeared a whole lot like desire if I hadn't known
better. "Just like a lot of other things in my life."

I would have challenged him to name exactly what those
things were, but just then a light went on in Doc's office upstairs.
We stood up in unison, but I grabbed my purse and was out the
door without a word, leaving John to pay the bill. I waited for
two cars to pass, looking up frequently as I crossed the street. No
sign of Doc at the window, but it was unmistakable: his light was
on. I ran to the door and reached to open it, but it was locked. I
searched my purse for my keys, scrabbling through the bottom of
the bag, but they weren't there. I knocked on the door, no, banged
on it, yelling, "Doc!" but there was no sound of footsteps on the
stairs. I tried to peer through the blinds, but they were closed tight.

John Quincy came around the corner just as I was dumping my bag upside down in one last feeble attempt to locate the keys. John tried the door as I searched past a brush, powder compact, lipstick, loose change, my billfold. "It's locked. You're wasting your time."

He knelt down to help me pick up the loose change. "Has he ever done this before?" he asked. "Gone missing, I mean?"

"Oh, not Doc. You're the one famous for that."

As I stood up, I realized that wasn't like me. "I'm sorry." I snapped the bag shut as the light upstairs suddenly went out. "That was a nasty thing to say." It had been traumatic, it was a part of my history, but that was the point—it was history, and I had to let it go. "Maybe we should just stand here. He has to come out sometime."

We stood for what seemed like an eternity, awkwardly shuffling back and forth, but still no sound of any kind and no Doc Philips.

John laid a hand on my shoulder. "Mercy, listen. There's something you should know. What happened a long time ago? My being gone, suddenly, without explanation—it looked like there wasn't a reason. But there was." His hand was warm on my shoulder. I reached up to brush it away, but when my fingers touched his, I just rested them on the top of his hand. Then he pulled me in next to him and was hugging me, standing right there on the sidewalk, my head on his chest, both his arms wrapped around me, and for just a moment I wasn't thinking about whether or not he was Tommy Taylor or John Quincy or why he was really in Bay City.

For a moment, it was just a lovely summer evening along the bay.

Then we heard the door unlock. The embrace came abruptly to an end as we looked up. Miss Perry stepped through the door. She jumped back slightly at the sight of us. "Oh, dear," she said, "you startled me. For just a moment I didn't recognize you." Then she turned and locked the door with a key as if she did it every day. "Okay, that's done, and now I'll just be running back home." She seemed well at this point, no sign of the morning's pale, weak old woman. Then she actually turned to go.

"Miss Perry, what are you doing here? How did you get a key, and where's Doc?" I always seemed to be the one asking all the questions. Miss Perry looked up and down the street as if searching for something.

"I think it would be better if we moved off the streets, don't you?" She pointed to her car across the street. I hadn't even noticed it I had been so keen on looking for Doc. "Why don't we all take a little ride, shall we?"

Miss Perry was wearing her suit, gloves, hat, and heels. She looked like she had been at a meeting of the needlepoint society, not "simply running a tiny little errand for Doc," as she said. Which I found so confusing that I sat quietly, trying to listen. "Apparently, Mercy, you and Mr. Quincy were out of town when Doc needed a favor. Oh, by the way, hand this key back to him when you see him." She took the key out of her jacket pocket and passed it to me.

"But why wouldn't Doc have just gone up to his office himself?"

"Well, I didn't ask him any particulars, Mercy. I'm sure he had his reasons, or he wouldn't have asked me in the first place."

"You've certainly turned the corner from this morning. It's good to see you doing so much better," and then almost under my breath, I added, "in such a very short amount of time."

"Oh, never underestimate the power of a good nap to set things straight again." Miss Perry drove back to the boardinghouse and parked the car in the back. We got out of the car and said good night to her on the porch, as she made it rather clear that she wouldn't be discussing her late-night errand with us in any way. I couldn't totally let her get away with that.

"Sam's looking for you," I called after her. "Something about you not having dinner ready."

"Good night, Mercy, Mr. Quincy." She nodded as she said it with a voice sweeter than usual. "And you might like to know that Doc is at home." Then she closed the door as if we didn't live there so that we were left standing in the dark. We could hear her humming as she walked away, and I assumed she went straight to her room to take off her hat and gloves.

"Now what?" Sometimes his voice was all honey. Other times it was just that boy in the woods, shooting his slingshot at whatever dared to move and saying, "Now what? What's next? What're we going to do?" It was the voice that I had heard, ghostly and moving against my ear as I had sat on the porch in the evenings and the Bittersweet blues fell across my shoulder. I didn't know what to do next, so I sat down on the porch swing to try to con-template things.

"Good question."

"Seems that Doc is alive and well."

"Well, alive anyway."

He came and sat next to me in the swing. "And that Miss Perry is in much better spirits."

"I'll say."

"And that I was called to Bay City and still don't know why."

Then we rocked, and I didn't comment for a while. Then I tossed him a question. "What exactly did Doc tell you when you spoke?"

He finally spoke up. "I don't think I'm at liberty to tell you about that."

"It looks like we are at a standstill. I don't know why you went away without saying good-bye and let everybody go on thinking you were dead for all those years."

"Not everyone."

"Everyone but your mama."

"She wasn't the only one who knew."

"Who, then? All of Bittersweet believed it was so."

He looked at me, and in that moment, eye to eye, I could see his very soul. It was a strange thing. Yes, there was something shift-ing in him, something fighting. One minute he was that old tree climber, the next—I didn't know him.

"People had to help me get away. You know some of the people."

"People I know? Like who?"

"Like Doc Philips, for one."

I still wasn't following what he was saying. But what I did know, sitting under that porch light, was that every word he was telling me at the moment was the truth.

"He always knew."

"Doc? My Doc?" I stood up and stepped back from him, trying to understand.

"They were only trying to help me, Mercy. They didn't mean for it to have to be a secret. That night they were just doing what they could to help me."

"They? Who else was there?"

He stepped forward. The shadow and light of the moon through the trees caught him and then caught him again and released him with every breeze. He was a man of light and shadow. John put his hands on my shoulders.

"Your father, Mercy. He helped too. He was the one who drove the car, who carried me out of Bittersweet."

There are moments when we remember the details. The sound of the moth's wings beating against the porch light, the crickets in the nearby grass, the dog barking in the night…and the sound of a deep and abiding trust being shattered. My broken trust of Doc was like the sound of footsteps on ice, like the soft crystal cracking just prior to giving way to the freezing waters.

TWENTY-THREE

Harry was baying at the door at my banging. A woeful sound, and it matched my mood. I yelled, "Get up, Doc!" I had left John Quincy standing on Miss Perry's porch and saying, "Wait, I can explain," but I didn't want to hear his explanations.

All this time he had known. Here, for years, I had taken care of his mail, his plants, his dog, his life, and now he had roped me into that…that book of his without asking my opinion, thank you very much. And all this time he had known who he was. He knew!

"Doc! I swear I'll break a window!"

The door opened, and he stood there as rumpled as he typically was these days. I didn't care anymore. I barged in before giving him a chance to invite me.

"Are you alone?" he asked.

"You knew who he was when you found him. You've known all along."

"I have." He motioned to the living room, where there was little room. Obviously he was in need of a maid. Papers were scattered everywhere, and I had to push some aside to sit.

"Here, here," he said. "Careful now." He gathered the papers into a neat pile, searched for a clear spot to put them, but found none. He ended up standing before me, holding the stack. The desk was covered, the floor was covered, the sofa was covered, and there were papers on the small chair, papers on the footstool. The only clear spot was Doc's chair, which I suppose he had been sitting in when I arrived. The place was so shocking, so cluttered, I was distracted from how mad I was.

"What's going on here?"

"I've been working on something."

He still stood before me, arms full of papers, looking like a schoolboy caught with the test answers.

I eyed him suspiciously. Doc Philips had possessed all the trust that I could give a person. Now I took it back.

"Do you know what I know?"

"Don't know."

"I know that you helped John Quincy escape when he was sixteen, and he just told me it was you who got him sent to a school for boys for his *safety*. A school for boys?" I was so mad I wanted to stand and pace the floor, but there was absolutely no room to pace. Every inch was covered in paper. "And you never revealed this to me, the one who has been your blind, faithful go-to girl all these years?" Harry came over and nuzzled my hand with her cold nose. I pushed her away. I didn't want anything making me feel warm and cuddly. She flopped down with a sigh at my feet when I ignored her.

"I tried to tell you, Mercy—remember? I tried to tell you who he was, and I couldn't."

"You tried way too late. Do you know how worried I was

about you today? That I was thinking I had to save you? Then I catch Miss Perry in your office—Miss Perry, of all people, running an errand for you, she said."

"She did run an errand for me. I felt it was safer that way than me going back to the *Banner* today."

"Where have you been all day?"

"Right here. Hiding out right here."

"I called. I came looking for you."

"But it's not just you now, see. It's him too. The him that I brought here, and I have to try to fix it." Doc looked downright haggard. His shirt hung from his back; he looked as if he'd lost weight. And it appeared that he really was afraid or that he had a reason to think he should be. For just a split second, I cared. "You helped him get out of town, and everyone—a whole community and me included—thought he was dead."

"I'm sorry for that, really I am. It had to be done."

"I was only fifteen, Doc. Fifteen. Can you imagine what it was like to lose a friend you'd had all your life without a trace or word? And to think my own father let me believe the same thing. Why, Doc? Why didn't he just tell me he had carried him to you? I've got a mind to drive to Bittersweet and call him out on this right now!"

Doc looked about him at the scattered papers, at the mantel— the only pictures being one of him and Opal on their wedding day and one from their fiftieth anniversary. "Sometimes a man has to make hard decisions. Some that are contrary to popular opinion. I was trying to protect certain people. I'm sure your father was trying to protect you."

"A boy being thought dead is not a popular opinion. That was a headline you had no right to run."

"Sometimes contrary to what everyone believes to be right. If I could have done it differently, I would have. Please believe me."

"There's such a thing as a sacred trust."

"I never broke our trust, Mercy. I never have. I've kept your little secrets, and you've kept mine." He moved to the mantel and straightened the photos by a degree. "And I've kept John Quincy's even up until now. And just so you know, you can check the archives. I never ran a story about him being missing or dead. I could have and would have sold more papers. You know I don't go for the quick and easy headline." He pulled a nasty cigar butt from his pocket and clamped it between his teeth. "It appears he's told you more of his story, and that is a good indication there is still hope."

Doc was like a second father to me. I was trying my best to stay angry, but the anger was defusing. The hurt, however, was not. And my trust meter was going down all the time. "Hope for what?"

"That he can still become the man he was meant to be. Spending time with you, Mercy, is helping him see that. I caught wind of that the first day he showed up when I realized he knew who you were. The way he looks at you and the way he looks at the world are two widely different things. You connect him to the good in him. I can understand why."

Something occurred to me out of the blue. "You legally changed his name?"

"I didn't have the power to do that. I helped it along. I had a few one-on-ones with the judge. For John's own protection."

"And is his name in the book?"

Doc looked stricken when I asked. His hand clutched the mantel tight until his knuckles were white. "It was."

"What do you mean *was*? It is or it isn't."

"We'll have to look together; we'll have to double-check to see if it surfaces. Something bothers me about him. Something I wasn't expecting when he made it to Bay City. He used to be something special, unique." He seemed to be talking more to himself than to me. "I've never seen anyone work so hard in spite of his circumstances. Who applied himself so diligently. And then there was that terrible night, that awful night, and…" He laid his head down on his arm draped there, and a sob escaped him.

I couldn't help myself. I went to him, laid my hand softly on his arm, and said, "What night? What was it?"

"Sometimes there is evil in this world. Sometimes man becomes the monster."

"I don't understand you. Talk straight. Just tell me what you are so worked up about."

"Tommy Taylor was beaten with a flatiron by his father. Beaten, I tell you, until the boy's foot was crushed and he would be crippled for life. Beaten badly all over. They had to get Tommy out of Bittersweet fast before his father killed him. Bay City was the only place they knew to bring him. And I was the only person they knew here."

"His daddy was a mean one, all right, but why? Why?"

"Because he had seen Tommy hiding money that he had been working for, that he'd been stashing for years, and he had earned every penny of it."

I stepped back from him, uncertain of everything now. Uncertain to the point I wanted to get in my car and drive to Bittersweet, to go home to Mama and Daddy and Ida and never come back to this place or to Doc's. I looked around the room, at Doc, at the wild mess and state of affairs. I thought of Tommy, or John—whoever he was—back to life from the near 'bout dead, and I didn't want any part of it. Not of that book that Doc was moving around now like sand in an hourglass, shifting it first to one place and then back to its original spot, like that would solve anything.

"And, Mercy, his father jumped on him while he was sleeping. The boy never had a fighting chance."

I crumpled to the floor, my hands over my eyes. Harriet moved over and dropped her head into my lap. She rolled her eyes up to me, always woefully full of love. This time I embraced her and leaned my face into her fur.

"Sit down now, Doc. Just sit down and start slowly, very slowly from the beginning."

"If you don't mind, I think I could use a little fresh air. I'll begin at the beginning while we take a walk around the block." At the word *walk,* Harry lifted her head from my lap and wagged her tail. "Yes, you too, old girl. We can't forget you." Then he offered me his hand and helped me to my feet. "Forgive me, Mercy. There were reasons for everything. But now I am old. And I am scared and confused."

"From the top," I said. "We'll walk, and you begin at the beginning. There'll be time for forgiveness later."

TWENTY-FOUR

Doc closed his front gate, and we both looked up and down the dark street and the sidewalk. Without saying it, we were searching for whoever had been following him. It was well after midnight, and not a single car drove through the neighborhood. I had to admit, as angry as I had been, as tired and confused as I still was, it was good just to be walking alongside the familiar shape of him, Harry sniffing at the bushes, her paws plodding along. The ritual of it calmed us both.

"I've been working on something," Doc began. "Trying my best to see how those names in the book affect one another. Trying to work out all the possible story lines. Tell me, do you think that one man's decisions, his choices, could affect, oh, I don't know, the lives of all the people around him? People he doesn't even know?"

"Well, if that's what you've been working on, I think you've made a mess of things." We turned the corner at the street sign and headed deeper away from downtown and closer to the bay. "I don't think I would know the answer to that any more than you would. Maybe go ask my daddy on that one. He might have an answer. The point is, on with your story, Doc. From the beginning."

We walked under the magnolias and oaks that lined the side-walks. The hanging moss moved a little with each passing breeze, scattering the light from the streetlamps and porches so that we moved continuously through light and shadow. Doc did as he had promised. He started at the very beginning. It was during the time when I was only a child of about ten, running through the woods with Tommy Taylor on the days that he appeared from across the creek or from nowhere. There had always been days that Tommy was just gone for a while. Then he would step up in front of my porch or find me at Aunt Ida's, looking for adventure.

"There was a boy who took to showing up in town. No one knew how he came, although when Old Whistler was driving the school bus, he saw the boy hitchhiking. He wasn't supposed to stop, you know, and so for a while he didn't. But the boy was too small to be out there like that. Whistler started picking him up regularly, and he knew what the boy was all about. Whistler took to giving him a lift when the bus had been emptied at the end of the day and he was on his way back into town.

"It was obvious he didn't belong around here. No one knew him. He didn't seem to keep regular school hours of any kind but came and went as he pleased, or at least as he could. Looking back"—here he paused and caught his breath—"maybe we could have done something sooner." And with that he didn't seem to be talking to me anymore. He was talking to himself, and I had no doubt that part of the conversation was due to the book, to what it could tell. I had held it in my hands, and just a moment in its presence was a lifetime fully lived. All time stopped, and all time moved forward at once.

"Go on," I told him. He tugged at Harry's leash, and we moved on.

"He was almost more shadow than boy, but he became so regular a shadow that, God forgive us, we no longer noticed him. We didn't really look at the boy, do you understand? But yet we used him."

"Used him?"

"For everything. Rake the leaves? He would do it. Carry groceries? He would do it. Cut down a tree, wash a car, patch a roof? Was nothing but a kid, I tell you, but he would do it. No job was too rough for him, and he never turned down the slightest nickel. It got to where the whole city saved up jobs. We'd not do things we disliked or simple things we seemed too busy for and just wait for the day he appeared. We didn't even really know his name. We called him the Bittersweet boy. To you he was still your Tommy Taylor."

"Tommy," I whispered to myself. Then the days of Tommy not being around made more sense. Made perfect sense. Three days and no sign of him, and then he'd be at my door calling, "C'mon, Mercy, let's go." And we'd be off. I guess our playing was the only childhood Tommy ever had.

"So that's how he came by the money? The money you said his daddy…" I couldn't bring myself to say another word. That kind of evil I couldn't conceive. "But his daddy never drank a drop. Or at least that's what I heard."

"Wasn't alcohol, Mercy. Was a wild, cold-blooded, premeditated rage. It was some kind of hate that had been eating at that soul forever. I guess it finally won out that night."

"He died, you know. His heart gave out years ago. No one seemed too sorry for it, including Tommy's mother."

"I would imagine so."

"So how did Tommy know to come to you, Doc? Why you?"

"Oh, you know Opal. She took more time with the boy than anyone else. Hired him to help her with her camellias." He glanced down at me and smiled. "You don't have to do a whole lot to camellias. I think she just wanted to visit with him. Give him someone to talk to." We walked on for a little while, Doc remembering Opal, and me as well. "She was good that way. Taking time. Knowing the right thing to say. I was just always rushing so. Taking care of the paper, gathering news, covering the story. All that was so important at the time. And it really was, but so was that small shadow that followed me around the streets all the time. He thought I didn't know he was behind me, but he followed me everywhere. I don't know how he had time to find work and to turn a dime. He seemed to always be there. Sitting as small as he could in the back of the courtroom if I was covering a trial. Or shuffling along somewhere behind me on the sidewalk, trying to hide in a doorway if I turned to catch him there. I never asked. I never tried to get to know him or to find out why the boy, obviously in need… I mean, you could look at him and tell. Why didn't I do more? We had no children of our own. I could have, I could have…"

We had stopped where the sidewalk ended down by the bay. There were no boats on the water tonight, but the moon was almost full, and it hung in the night sky so that Doc and I just stood there looking at it. As mad as I had been earlier, I wanted to comfort him now. He seemed tired, forlorn, or vexed, as Mama would say.

"Let it go," I said, even though a part of me, a small but persistent part of me, was still reeling at the news. I had left a certain someone standing on the porch, saying, "Wait, I can explain." Well, there had been plenty of explanation, but the reasons were weak. His daddy had been evil, or possessed by some kind of evil, to do what he did. Apparently, Doc had rescued him, but that was a long time ago. Maybe this John Quincy felt like he owed Doc something. I wasn't sure of that, but I knew that Doc thought he owed John Quincy everything. A past he couldn't remake.

"I could have taken him in, Mercy. I could have made him my own."

I didn't comment, because he was right. Comforting was one thing; lying outright was another. It might have made all the difference in the world. It might have at least saved his foot.

"Seems like you did an awful lot for the good in the long run." I could offer him that.

"Does it? Does it seem that way to you?" His eyebrows knotted up as he looked down. It was like in his office after a witness of some kind of story had left. "Tell it to me straight, Mercy. Is he who he says he is? Is he your little Tommy Taylor all grown up with just a season of a dark past?"

I looked up at that white-haired old man. Eye to eye—truth be told without twisting it.

"No, he's not, Doc. He's not that man at all. He's two men. One that's still there from the past, and one that's let something dark get under his skin. You gotta be careful and know which one you're talking to."

We looked out across the bay and realized how late it was getting. The moon was actually beginning to set out over the water, which was an amazing thing to witness. What I tried to explain to Doc was that this John Quincy was not the Tommy Taylor I had known. And the more I was around him, the more certain I was of it. Granted, it was the same body, still broken to some degree from that horrible night, but it was as if the evil that had taken his daddy had twisted not only Tommy's foot but also his life somewhere deeper. It had shaped him into something else. It was as if his soul had split in two.

"That doesn't mean he's a bad man," I added. "But he's got a dark bad moving through him." I couldn't quite put my finger to it. "And he's hiding more than his past."

We wandered down the dock, the sound of Harry's nails clicking on the boards. "What we have at our disposal, Mercy, or at least in our temporary keeping, is something too sacred to just toss to the man. I have to come completely clean with you, Mercy. I feel it's my fault, this life of his. I wanted to bring him here, to use the book somehow to reshape his past. That's why I searched him out."

"Why didn't you stay in contact? Why did you send him to a boys' home of all places?" A lump of anger rose in my throat. "You said yourself that he was exceptional, that he was unique. And he was, Doc; he really was."

"I didn't know what to do. Not really. Opal wanted us to keep him." He stopped walking and turned to me. "And, yes, maybe that would have been the right thing if we could have done it legally. If his father would have stayed away. But after that night, because of that night, I knew he was a madman. Someone capable of anything. I felt like all of us—Tommy, me, Opal—would have ultimately been in danger. The judge made the arrangements. It wasn't a bad place. It was just—a place. You know, for boys."

"You weren't the one who had to stay there. You don't know if it was a bad place or not. A place for boys is not a family."

"I had no contact after that. Not until I tracked him down and we spoke. A few hushed phone calls about the book. Telling him that he might have an opportunity to change things, that perhaps I had in my possession something that could show a man his past and his future possibilities. It was wrong of me, I know.

"The first time I saw him again was out that window when you arrived. I hadn't personally seen him since we helped him get away. And that was no quick arrangement. It took a few months. He was a mess, had to be doctored, and then we had to decide what to do next. We kept him hidden while we tried to figure things out. Until the proper arrangements were made. The day you picked him up from the train and brought him in, it was as if I was meeting the man for the first time."

The moon was sliding slowly into the water now as if we were watching a white sunset. Harry had decided it was time for sleep, regardless of her location. There were the sounds of the gentle lapping of the water against the pier pilings and of the dog softly snoring. I felt Doc's regret rising in him like the tidewaters of the bay.

"What kind of man am I to do such a thing? Dear God, what kind of man turns a cold heart like that?"

Doc had been my hero for a long time. He had that hero air about him, and everybody felt it. And expected him to carry on that way. But in the end, like everyone else, he was just a man. "A human one, Doc. You're just human."

The moon disappeared into the water's black edge. We didn't rush away. We had nowhere to go and no one to rush home to. It was so late now that the hands of the clock had moved over to predawn. Neither of us was going to get any sleep.

TWENTY-FIVE

Doc walked me to the gate. For the first time I realized that in a few hours the *Banner* was supposed be tossed up on the porches, and we'd skipped right through the day without it. "Doc, the *Banner*!"

He broke a smile for the first time that night. "Old Doc hasn't forgotten everything. I called you to send you for my ace in the hole. You weren't back yet, so I sent our ever-trustworthy Miss Perry to get my emergency layout."

"What's that?"

"Life can get in the way of that paper deadline at any given hour. I keep a few extra dailies all laid out and ready to go just in case. Old news, small bits of interest, some larger than normal photos, a lot of editorials, and a few free ads. It's not award-winning stuff, that's for certain, but what would the people do without their morning news? Far be it from me to break the tradition."

"Why'd you never tell me about this?"

"Thought I'd wait till you realized it was going to be a black-out morning without it. The importance has a little more impact, don't you think?"

"You are making me mad again."

"No time for mad this morning. We've made up our minds now. There's only one thing left to do."

With that, Doc waved at me in the early morning light and walked away. He was right. We had decided, come what may and however the winds blew, we were showing John Quincy the book, and the three of us would try to decipher what it contained. And we would tell him the truth: that at one time his name had been found there but that now Doc couldn't find it anywhere. Doc had told me this gave him a concern that rumbled in his soul.

When I walked into the house, I could smell coffee and was ever so thankful—until I realized I was still wearing my clothes from last night. Miss Perry held certain opinions, and the way a lady should and should not conduct herself was one of them. Me coming in dressed in last night's clothes fell into the wrong category. I tried to tiptoe past the dining room without a word.

"Good morning, dear." Her voice came out smooth.

"Be right back!" I continued up the stairs. "Just out for some early air."

An arm reached out and grasped me, and I stumbled. John Quincy was waiting for me at the top of the landing.

"There, there. Didn't mean to scare you." He didn't let go of my arm.

"First the kitchen and now this. I'm not certain you're not out to scare me to death."

"You didn't come back."

"I did." The night was wearing on me. All I wanted was a bath and my bed, but the day was just beginning. "I'm back. I'm right here."

"I meant last night. I waited up for you."

"You knew where I was, and you knew why."

He walked to the edge of the stairs, looked over the railing, and came back. He put his finger over his lips to signal for me to be quiet. "Can I come in for a moment?"

"It's against the rules," I whispered.

"Just for a minute, Mercy. I need to talk."

"Oh, for just a minute." I unlocked the door, and he walked in behind me.

Thankfully there was nothing scattered about the room. Obviously I hadn't been in a messy mood. I was capable of that too. "Sit there and say it, but hurry. Doc's waiting, and we've got to put out a paper in the middle of everything. You'd think the world would just stop making news for convenience's sake, but of course it won't do that."

I opened the window and leaned on the sill. He took the small chair by the desk, put his elbows on his knees, his face in his hands. I sat there watching him, still thinking he was beautiful. This wasn't my idea of hurry. I turned to the magnolia tree, in full bloom now, the soft, lemony scent drifting toward me.

"I tried to tell you last night that I was in a situation. I was hurt bad. Almost dead, really." He leaned back, his hands on the armrests, and crossed one leg over the other so that he looked like a dictionary picture of calm. If you had taken a picture, that would have been the only thing you would have seen. A calm, collected, successful man. But I knew now that there were scars that ran deep and wide. Physical and otherwise.

"Doc told me everything. You don't have to say anything else."

"But you meant so much to me, Mercy." His gaze was level. "There was the dark place called my life, and then there was you." I looked back out to the magnolias and felt the heaviness sitting in the air. It felt like another storm was coming on. A big one. We had suffered enough of them this summer. Part of me wanted to tell him about the entire night. About watching the moonset and about Doc's regret. The other part only wanted a bath and breakfast.

"I thank you for your kind words." I stood up. "And I'm so sorry that...that something hurt you."

"It wasn't a something," he said, his voice turning to ice. "It was a somebody."

There were things I could have said to him, but I didn't think any of them were words he wanted to hear. "Doc will be waiting for us. Why don't we have breakfast and walk together?"

The icy look passed. He gave me a weak smile and walked to the door, cracked it an inch, and peered into the hallway, then walked slowly backward out of the room, smiling at me with his finger to his lips. I wanted to curse the flutter in my heart.

DOC'S JOURNAL

I may never know if what I intend this morning is the right thing. What the book has shown me each time is that a choice made opens one door and closes another. What I have not discovered is if different choices sometimes find their way to the same eventual end. If a man lives in one part of the world and travels forever, will he eventually return to the place he was born as if he never left? If this were his destiny, would it so find him, pluck him up, and return him to its nest? All of my worrying and calculations have been for nothing. Pages and pages of trying, but none of it matters. I have surrendered to my lack of knowledge. No, that is wrong. It is my lack of knowing that brings me to my knees. Knowledge and experience I have plenty. But the knowing of the future, the real knowing, is beyond me. God knows I've tried since I laid eyes on John Quincy again—or for the first time, depending on your point of view. What has captured me has been my state of conviction that I once had the power to effect a different kind of life for him and that now all of that is lost.

    We will know soon enough if I have managed to play havoc with lives because of my own selfish concerns. The bell rings downstairs. They have arrived.

Twenty-Six

John Quincy

To open a book, to see one's past and one's future, to see the days of one's life captured and painted with such amazing, precise movement—could it be compared to the internal workings of a clock? Yes, the movements, perhaps, of a great timepiece, only the calculations are offsetting. Anything can trip the mechanism so that time rushes forward or backward, so that the choices made create new doorways, which open onto new corridors, which enter into rooms containing years. It is madness. Wonderful, delicious madness, and that is exactly what I felt as Mercy closed the book. We were huddled around Doc's desk, and the thing that it was lay before us. I looked at the window, trying to focus. Doc had drawn the blinds as Mercy had brought the wrapped book to the desk. When she uncovered it, suddenly light—but not light as I have known it, not the kind of light that we are now so accustomed to—saturated us. It was the light of a thousand days, a thousand suns. When her hands lifted the book from the box, they literally disappeared into the light. I wanted to ask, *Is this true? Are we really seeing this?* But I couldn't bring myself to form the words. We were all bathed in that incandescent, brilliant light. And a shadow passed over me, a sense that at any moment Cilla would walk through the door, snatch the book away, and disappear into thin air. Then I touched the pages of the book before me, and the fear of her presence receded.

Name after name of people and the stories of their lives surfaced. But those stories appeared to have no end and no beginning. They were eternal, forever stories and the weaving of them just as far-reaching. It was as if every person's actions overlapped into another life and another and yet another so that lives were not at all as we saw them—short, independent stories—but were layered over one another in what appeared to be infinity. The words were strange, alive and moving. Yet, even so, I could understand them.

When Mercy finally closed the book, it was as if a star had collapsed upon itself. A sudden greater flash of light occurred, and then nothing but the darkness. And that dark was complete. We were not actually sitting in the dark at all, but by comparison all other light was like unto darkness. Mercy moved to place the book back in the box and into the cabinet with me wanting to shout, *No, stop, I must see more!* But I could not speak. Yet she turned back as if she'd heard me, leaving the book as it was.

Doc stood and walked to the window, opened the blinds just a little. I couldn't tell the time, and the truth was, time at the moment didn't matter when I had just witnessed the depth of days. Even the concept of time as we thought of it was so absurd to me in that moment that I laughed aloud.

They looked at me and smiled. Obviously, they had experienced this many times in these few months. They had been touched by this and knew what to expect, but for me, it was so surprising I might as well have been sitting on the moon.

Mercy walked to the window and peered out. Without her asking, Doc looked at his watch and said, "Two thirty-two." She nodded and came back to where I sat, taking the chair next to me. Doc returned to his seat as well.

We sat in that bubble of quietness, me contemplating time. The times I had just witnessed. At once time was of all importance and no importance at all. And again I laughed to myself that I had ever been affected by it. Been worried by the measure of days. It was clear to me now that there was no end and no beginning. There was no unilateral line of time. It came in pockets, like air below some great volcanic ocean.

"Mercy, your heart…" I couldn't form the words, but I knew what I was trying to say. That I could see the heart of Mercy. "You are…"

"You've been affected." Doc spoke, his voice low, reassuring and at the same time demanding to extract me from another dimension. "This will pass in a little while. Mercy, perhaps some coffee would do us all good."

I don't want it to pass, I wanted to say, but I just looked at Mercy, watched her leave the room, all the while longing for her to stay. Her presence gave me a comfort I wasn't prepared for. A balanced sense that we were in this together and that as long as she was by my side, everything would work out all right.

"We've both been affected this way by the book." Doc pulled out that old cigar stump of his from a pocket and put it in his mouth. "The night it first appeared on my desk, I was lost and found all at once. Lost in one world and delivered from another. The hours of the night came and went, and as soon as it was fair to do so, I called Mercy and told her to come right away. The book affected her as well. Each a bit differently, I suppose, but both of us affected. Now I know what to expect, or more, how to…" He searched for words he couldn't find and then settled on saying nothing more on the subject.

"Coffee's making." She stood at the doorframe, and even her voice was something I wanted to lean into. I almost got up, took her by the hand, and led her back to her chair so she would be nearby. "And the *Banner*?"

"Rip the wires, Mercy." He rocked back slightly in his chair. "You choose the headline. We'll run something international. Lots of national news too. Grab some human interest pieces, little things, from Anywhere, USA."

Doc Philips was watching me, searching me for something, but at the moment I felt much like a blank sheet. That what had come before was of consequence to another person in another time and what lay ahead was in a realm of possibility I could not contain.

"Mercy took the news about me moving you away pretty hard last night."

I nodded, my normal senses just beginning to return around the edges.

"I want to tell you that I'm…that it has recently come to my attention…" He cleared his throat and looked away. Finally he said, "I could have done more."

There was a rush inside my soul then of something I couldn't reach. A deep-seated pain like that of a wounded animal. I wanted to tell him, *No, you did enough. You did everything and more than a man, no relation at all, no connection, should have done.* But the pain of the past engulfed me so that I looked at my hands. I never said a word, and again time seemed to fade into a deep recess beyond me, as if I had fallen asleep, but I knew that wasn't true. Mercy reentered the room, holding a tray. I wanted more than anything to kiss her. To hold her. And to cry. And these desires, these feelings, were such a sudden surprise to me that I placed my palm over my mouth and left it there. Obviously, I had been affected by something I had seen or felt and now had no memory of it. I couldn't say it was a bad sensation, but I felt…*influenced.*

Mercy poured the coffee, looked at me, and said, "Sugar, yes?"

"Oh…yes, please," I said. As if we were having tea with the Queen of England.

"Feeling better, I hope." Mercy passed a cup to me, made one for Doc, and offered it to him. "Not that it's really a bad sensation, but it is different."

"I believe I feel myself returning." I took a sip of the coffee. "And now? You've called me here for some purpose related to this, which I can't imagine. It doesn't seem to be anything…"

From the moment Doc had told me about the book, I had been beside myself to touch it. Immediately I knew that if his story was true, the book was worth more than gold. And that something worth more than gold, something priceless, could bring a very high price indeed. The problem was, I had mentioned it to Cilla, and in only moments she had been feeding on the possibilities of what the treasure could produce. And she had been certain Doc Philips wasn't just an old fool losing his mind. She had made certain I got on that train to Bay City.

"There are lives living in those pages, but there appears to be a pattern to the names. Some type of equation of sorts with words. I've tried to decipher what it is, but apparently it isn't in me to do so. I keep overlooking something of critical importance."

"It's not you, Doc," Mercy said. Then she turned to me, apparently deciding that Doc's explanation was taking too long to get to its destination. I agreed with her. "The book came to Doc, but he can't do whatever he's supposed to with it because he's not supposed to do it alone. None of us are really, don't you see?"

I was reaching for the book, and the moment my fingers touched the edges of the book, again time fell away. I could hear Mercy saying something. I could hear the rhythm and rise of her voice, but the words were like a distant sound of moving water. Then two things happened at once. The truth of the matter exploded inside my mind, and the window behind Doc shattered into a thousand pieces.

Twenty-Seven

While we had been locked away in Doc's office above the city, we hadn't been aware of the news developing in our immediate surroundings. A tropical storm of major proportions had developed in the gulf and then whipped its way across the bay, casting off waterspouts and tornadoes in the process. Surely there had been a howling, the sound of tropical gale-force winds picking up throughout the day. But the book was like that. It had the ability to carry you away so that places like Bay City and Bittersweet were just a rustle in memory. I vaguely remembered thinking of a storm when John had been in my room, but the fact that we were going to finally open the book to him had replaced any concerns I might have had. Doc had said we would simply suffer the consequences if it turned out to be the wrong thing to do. I had not argued with him, because even though I was a part of this, the book had appeared there to him, not in my room at the boardinghouse. It wasn't mine to direct or decide what was the best course of action.

Neither Doc nor I had slept all night, but the book electrified our senses so that sleep, at least immediately, was not a necessity.

What was necessary was to understand exactly what was in our possession and why we had it. What was its purpose, and how would we know we had completed whatever task had been put before us?

We didn't know what John might be able to add to the picture, and maybe in the long run he could add nothing at all, but we had to try. We had apparently spent a full day with that book opened before us.

John Quincy had no time to explain anything, because the second his hands touched the paper, the wall of glass behind Doc exploded. A waterspout must have caught at just the right angle, because it blew the window to smithereens. Thankfully, the blinds were almost closed, or the glass would have caught us full force. We could have been cut head to toe. As it was, Doc hurried us out of the office, exclaiming, "Downstairs, now!" We moved as he directed us. The wind howled around the building and into the room, the shattering glass falling to the floor and scattering about. A few pieces managed to escape, and one caught Doc's cheek, another his arm, as he was the one closest to the window.

We rushed down the staircase to the kitchen below. Then I cried out, turned, and ran headlong back up the stairs and into the office with Doc calling out for me to stop. I couldn't leave the book upstairs in the storm. What strikes me now, of course, is the book itself was more apt to take care of the three of us than the other way around.

I ran up and grabbed the book and the box and turned quickly to retreat. That's when I found John Quincy standing there, watching me, his face a mix of emotions I could not read.

The wind gusted and snapped at the windows, rattling the blinds wildly. Another piece of glass broke free from the shattered window and fell to the floor. I could hear him calling my name, and yet I was frozen there, wondering if John was my protection or if he was a threat. Finally I asked, "What is it, John?" but with the sound of the wind, my words came out more like a whisper. He put out his hand. For a moment I thought he wanted me to hand him the book or that he might take it from my hands and then be gone forever, never to be heard from again. This disappearance of the Bittersweet boy would be for good. When I didn't move, he came toward me, put his arm around my shoulders, pulled me through the office door, and led me down the stairs.

Doc stood watching us. The wind howled wildly upstairs, the shattered glass still dropping and breaking. Doc walked to the windows and peered through the blinds downstairs. A steady rain blew in sideways gusts up the street. The streetlight was waving back and forth, looking as if it might fall from the cables.

"Looks like we're in for a little rain. Any cake left in that kitchen? We should move into there, where there's less glass to find us."

"Tell us what you think," I said. The rains were pouring, and I looked at the clock on the wall. I was concerned about our deadline. My nerves were on the edge of my sleeve. I was in no mood to pussyfoot around with this man anymore. Maybe we could get down to the business of what came next and then get back to our normal lives.

Then I realized that when that happened, when it was over, the book would be gone forever. And so would John Quincy.

I put the book in its box, locked it, and held it in my arms for safekeeping.

The rain and wind came in waves outside the building. We could hear it pouring, the water beating against the building, then a slight pause before it slammed into the building again.

"It's just a tropical storm. Just a little damage," Doc said. "We've weathered worse, haven't we, Mercy?"

I didn't answer him directly. I continued to hear the glass popping and dropping in little pieces upstairs and shards getting blown across the room and hitting the walls, then falling like crystals to the floor. We were held together like shipmates in tight quarters, the dark afternoon raging outside. We were safe, dry, and in possession of a book that told eternal stories. A book full of living legends and small stories unfolding, simple lives and those full of adventure. I held the book closer, tighter to my chest, and closed my eyes. Then all I heard was a quiet peace. As if I had been taken to another place.

"Mercy? Mercy?"

I thought John was calling me. I opened my eyes, but he and Doc sat at the little table, studying the book, the sound of the wind and the rain still drumming outside.

"I can't say that Mercy and I ever made much headway understanding what the purpose of the book really is," Doc said.

John Quincy ran his fingers over his brow. "I understood everything for a moment. Now I can't remember a thing about it."

"I think these names are just of people in Bay City." Doc pointed toward the box. "Now, why would it just be Bay City? Why would that be true? With a book such as this, we should be able to see the entire world. Perhaps the book then is only *for* Bay City."

Doc was right, at least from the names I had recognized. I was the only Bittersweet name on the list, well, with the exception that Doc said John's name had once been there—but it never occurred to me to ask, *Which name?*

"Doc, you said you saw John there, but then you couldn't find his name again."

"It doesn't mean anything. You know from trying that we can't summon lives at will. We can't really turn pages as planned. It shows what it wants to. We could be standing side by side and you see one thing and I see another."

"But you did see him there."

"I did."

John Quincy leaned in closer, I suppose hoping that Doc would be able to shed some light on something for him. Maybe tell his fortune for him, show him his future. It was tempting, I knew. I had tried to get Doc to share with me what he saw of my life. He simply said, "You were born in a lightning bolt. And you are a good soul." That was the kind of thing Mama would tell me; that wasn't my future. When Doc realized I had stepped into his life, he didn't ask me anything like that at all. He just said, "Did you see Opal?"

"I saw it all, Doc," I had told him. "And you were the cutest little boy."

But the seeing faded right away so that the experience was left just under the skin; a better knowledge of a person lingered but not the details.

"What I'm wondering now, Doc, is which name of his did you see? What part of the man's life?"

"John Quincy," he answered. "Who, of course, is now in Bay City."

I had a notion. "If the book is only for Bay City, then it means something special is coming here to this place. Maybe something is supposed to happen in Bay City," I said.

"Or maybe something already happened," Doc said, but he didn't seem too happy about it.

The wind had dropped outside now to a regular off-the-bay howl. I placed the book gently down on the table and walked over to the little kitchen window and peered out. The rain had gotten softer and was coming straight down now instead of blowing sideways off the bay. Marie's sign lit up, and my stomach growled at the sight of it. I had been up all night and day and didn't even remember eating breakfast. Suddenly I was starving. I glanced over my shoulder at the book, then returned and picked it up again. This desire to keep it with me, to keep it safe, was getting stronger. Safe from what exactly, I didn't know, but just safe. Apparently, Doc had felt the same way the last few days. I guess that's part of the reason he'd had those terrors and kept moving it around.

"Maybe something in the past is here; maybe…a chance for the town to do something different. Maybe something it should have done a long time ago." Doc was muddling through his mind, trying to figure something out, and I had a good idea of what it was.

"You can't change the past, Doc. The past is the past." But as I said it, John gave me the oddest look.

"So, if the book were taken out of town, most likely the names

in it would—what, change? Do you think they would change?"
His voice took on a new note of enthusiasm. "Just for the sake of
hypothesis, say, if the book were taken to Bittersweet Creek, do
you think the names would be different?"

John said this slowly, like he was working out details in his
mind. He was either contemplating or calculating. I didn't know
which one, but neither one of them felt right. Then he looked at
me and grinned his old Tommy Taylor grin. In spite of myself, I
smiled at him, but I clasped the book tighter to my chest. I didn't
know exactly what it contained, but I knew that losing it would
somehow change things for everyone. And not for the better.

"No, John. It's not supposed to leave Bay City, understand?
And don't even think about it!"

"Why, Mercy! There's no call for that. He's simply trying to
figure things out. Let the man work through the confounded
thing step by step, would you? Let him apply his logic. This is
why he's here with us. To look at options we might not even consider. To see things that we can't. Suppose he's right? Suppose the
book changes every time it crosses into…"

"A jurisdiction," John offered.

"Yes, exactly—a jurisdiction."

I glared at him. I *never* glared at Doc. But maybe they had a
point. I just wasn't in the mood for the book to be taken anywhere. No, it was more than a mood. It's what Mama would
call—

"I got a powerful leading about this," I said. "I don't think it's
right."

"Mercy," he chided me, disapproving. "Let me see. If we took the book and drove to…" He pulled out that pocket watch in spite of the clock on the wall. Then there was a loud banging on the door and a voice that came along with it.

"Mr. Doc? Mercy?" It was a heavy, lilting, beautiful Italian accent. "Are you okay in there?"

We filed out of the kitchen as a group. Doc answered the door to one of Marie's sons. "Do you know about your wall?" He pointed upstairs.

"You mean the window?"

"It's missing. Glass is everywhere. Look, Mama is so worried." He pointed across the street. I stepped out on the sidewalk and looked in her direction. Marie stood on the sidewalk in front of the restaurant, her hands wringing her apron. I gave her a little wave.

"Oh, poor Mama Marie," I said. "Tell her we're okay. We're all okay."

He yelled from the sidewalk immediately, "They're okay, Mama. They're all okay." Then there was a rush of Italian from across the street and Italian from our corner. He turned back to me. "Mama says you have to come eat. She says eat first, clean later."

I couldn't agree with her more. Still carrying the box, I walked back in and picked up my purse without another word. The men, as I saw it, could do as they pleased, but as for me, I was having Mama's special spaghetti.

"Mercy, the book," John said. "Don't you need to"—he paused, trying to be careful with what he said, as Marie's son was still standing by the door—"return it?" He motioned up the stairs.

"No, I don't." I looked at Doc. "The glass is blown out. The whole wall's missing. I'm not leaving it."

Doc nodded at me, closed his pocket watch, and put it away. "Very well. Seems like a dinner of no small proportion is in order."

And that's how the three of us made our way across the wet street, the thick, misty rain still hanging in the air and the sound of our shoes crunching on broken glass as we crossed into the warm light of Marie's presence, where I felt anything in this world would be safe.

TWENTY-EIGHT

John Quincy was walking me home. Or you might say we were walking home to the boardinghouse together. Harry had missed her walk all day, and Doc went home to get her, but not before we had consumed double helpings of Marie's spaghetti followed by her famous cheesecake. Then, full and sleepy, the three of us had gone together to pull the wires, find the news, and write a few small stories that would make up a small *Banner* edition. It was John Quincy's first time at actually doing anything since he came to town, and he fell into rhythm so smoothly, working side by side with us and following Doc's instructions, that I didn't even think it odd to have him there. Herman's work was getting easier and easier with so little for him to typeset these days. The paper had been losing pages.

I walked slowly toward Miss Perry's, satisfied with the knowledge of at least one more skeletal edition making the rounds in the morning. And also because Mama Marie's food left a lasting impression of well-being.

The box was still held tightly in my arms. It would be tomorrow morning before the glass company would repair Doc's office, but they had arrived as we worked to temporarily cover the large wall of windows with plastic. Living in a hurricane alley where tropical storms, waterspouts, and gale-force winds were expected, everyone stayed prepared.

"I said, do you believe me?" John questioned.

"About what?" I was sleepy and didn't want to think anymore.

"I'm just trying to figure this out."

The magnolia leaves were reflecting the water they still held, shining in their dark green essence as we walked beneath them. There was a soft dripping sound as water fell from everything around us. The white fences that lined the yards and walkways were all washed clean. I looked up at John in the glow of the amber light that seemed to always hang in the air after a storm. The handsome just never rubbed off of him. I kept hoping it would. Not in a mean way, but just in a don't-let-me-be-affected way. Don't let me trust a man who should be kept away. Then just underneath the warm, full feeling on a beautiful evening, I heard the uneven, hobbled steps of John Quincy and remembered where he'd come from and who he used to be. I thought of the pain he'd been through, of his being shuffled away secretly, spending those years at a home for boys. There must have been a number of lonely years between then and this moment. Now that I thought about it, who did he have in his life besides…well, me? With the exception of Doc, I was his only connection to what used to be.

We arrived at Miss Perry's. I turned to him. "John," I began, then I didn't know exactly how to venture forth. To tell him maybe I hadn't given him a fair chance since he'd showed up here. That maybe a part of me was still hurt by the fact that he never let me know he was still alive. Or by the fact that apparently he had never intended to do so. He could have sent me word by his mama. He could have sent me an arrowhead. Anything, anything at all, and I wouldn't have been so shocked by all of this. But there was more. And maybe one of the reasons I didn't want to trust him was that he had showed up not looking anything like that scrawny, scratched-up boy I used to know. And that wasn't his fault, either. I turned around without saying a single one of those things. I offered him a nightcap instead. "Hot chocolate?"

"You were reading my mind."

I hadn't really said the things I wanted to tell him. Or even apologized for the way I had been short-tempered with him and distrusted him from the moment he stepped off the train.

He held the gate for me, and we walked up the porch steps, the scent of jasmine and honeysuckle encircling us. It was hard to stay mad in that kind of air.

"I was mad at you for not sending me word. For not sending me some kind of signal to let me know you were alive."

I opened the door, and John followed me into the little kitchen, where I flipped on the light, got out the milk, and started making our cocoa. He sat quietly looking into the dark backyard.

"It wasn't easy for me. Well, I've told you that. But in other ways a boy gets lonely."

I stirred the chocolate and milk and didn't respond.

"I wasn't the kind to make friends after…the things that had happened. I guess you might say I wasn't the most trusting soul, but like I said, I was a lonely boy."

I put his cup down in front of him and sat down with mine on the other side of the table.

He picked it up and sipped slowly. "I was lonely for you."

I tried to hide my expression when I drank. I needed a shield from his eyes watching me. "You were just homesick for the good things. That's what I was to you—home." I put the cup down and laced my fingers under my chin. "So tell me truly, what is that life of yours like now in the big city?"

"Tomorrow, Mercy." He ignored my question and pointed at the box on the counter. "I want us to take that tomorrow to Bittersweet."

"You can't erase the past, John. I'm telling you."

"Why would I want to do that? It's got you in it."

I hadn't taken a solemn vow out there by the gate, but I had purposed in my heart to at least give him a chance. To look past the things that made me ill at ease and to remember all the good things Tommy Taylor had once been. To believe that somewhere inside the man before me, the good heart of that boy still lived.

"Well,"—I raised my cup—"here's to Bittersweet Creek." And just like that, my heart went out to the man before me, and the die of a thousand years was cast.

Twenty-Nine

John Quincy

That book was like nothing I have ever seen, and it was so much more than I had expected. Old Doc had whispered on the phone that he had something he believed would interest me. A project that he said was extraordinary. Something that could possibly reveal the path of a man's life to him—both his present and his past. I had hesitated then. Our conversations had been few over the years until finally there were none at all. The memory of them was practically nonexistent, so why now his sudden phone call requesting that I come to assist him on a matter? Was it to pay him back for his time and trouble in getting me patched up and out of Bittersweet? Was this when somehow my check had to be cashed in return? Regardless of what I tried to ask, he couldn't, or wouldn't, tell me anything more. Just that the matter was of great importance. When I didn't answer, he finally had added, "And a man's future. This book...this thing...somehow knows a man's future." I told him I would think about it, but Cilla heard every word I said. I put the phone in the cradle, and she questioned me for over an hour. "Tell me again about the book," she would begin. "Tell me everything again." She was such a twist, that one; but she'd been in and out of my life for years, finding me every time I moved on.

What I hadn't counted on was that little Mercy Land would meet me in the rain. I didn't even recognize her all grown up, but when she told me her name and I looked closer, of course it was her. Those big Land eyes staring back at me through that young woman's face. Later, when she got riled, I saw that spitfire Bittersweet Creek girl was still in there too. She'd been mad at me for good reason. It would be better for her if she stayed mad. Mercy had always been able to look straight down into the cracks in my soul. Now I'm trying to keep those covered up. I keep asking her to trust me when I don't even trust myself. Then I tell her not to in a moment of honesty. But I hadn't known when I bought the ticket and got on the train that she would be a part of this. All I knew is that I finally had a chance to get what I felt like I deserved. A long overdue debt might somehow finally be collected. And there in the background, Cilla was more than willing to help me, no, *require me* to cash in on that possibility.

I was delirious after they opened that book to me. A madman touching another world. Drinking in more of it than I could hold. Traveling through lives and ages in only minutes and everything moving as if it were light itself. And exactly what are the limits of its possibilities? Can a man make a choice that will change time itself? Change the outcome of a man's bad hand? Could he really repair the past? I plan to find out. And if it's so, I know what other men would pay to have that power to affect their destiny.

I've talked Mercy into going to Bittersweet with the book. And a tiny place in me regrets the game. But it's a tiny part that I am willing to silence. I know what I would give to change what happened to me.

Everything.

THIRTY

I'm trapped in my dream again. Over and over I'm calling to that man, but my voice isn't reaching him. There he is, papers scattered all about him, blowing from that wind, the very light of them disappearing on that empty street. And he looks lost beyond lost. He looks hopeless. As if the truth of the matter has just fallen onto his shoulders but it was a moment too late. Then the only thing in my dream is the book. I see it rise before me, replacing the man. It opens of its own accord, and a name begins to surface.

I opened my eyes, and there was the box on my night table. Somehow even in my subconscious mind, it had reached out to me. When I came in last night, I put it in the dresser but eventually wasn't happy with that. Then I hid it under the bed but got up to move it again. It wasn't until I put it right in front of me on the nightstand that I could sleep, knowing that it was within reach. I was watching over it, my eyes getting heavier and heavier until I finally drifted off to sleep.

Last night's bargain rose to the surface of my mind. It was a Bittersweet Creek day, and I hadn't even told Doc. He needed to be prepared. I decided I should call immediately, so I put on my robe and slippers and stepped into the hallway, careful to use my key and lock my door behind me.

I tiptoed down the hall, trying to get to the phone quietly without alerting Miss Perry. I had just made it down three steps when I heard John's voice in the hall. I paused, surprised that he was awake at this hour. Generally people slept a little later around the boardinghouse to give Miss Perry ample time to ready herself and make breakfast.

Then I realized John was having a one-sided conversation. He was on the phone in the hallway directly below the staircase. Who could he be calling at this hour? Or maybe he'd had the same idea I had. Maybe he was speaking to Doc to let him know about our plans. I sat down quietly on the top stair to listen. If that was what he was doing, it would save me a phone call, and I could get dressed.

It only took a moment for me to realize that wasn't the case. Whoever John was talking to wasn't in Bay City. That much I could gather. I heard him laugh softly, and then he answered a question.

"No, I'm not certain. I'll know more tonight." There was a pause. "I don't believe that's going to be a problem. Trust me. No, I wouldn't advise that right now. No, look"—his voice took on a harder tone—"this isn't your concern right now. I'll let you know if there's anything you can do." A pause again and then, "I understand."

I waited for a good-bye, but it sounded as though he replaced the receiver. Then I heard him approaching the stairs. Trapped!

The only thing I could do was turn around and call Doc as planned. He started up the stairs without noticing me at first.

"Good morning," I said, cheerful as you please. "You're up early."

"Ah, business from Atlanta."

"I see." We stood there awkwardly for a moment. Me pretending not to have overheard his phone call and him fully knowing I did. "I'm calling Doc to tell him we'll be going to Bittersweet Creek today. Is that still the plan?" I pulled my robe tighter around me, feeling a little plain, my hair a mess. "We aren't going without him. We can't take the book and leave Doc behind."

"No change of plans, and I wouldn't think of leaving Doc behind." He continued up the stairs as I walked down them. Then he turned, laid his hand on my arm in passing. "And thanks, Mercy." I didn't know what he was referring to. Then he added, "For everything," and without a pause hurried up the stairs. I heard the door to his room open and close before I reached the telephone.

Our breakfast was unusually quiet. Miss Perry had tried to get John Quincy to tell her more about the big city of Atlanta or other places he had lived. He was so noncommittal about everything that she finally stopped asking. My mind was focused entirely on the book that lay in my lap just below the table's edge. More and more I was tempted to open it, to study it on my own. But Doc and I had agreed that it was dangerous to do so. The book was enticing in such a way that the journey could go on forever, one life to the next, to the next. It was a wild labyrinth of stories, hard, fast, and true. Some broken and then mended. Some stellar, like fine handblown crystal that never dulled. And in that way, it was like an eternity every time you tried to read it. And once inside those pages, you didn't want the experience to end. If I opened it alone, I might never come back.

Sam sat next to me at the table. He eyed John suspiciously, then left the table without a good-bye and went back to his room. He was a fisherman by trade, but arthritis had hit him so hard that the deep waters were no place for him. So he was landlocked in a boardinghouse, and he hated it. By association, he seemed to hate all the rest of us and everything related to daily living. Although the grouch left, we weren't far behind him in mood. We sat silent and brooding, each lost in our own thoughts. I excused myself and went to my room. I sat there with the book in its box, wanting to open it, my fingers trembling. There was a soft knock on the door.

"Mercy, are you ready?"

It was the man with nine lives and two faces. Just when I was ready to forgive him, to trust him, something always popped up, like that phone call, that made me know I needed to be careful. His company was pleasing, but he was up to no good.

"Coming," I called out and took the tiny key from around my neck and locked the box. I picked up my purse, the treasure box with the book, and opened the door.

DOC'S JOURNAL

So the Bittersweet boy is determined to take the book out of here. To take it home and to try to set things right. I saw it in his eyes yesterday. Mercy was right, and I knew it. Forgive me someday, Mercy, for not telling you all. She protects the book now, carrying it about with her like a guardian angel. That doesn't surprise me. It was always safe in Mercy's keeping, and it was the reason I gave her the key. She is without guile and blind ambition. Most men and women would be tempted to alter the course of their lives through that book. To benefit from twisting time to and fro like a snake that might be handled. I'm no different, I'm afraid. Not in the end. And Mercy has been right all along. Anyone could smash that box, break the lock, or tear it apart piece by piece. Anyone, that is, but me. It was Opal's gift on our wedding anniversary. *"For your journal, love, so you can keep it safe from me."* Then that sound of her laughter, like water for my soul. Oh how I miss Opal's laugh. That was in the early years of our marriage. And the treasure box has held many journals since then, but it was never locked. That was just Opal's idea. I hid nothing from her. But when this book came upon me, so obvious at first glance that it was worth protecting, I knew the box would hold it. And I gave Mercy the key right away. I wouldn't bust it open for anything. I wouldn't.

THIRTY-ONE

The ride to Bittersweet Creek was a quiet one. I drove, and Doc rode up front with me. The box containing the book was between us on the car seat. John Quincy sat directly behind me. I glanced in the rearview mirror from time to time and watched him. He was usually in profile, staring out the window. Once I glanced up and caught his eyes watching me. *You won't change things,* I thought. *You're going to wind up right back where you found yourself.* Ida always said the road to regret was a futile journey. Sometimes she just made plain good sense.

"Unless we want to spend a portion of the day visiting with my folks, we'll have to make sure my car isn't seen all over the place. Any ideas on where we're going?"

"Other side of the creek, Mercy. My old stomping grounds."

So that was it. Open the book at the scene of the crime. I glanced over at Doc, but he was looking straight ahead. He didn't say anything. Maybe he was thinking of what was going on back at the office with all the repairs. Of all things, Doc had called on Old Whistler to keep an eye out, as he told him, on the installation of the new window. Doc was getting in the habit of calling on people for odd favors at odd times. Maybe the book had affected him in more ways than I was aware of. First Miss Perry, now Whistler. Or maybe he had seen who he could trust and who he couldn't. Of course if that was the case, I sure wish John Quincy's name had surfaced again. It certainly would have made it easier if Doc and I could have seen where the two-sided path that John was walking down was going to lead him. And where it was going to carry us.

I turned down the third dirt road along the creek. It was still wet from yesterday's storm that must have passed through after it cleared the coast. Which made me think that I should check on Mama, Daddy, and Ida Mae. Just in case they'd had some damage of their own. The winds could spin off tornadoes all over the place.

We passed a few shacks built up a little on pilings that saved them when the waters rose and the floods came. And eventually the water always rose. Water rising wasn't something we had to worry about too much on the other side of the creek where the bank was higher. Here it was muddy, flat, and lonesome. That's how I always felt about it. Like a place that had been left behind.

"There, through the trees." John pointed to what was left of his old house. If there were ever a place that looked lonesome and forgotten, this was it. And oh so sad, like nothing good had ever happened in it. The porch sagged, and the tiny roof had fallen in so that part of the roof met the porch. The woods were so overgrown around it that vines had attached themselves to the house, working their way into and across the windows. I parked the car as close as I could. Before I opened the door, I looked at him in the rearview mirror and said, "Are you sure about this?" He didn't act like he had heard me at all. He opened his car door and said, "The book?"

I laid my hand on top of the box. Doc looked at me, and I searched his eyes for some kind of signal that would say everything was okay. I didn't find one.

"We'll know soon," he said and opened his door.

That wasn't the reassurance I had hoped for. But I agreed with him. We'd know soon if the names appeared and if John Quincy could find his past and change his history. I picked up the box, testing its weight to see if maybe it was lighter, to see if the book had disappeared. Then a fear came over me so strong that I wanted to put the box back in the car and drive off, leaving Doc and John standing there in the woods. I feared the book would turn to dust and with it every person listed there. That it would be like Daddy's sermon on manna. Not the receiving of the good stuff but the things that came after. The part with the hoarding and the maggots.

John stood on the porch of what was left of the house and shoved open the door with his shoulder. From the looks of things on the outside, the state of affairs inside had to be pretty nasty, and I wished I had on my work clothes and boots from home. Doc was waiting on me. I stepped out of the car onto the wet earth.

Doc looked over his shoulder and then leaned down to me, whispering, "Just remember, no matter what, that you are the keeper of the book now."

"What are you talking about?"

"If there need to be adjustments, just do it," Doc said.

"It's not mine to—"

"Don't argue with me." Doc looked up at the house. There was no sight or sound of John. We made our way through what had once been a yard. An old azalea bloomed, a few pink flowers opened, and I suddenly felt so sorry for his mother. All these years over here with no one, and her only son sneaking around from time to time to see her.

"I don't like this place," I said, and we stepped carefully up onto the rotten boards. I walked ahead of Doc into the house, and there stood John in the middle of the tiny room, or what was left of it. The vines had grown through the broken windows, and obviously animals had moved in. Maybe possums or raccoons. There was the smell of old, wet wood. Without realizing it, I had clutched the box tightly and held it to my chest with both arms wrapped about it.

There John stood, eyes closed like he wasn't even with us. Sometimes you can see the pain of a person's heart. Sometimes it is so strong it becomes a tangible thing. I could have sworn that a dark cloud encircled him. Something so wrought with old hurt that I caught my breath. He must have heard me, as he opened his eyes and turned his face toward me. "Don't feed that thing," I said before I knew it. The words had formed and come out of their own accord. Tears had sprung up in my eyes, and I didn't care; we were in an awful place, and I felt that clutching the book was all that kept me upright.

Doc laid his hand on my shoulder, ushered me another step farther into the room. He looked around the floor, strewn with pieces of things. Broken glass. Old bits of paper. "We'll need a place to open it. Some place"—he was apparently searching for a word instead of *clean*—"safe."

John looked around for a moment and said, "Maybe this wasn't such a good idea after all." Then he put his hands in his pockets and walked out of the room. I had been to his house only once in all those years, and it was only for a few minutes while I waited for him outside. While none of us had a lot, I always felt his home had an extra slice of sorrow. A place the sun would never shine.

I looked at Doc and mouthed the words, "What now?" then stepped over the debris and walked around turned-over furniture and other things that had been abandoned. John stood in what looked like a little bedroom. An iron bed was still pushed against the wall, but the mattress had been eaten through. It smelled of animals.

He moved his foot about, going through the stuff on the floor. "You know I own this place outright? I guess I should clean it up a little." He looked at me and smiled weakly. He knelt down and picked up something, scraped the mud from it. Then he stood and laid it on what was left of the windowsill. "I never even came back and got her things." He knelt down again, picking through the trash. "Not very good of me, huh?" His fingers traced through the dirt, searching for anything worth keeping. "She was always good to me; I want you to know that. She was just a scared woman. Tired and very scared." He stood up as Doc stepped into the doorway.

He said, "Let's go for now. This is something I need to do, but I can do it alone. There's no reason to drag the two of you through"—he looked at what was left of his yesterday life—"this mess."

Again the silence fell on us, and no one said anything until we'd all gotten safely in the car. I placed the box on the seat and reached for the car keys.

Then Doc stopped me short, saying, "John, there's only one way for you to know for sure if this book will let you reach the past from here. If that old number can be dialed. It's why you came here. If you don't try, you'll always wonder if things would have been the same."

Doc had lost his mind. We had almost made it out of this sad place without a horrible incident.

I looked at the reflection of John in the mirror. It was as if a rock had hit the water, rippling the reflection on the surface until it began to calm. Only this time the image never looked the same. "You're right. Open the book."

"Mercy, the key, please."

Sometimes good people need to leave well enough alone.

THIRTY-TWO

It could have been a day or a lifetime. If we hadn't finally driven out of those woods and found somebody, we would never have known. You just can't open up another world and expect it not to open you up as well. I reached to my neck, and there was the key on its chain. I reached out to feel for the box without looking. It was still there.

Doc had both hands on the dashboard as if bracing himself from something. I was driving the car down the back roads of Bittersweet. That much I recognized. I knew the old houses, the way they leaned on their pilings. The way they stubbornly sat there, defying the creek to rise again. There was the water to my left. That meant we were on the other side of the bank. That meant I was driving toward Aunt Ida's of my own accord. Some part of me had just steered in that direction.

I looked in the rearview mirror for John Quincy, but no one was there. I slammed on the brakes in the middle of the road, turned, and looked in the backseat. He wasn't there.

"Doc?" I reached out and grabbed his shoulder and shook him. He still seemed dazed. "Where is he? What have we done?"

"Let's go home, Mercy."

"But I don't remember. Just the car, just pulling the key from around my neck, passing it to you. That's the last I remember." I let off the brake and accelerated. "Did we…do something to…kill him?"

"I don't know where he is."

"I'll turn around. I'll go back."

"That's just it. You can't go back."

"Then where is he, Doc?" My voice was climbing higher and higher, and I surely didn't like not remembering where'd I'd been or what was happening.

"You closed the book. I told you that you'd do it, and you did." He sighed like a weary old man. A deep, exhausting sigh. I rolled my window down and felt the early night air dropping down.

"You're not answering any of my questions to please me. Not a bit."

"I told you that you had the power to keep the book. I don't remember anything more than this: I opened the box with the key. John leaned over the seat, and the three of us looked into the book as I opened it. Then it was like there was the sound of thunder. You took the book from my hands and closed it and locked it away." He turned sideways in the seat. "Whatever it is, Mercy, I think it is safe with you. I really do."

"Doc! Forget about the book for now. Where is he? I mean, for goodness' sake—for all we know he's in the book! You ever think of that?"

He turned back around to face front and rolled his window down as well. The wind whipped through my hair. "I thought I had everything figured out that I possibly could. None of it made any difference."

There was a foggy mist forming on the surface of the creek. Doc and I drove over the bridge where John and I had stopped only a few days before to look down at the water. I drove slowly past Mama and Daddy's. Besides the flowers being beaten down, some from the storm, everything looked all right. Ida's was a different story. She was standing outside next to the road by her mailbox, looking like for everything that she had been expecting us to come this way.

Ida's house had never looked better. I was still in a woozy state. And as much as I knew Doc wanted to go home, he was in no place to argue with me about where I went. We were still missing John Quincy and didn't have a clue what had happened to him. For reasons I didn't know, Doc was opposed to going back to the old house to look for him, which seemed to me the most logical thing to do. The only right thing to do. We were about to get into our first real argument since my employment when I spotted Ida. How in the world did she know we were out here? I pulled onto the grass next to her little cabin.

With her hands on her backside, she leaned way over toward me in the window and looked across at Doc. Then she said, "Uh-huh," nodding her head. She straightened up and continued nodding and saying, "Uh-huh. That explains it. I knew it. I just knew it," as she turned around and left us, walking toward her house. I had no choice but to get out of the car and said, "C'mon, Doc, it's only for a minute." And then the idea of saying anything was only a minute, the idea of a minute itself, seemed particularly child-like. And it made me turn around and get the box out of the car. I couldn't leave it.

"Why this misery, Mercy?" Doc asked me.

"Get out of that car, or I'm gonna give you some."

It sure was difficult being everybody's everything. I turned around and looked across the creek, half expecting the younger version of John to be standing there at the water's edge, saying, "C'mon, Mercy. Let's go." But it was smooth as glass, with the mist getting thicker and still rising.

Inside I begged Ida for hot chocolate, and she complied. Doc shook his head that he was just fine. She eyed him. "Piece of cheese then?" she asked.

"A piece of cheese would be very nice, thank you."

Cheese? I suppose he was just trying not to hurt her feelings. I had to admit that through other people's eyes, maybe Aunt Ida was as peculiar as Daddy had always said she was. Actually, he said a lot of things about her. One of them was that she talked in rid-dles that hurt his head. I had understood her all my life, but then, she was the second person I had ever laid eyes on. That had to count for a lot of understanding. Aunt Ida brought Doc a slice of her hoop cheese and put it on a plate in front of him. Then she added a piece of bread, and he really did look pleased. Said some-thing silly like "Oh my" and took a bite.

Then she pointed at the box and asked, "What's that?"

"The big secret," I answered. I stood and walked to the screen door and looked outside toward the creek. Not a sign of anything happening. Not a sign of anybody.

"The secret, huh? In a box the size of…"

"Smaller than a breadbasket." I filled in the blanks for her. I could smell her gardenia bush on the porch. She brought my cup to the table and set it down, then she laid a hand on top of the box, and I flinched. She caught that too.

"Not meaning to make you nervous, girl." She scratched at her neck. "Just wondering why it's locked."

She already knew I had that key around my neck, had seen me fiddling with it on my last visit. She hated secrets between us, and I hated keeping them. It would be so much easier to simply show her. I placed my hand on my neck. Of course there were other secrets that had been kept. "Aunt Ida, did you know that Doc helped Tommy Taylor escape when he was a boy?" She gave a grunt but not an answer. "And did you know that someone from Bittersweet helped him get to Doc's?" I pulled up a chair and faced them both.

"Wait," Doc cautioned and then glanced at Ida and swiftly back at me. "Perhaps in a little while." He took a bite of his cheese and studied Ida fiercely. She pulled up a chair and sat down. I took another sip, and the showdown began. It was what I'd heard of those bullfights in Spain when the bull charged into the ring. We were all determined to win this. I got up and left them there, walked to the screen again. The last bit of sunlight was filtering through the trees and across the water. "This isn't over, you two. Not over by a long shot. I'll get to the truth, and I'll talk to Daddy.

Me and him's got a meeting coming." I turned back to the door, searching the road and beyond to the banks, watching for him to walk through those trees.

"You lose something out there?" Ida never took her eyes off Doc.

"Yes," I whispered. "A long time ago." I made up my mind that with or without Doc, I was going back over there before I returned to Bay City. It was impossible not to.

"Seems to me when that lightning bolt shot through the trees like it did a little bit ago from that spot over the creek, something was bound to disappear. I just didn't know what it would be."

I turned to face her. "Lightning?"

"Light, lightning, whatever you say. Could have caught the whole place on fire. Ashes to ashes."

"Dust to dust," Doc said, and Ida stood up like she was ready to fight him.

"You making fun of me? 'Cause if you are, you're barking up the wrong tree."

"Wouldn't think of it. I was thinking you were right. Ashes to ashes it is. All but a breath. All but a blink and it's gone."

She sat back down and started bargaining with him. "Well, seeing how I gave you the cheese and you ate it, how 'bout you let me see what's in that box there?"

"Miss Ida," he began.

"It's just Ida."

"Ida, it's not that simple. It's a rather complicated issue."

"Ha, you be thinking I'm simple as pie. Let me cut it for you, Mister Philips. You done bring that suit boy from 'lanta down here to fix your plan, but he's just an upside-down man. So your planning is poo." She pushed her chair back as she stood up. "You got lightning in a box that don't belong to you." Then she pointed up toward the heavens. "Think you got a doozie do-good going on. Better get busy 'fore you're gone, gone."

Aunt Ida was talking that chatter talk that came over her sometimes.

Doc looked at me and said, "My head hurts."

In spite of everything, the wild time and the unknown of the last few hours, with one look at Doc's pitiful face, I busted out laughing. Then Ida laughed too.

I put my cup on the table and picked up the box. "I'll tell you all about it soon as I can. Oh, and don't tell Mama and Daddy I came around today, okay? Hopefully they haven't seen me. Just no time for a good visit."

She zipped her lips, and I kissed her bye. "C'mon, Doc. Let's go home."

THIRTY-THREE

The crickets were getting louder by the minute, and the bull-frogs were calling out from the waterside. By the time we got to Bay City, the night noises would change. They'd be infused with birds calling out even in the late night, the sound of the streetlights changing, and the occasional car passing by.

I drove as quickly as I could back over the bridge. I turned on my brights, looking for Tommy's—no, that wasn't right—*John's* road. I was looking for the low side of the creek road, hurrying back to where we'd left him. The book, the whole experience had left me in a daze. My car had already pointed to Ida's of its own accord. Now the edges of that had worn off, and I was nail-biting mad that we had somehow left him in the middle of such a desolate place. Not that there weren't people up and down the creek on the low side too. Not that he couldn't have reached someone. But that place?

"We might have done him wrong," I said.

"Oh, we did him wrong. That's what I was trying to repair."

"No such thing, Doc. You were trying to fix your own guilty conscience. I wasn't raised on the Bittersweet for nothing. I know the shade of an animal when I see it. Spots, stripes, or feathers, it makes no mind to me."

"You're starting to sound like your Aunt Ida. It's alarming."

"Well, I'm just like her, don't you know?" I said, and at that moment—blood kin or not—it was Aunt Ida's wild courage that ran through my veins. I turned down the next road on the right and hit the gas pedal. For a moment the rear tires spun out in the dirt, then they lay down, and we took off, speeding through the trees and past the old houses.

"Mercy!" Doc said, his hands back on the dashboard. I ignored him. I was on a mission to save a man, and I guess a part of me was hoping that the man would be my old friend. But the other part of me didn't care. The other part of me had begun to see that they were one and the same. And I could call him by any name in the book—he was both the old man and the new one, he was what he had become from the seeds of the past and whatever polluted present he had created. All of it had brought us together in this moment we were standing in, this tiny stream called *now*.

I pulled up at the house. Even the light seemed thinner here, the trees all overgrown and the darkness looking as if it rose up from the very ground. "Hand me the flashlight out of the glove compartment."

Doc did as I asked, but he said, "Mercy, I have to tell you the truth: I'm afraid. There is something dark about this place. Really, tangibly dark."

He had sweat on his brow and on his upper lip, and his hand shook a little when he passed me the flashlight. "Me too," I said. I looked at the dark, broken-down old place, at the vines encrusting it, and wondered if we'd find John inside. And if he was there, what condition would he be in? What would be left of him? "We'd be crazy not to be afraid right now. It just makes good sense."

"Lock that door." I locked mine and closed it, tried to find his face over the roof of the car, but it was already too dark. All I saw was his outline. "We're leaving it here." He didn't bother to ask what; he knew. This was one time I felt like the book would be safer locked up out here than going back in that place with me.

I turned on the flashlight and cast the light in front of us. The dark seemed to eat at it, swallowing it as we tried to find our way and move forward. I slapped my palm against the base a few times, thinking it might be the batteries, but they were new. I wished I had Mama's water-walking, door-kicking faith. I tried to imagine what she'd do in a case like this when I stepped up on the porch and heard the wood groan. Then I reached out and grabbed Doc's sleeve as we inched forward. We might as well have been five years old the way we were shaking and creeping. *Get hold of yourself, Mercy Land,* I said in my sternest silent voice. It usually toughened me up a little, but this time my knees shook in response. You would have to stand right in this place—so thick with sad and bitter that the stars couldn't even shine through—to know why we trembled so.

"Anybody home?" I called out in a weak voice. "John, are you in there?" Doc slowly pushed the door open that was standing ajar. We took one step inside and stopped right there. I shined the little light around the room and from corner to corner. It was the exact same mess we'd left. Then I thought of something and tried, "Tommy?" in a whisper.

"Do you think we have to go further?" Doc asked me.

I clutched his arm even tighter. "We do, Doc, oh, we do. We have to go all the way in." By now I didn't think I could even breathe. I wanted to throw down that light and run, run for my life. To drive out of there and never look back. I guess that's the way Tommy had felt. And I began to understand how he could leave like he did. How he could go for years and years and not come back to this. How he could never, ever come back to this.

I started to call him again, but even the sound of my voice felt leaden. Our footsteps shuffled along, and I kept shining the light back to our feet, but that left everything around us in the darkness so thick it felt like we were breathing in dark. We would stop so I could shine the light about the room again just to make certain of…well, just to make certain. We didn't speak but moved together, waiting for some dark and unseen predator. We felt as if something lurked just beyond our sight. Something that would grab us and we would disappear from this earth, never to be heard from again.

We wanted to hurry through the house, to be through it and out of there, but instead we ever so slowly stepped toward the back of the house. I held the light up and shone it around what must have been the kitchen. The back door was ripped from the hinges, and here the overgrowth had taken full liberty and moved into the house. Kudzu and poison ivy climbed the walls. We backed away and shuffled to where John had knelt down on the floor, rummaging through the refuse there. I shined the light across what was left of the bed and released Doc's arm to kneel down and sweep the light under the bed.

"Nothing," I said, quickly clutching his sleeve again.

We stepped back into the little hallway. I heard a shuffle of some sort and snapped around to shine the light in all directions. The swiftly scattered light made things look even more frightening, so I stopped.

"I heard it," Doc whispered.

"Probably just a rat," I said, and we moved slowly to the other room.

Here, the room was as if someone had just left it this morning. A small bed was against one wall, a tiny chest beside it. The bed was made, a quilt covering lay on top, neatly folded at the foot. It wasn't animal eaten. The floor was swept clean—no leftover trash, no animal droppings or nesting. The windows were opened to the night with the glass intact. There were no trees crashing through, no kudzu or other vines invading the space. We stepped inside, and I was so surprised I dropped Doc's arm. Pictures from catalogs were on the walls. A small collection of rocks and an old slingshot. I moved toward them and saw someone else in the room and let out a scream. The flashlight fell from my hand, and I heard it rolling across the floor, and we stood grasping at each other so hard and fast our knuckles were white.

"It was a mirror. Only a mirror."

"I know," I answered. "It just took me by surprise is all." The light rolled on the floor casting odd images as it moved. Then it hit the small bureau, where it came to rest. We could see the large, shadowy outlines of ourselves.

"Don't touch anything," Doc told me.

"This room— How did it get this way? Why is it like this?"

"It's not natural…and he's not here." For the first time today,

Doc had begun to sound like his old self. Factual and logical. He stepped away from me and picked up the flashlight. I followed in his shadowy wake, my arm outstretched and reaching for him. I passed my image in the mirror again and shuddered. It looked like someone trapped in another space. The effect of the whole house, including this room, made me want to run to the car. "Doc?" I whispered, urgent and fretful. I didn't care how much better he felt; I was more put off by the eeriness of the room than I was the rest of the entire house.

"Doc, let's just climb out the window," I said, eyeing the outside like it was the greatest drink of water a thirsty girl could get.

"What we're seeing isn't natural. This could just be an echo from the book, like a photograph our minds took. It's not real. The windows could actually be jagged glass. We have to go back."

We didn't speak another word. I clutched Doc's arm, and he led the way out, holding the light in front of him. Something scurried through the front room, but Doc never wavered in the direction of the flashlight or his steps. We were focused on one thing: getting out of there.

I didn't speak until I had unlocked the car and was safely behind the wheel. I reached for the other door lock and popped it open, and Doc got inside. I had the car started and in reverse before he closed the door. I tapped the box beside me one time and then made a circle as wild and fast going out as I had coming in. It wasn't until we were off that dirt road and back on the highway, my headlights pointing brightly in the direction of Bay City, that I dared to speak.

"I don't like it, Doc, I don't like it a bit, and we still haven't found him."

"I think he's going to have to find us."

Twelve miles down the road we flew past a hitchhiker on the edge of the highway, his thumb stuck out to the wind. I slammed on the brakes. It was John Quincy, as if Doc's words had manifested him from the very air. I looked at Doc, too surprised to even back up. Then John's face appeared next to my window and that honeyed-up voice said, "You folks going my way?"

THIRTY-FOUR

The John Quincy that slid smoothly into the backseat of the car was full of a kind of exuberance I'd only seen when he was another boy a long time ago on a good fishing day. He hung over the seat in between Doc and me, talking a mile a minute but not a word about what had taken place at the house. Not a word about where he'd been or what had happened to him. First it was something about Howard Hughes—had we heard he'd made news by breaking that old world record? Then it was about a new jazz player he'd heard of in Atlanta, which was a terrific town by the way in case we ever wanted to try it out. Apparently, Doc and I were in silent agreement that questioning him at the moment was not the best thing to do, so we let him ramble on hard and fast. He leaned so far forward that I started driving with my left hand, my right resting on that box like it was a heartbeat. Then I noticed that Doc's hand rested on the other corner. Whatever it was, we were both thinking the same thing: something had happened.

This man seemed...electrified. Like that room back there in that dark house, it left me uncertain. What troubled me was that the book had been opened for perhaps a different purpose than it was intended. The book was intended for something beyond

measure. Not just one man having a better go of it. Maybe I
shouldn't have passed the key to Doc in the first place, but there
I was—both of them asking for it and the book. It didn't belong
to me. It didn't come to me first. If it had, maybe something
would be different. If only we knew precisely what to do.

A few miles down the road he leaned forward again, tapping
on the back of the seat with his hands as if he could hear music,
rattling off something about boxing and seeing Joe Louis in a fight
last year and wasn't he just great? Then he asked Doc if he liked
baseball, but before Doc could answer, he was off again on another jaunt about what was happening in the leagues. As desperately as I had searched for him, now I just wanted to kick him out
of the car and leave him on the side of the road.

When we arrived in the city limits, he read the sign aloud as
if he had never seen such a thing: " 'Welcome to Bay City—A
Place of Refuge.' Well, ain't that sweet."

His speech, his energy was part boy, part man, and part something unknown to me. That something felt a little dangerous.

At the second traffic light he said, "Hey, if you don't mind, I'll
just hop out here. Think I'll take a little walk down to the club and
see if there's a horn playing somewhere."

I didn't know what to say. I wondered if he even knew where
he was for certain, if he remembered his things were at the boardinghouse. I got the feeling that no matter how wired he was, he
needed some looking after. Some direction and someone to make
sure he wasn't traveling all over town blabbing about the book.

"John, wait." I looked at Doc, trying to let him know what I was up to. "Why don't Doc and I come with you? We'll all find a horn together, how about that?"

"Smoking, Mercy." He thumped the back of the seat hard and leaned back. "Just a smoking idea."

"Uh, no. This old man has had enough for one day," Doc said. "How about delivering me to my house before the trumpets start blowing?"

I drove to Doc's, thinking there was absolutely only one place with horns anywhere around, and that was the Bay City Club Dance Hall. I watched John in the rearview mirror, all smiles and arms outstretched over the back of the seat, fingers tapping out music I couldn't hear.

When I pulled up at Doc's driveway, I put the box in my lap and got out of the car. "Be right back," I said as Doc got out. There was something I needed to tell him. And I needed to leave the box with him no matter how much he protested. I had the key. The book was safer with him right now than with me. I was getting a little weary of the trouble. No, a lot weary. It was wearing on me. Then I realized I was wearing dirty clothes and flat shoes and was as unattractive as possible for a dancing kind of place. Maybe a quick change would be in order before we had to give it a whirl.

"Good night," Doc called as he opened his gate. I rushed after him.

"No, no. Here, take this." I pushed the box toward him before he could say no. "I don't want to keep it tonight." I thrust it in his hands. "It's okay; you'll keep it safe." He looked down at it like a man holding a newborn for the first time, like it was some-thing fragile that he could break or lose at any moment.

"C'mon, c'mon. Time to shake a tail feather." John was now jumping into the front seat.

"Somebody's got to watch him. I mean, just look at him." We both turned to see him grinning through the windshield, beating on the dash. "Something's up."

"Out of order," he said and carried the box forward. As he closed the gate behind him, he said, "All is out of order." I think he was really talking to himself. He was trying to work it out in his mind as usual.

I pulled up at the boardinghouse and asked John to give me a few moments to change. He didn't even bother coming in. Just got out and stood next to the car for a moment. Then I heard him shuffling—dancing, if you will—and something about the sound caught my attention, but I was rushing at full speed through the foyer and past Miss Perry, waving off her questions, racing up the stairs and into my room. I grabbed a dress and hurried down the hall to freshen up as best I could. Then I pulled the dress over my head and put on my best shoes, which still were really not built for dancing. They were church shoes.

Somewhere a little voice inside was asking me about this whole idea. Was I really keeping an eye out, or was I looking forward to getting out of these four walls with the man who— I stopped in midthought. "I don't know the man," I said aloud. "I need to remember: I don't know that man downstairs." Then I powdered my nose and put on lipstick. "Out for a little while," I said as I hurried past Miss Perry, who was trying to say something, most likely about her curfew.

John Quincy let out a low whistle. He made big sweeping gestures as he hustled around to open my door for me.

Yes, I very well needed to question my motives. Apparently it was too late for guarding my heart. It was gone. I knew it, and I wasn't fooling myself. A little perfume, a little lipstick. No doubt the handsome man sitting next to me needed help and needed watching over, but I knew myself well enough to know my best dress, my best shoes—I was finally getting an escort to a dance. I was leaving Old Doc and that beautiful book and all that it brought with it behind for the night, getting swooped up in whatever energy had gotten into the mysterious John Quincy. If only for one special evening. A girl could ask for that, right? Just to pretend for one night?

I was about to find out the answers in more ways than I had counted on as a clap of thunder rolled across the sky.

"Awww, come on," he said, looking out the window at the sky. "Haven't we had enough already?"

I pulled up to the dance hall, and we got out of the car. The band was already playing, and John was smiling because it had horns. We opened the door as they hit the first notes of the next song and the first drops of rain fell from the night sky. Just inside the door a small stairway led down to the dance floor, where the lights were low. The band was on the stage directly across from us, wearing black suits and white ties, their horn section gleaming in the spotlight, and the drums pounding.

Not a moment wasted, John grabbed my hand, led me down the stairs, and then without hesitation literally swept me off my feet onto the dance floor. We were already three turns around the dance floor, moving in a slow, close waltz. The feeling of him holding me was better than I'd hoped for when I realized something of paramount importance: I knew why the sound of him dancing had almost stopped me in my tracks at home. His limp was gone. I had doubted he could even dance before; it was too pronounced. Not like this, not in a wild whirl, his feet moving for all the world like a man who had never missed a beat. A part of me screamed, *Stop!* A part of me screamed, *Ask him what happened, then go tell Doc!*

But the other part willed it all away, refusing to think of the past or bad, dark places or occurrences that defied things as sure as gravity.

I was determined to forget about my old friend Tommy Taylor. I wasn't even interested in him anymore. Not where he went, what happened, or what became of him. The only person I had eyes for was the man holding me, moving me to the beat of the band. Well, as Aunt Ida would say, I was no fool. I knew when I stepped under those lights, when I looked up at his face as he wrapped his arms around me, that I was a goner. And that wasn't good.

There are times when you come face to face with yourself in the mirror—and not the kind on the wall but the kind where internal truths are evident. I had one of those times right there under those white lights. I was a lonely woman, a part of me indeed fearing that Miss Perry's lot in life would someday be mine. Old and alone. I could see myself huddled in a corner, maybe back on the Bittersweet. Someplace safe and familiar where I could live with an old, stray cat. Just me and the cat. My future didn't look too bright. Doc couldn't live forever. And after working for Doc at the *Banner,* what else would I ever do? Maybe get a job at the courthouse filing other people's marriage certificates? Stay on at the boardinghouse until Miss Perry faded away? For all my play at big and brave, at faking a kind of contented, secluded life that I preferred, I was only lying to myself. And this night that didn't bear logical reason, that was tinged with something that felt off course, might be the big night I remembered for the rest of my life. The night I got to dance with the most dashing man in town.

This realization fell on me with such fullness that I staggered and missed my step so that John caught me. If I asked him about his foot, I felt like some spell would be broken. And that with it, the way he danced with me, the way he led me carefully off the dance floor and to the edge of the hall, where we stood together, would be lost as well. The fact was, he still had his arm around my waist, and I could feel the heat of his hand through my dress. I didn't want to say anything that might cause him to leave. He was leaning in close, whispering something as we moved in rhythm with "Begin the Beguine" so that I tried to get closer to hear him. I could feel his breath warm on my neck.

I wouldn't have moved in an earthquake, but just then something more dangerous walked in.

She entered the room like smoke moving just ahead of a fire—a forewarning that something was coming that would scorch and burn. Just inside the door, she closed the umbrella that she

carried with her and untied her coat. She glanced over her shoulder, and someone appeared to take both it and the umbrella away.
There was no coat-check man, no coat checkroom, but for her,
well, there was probably nothing she couldn't have or manifest at
the bat of an eye or a toss of those platinum waves.

An audible sigh rippled through the room at the sight of her.
I think it was women wishing they looked like that. For the men,
their sigh might have been more appreciation for the way she wore
her hair. She walked slowly down the stairs. Surveying us all like
prey, her eyes searched until they latched on the one thing she
wanted—the man standing beside me. John dropped his hand
from my waist; the fairy tale was over as quickly as it had begun.

Dancers stopped dancing as she walked straight through the
middle of that dance floor, paying them no mind, as if they were
not of substance at all, nothing but a vapor. She glittered when she
moved, her eyes only looking forward. Her dress sparkled, and so
did the diamonds she wore around her neck, her wrists, and her
fingers. I had never seen a woman so covered with ice. The closer
she drew to us, the more I felt myself growing uglier, plainer. *Land*
was befitting at that moment. I was nothing but a lump of drab
dirt.

The scent of something preceded her, something so thick and
intoxicating that even I breathed deeper and half closed my eyes.
Then she was standing directly in front of John, and I was nothing but a washed-out afterthought.

"Hello, tiger," she said and kissed him full on the lips. "I just
couldn't wait any longer to see you. What's new?"

Without even a nod in my direction, he wrapped his hands

around her waist and moved her across the dance floor. They both shimmered, caught in the light cast by all her diamonds. With every twirl of her skirt, they became a beautiful blur of laughter, moving forward through people as if they were gods dancing among mortals made of stone.

THIRTY-FIVE

My windshield wipers were working overtime to bat back the rain. It was coming down so thick I couldn't see, and my crying wasn't helping. There was no way I could go back to the boardinghouse tonight. I couldn't face Miss Perry or my lonely room, and Lord knows I couldn't bear to hear John Quincy come up those stairs. Not tonight. Of course, who knew where he'd end up, and the thought of that made me actually sob. For the second time I was headed to Bittersweet, driving fast on the slick roads. If only I could get to Aunt Ida fast enough. I'd tell her everything. I would. Maybe she could fix things.

I turned left onto the creek road, the entire day on my mind: the old house and the horror of it, the way he had just appeared on the road, the lame foot gone, the wildness of John Quincy, and then—"Hello, tiger." I hit the accelerator, hoping that speed would help take away the pain, that the faster I could go, the greater chance I had of leaving it all behind. The last thing I remembered was the tires spinning out of control, the car crashing through the trees and sliding wildly down the bank toward the muddy water before a loud crash, and then nothing.

I woke up with my head on the steering wheel. The car was pitched forward into a couple of pine trees, the engine still running, the lights shining eerily through the pines and down to where they disappeared above the water. I sat up slowly and turned off the engine. Then I carefully opened the door and fell out, sliding as I did in my dress along the wet mud and pine needles, sticks, and roots. I was scratched to the nether regions. I tried to look back behind me, to judge where I was, and then I slid the rest of the way down the bank until I fell into the edge of the water.

Sometimes life can bring people a kind of misery that is brand-new, and at that moment anything familiar, anything at all is a reassurance. Right then all I wanted was what I had been born straight into. I crawled along the banks of the Bittersweet until I could stand, my feet scratched and probably bloody. The water moved about my knees, and I walked in the direction of Aunt Ida's, deciding that I'd follow the curving bank of the water and crawl out where the bank was lower, below her house. The rain hadn't stopped completely, but it had let up to a steady drizzle. Occasionally I'd see shining eyes in low bushes at the edge of the water and figured it was raccoons. I didn't hear the bark of the wild dogs that sometimes roamed the creek, no owls in the rain to call out, and no stars. But the dark was bearable and not unfriendly. I tried not to think of anything but reaching a place that was warm to my soul.

"Aunt Ida! Aunt Ida Mae!" She opened the door before I

reached her. I was sobbing again by the time she had thrown open the door and held out her waiting arms. After she washed me and dried me off, put ice on my banged-up head, and made me hot cocoa, I sat with her in a pair of her flannel pajamas, my hair hanging wet, and tried to tell her everything that had led up to my condition.

When I thought of them glittering on the dance floor again, my tears resumed. Ida spoke. "You are Mercy Land, born in a lightning bolt. Twenty-seven," she said, "loved by everyone."

"By everyone? I don't use the love word loosely."

"Loved like outta your mind sometime." She gave a hard pat of the hand to my thigh. "A mighty good girl."

"I'm not so good," I said. "I have very dark thoughts right now."

"The world has dark thoughts." She cocked an eyebrow. She rocked awhile and thought a bit, then continued. "It's them that acts on them that will have the reckoning."

I got out of my chair and threw myself at her feet, forcing the rocking to a stop. "I'm in love, Aunt Ida," I said.

"I know," she said. "I know."

"Tell me what I should do." She reached down and stroked my hair, not answering. "Deliver me, Aunt Ida. Please deliver me."

She lifted her hand, moved me away, and stood up. "We love and we lose and we go on." She tried so hard to be tough, to lead by example, but there were tears in her eyes.

"Deliver me," I whispered again, "please."

She came back to me with open arms and knelt beside me. I

laid my head down on her shoulder. She rocked me softly back and forth, holding me there, whispering, "Not my power to deliver, Mercy."

She leaned back, held me at arm's length. "You've crawled right up out of those banks of the Bittersweet and gone on to breathe."

"But I don't feel like breathing. I feel like killing or being killed. I think I will not survive this affliction."

"You need to sleep now. Tomorrow we'll find Johnny Cakes to pull that car out and see about the damage done."

"No, Ida." I wiped my face with the hem of the flannel shirt, picked up my cup. "I have to tell you some things."

"The special box?"

I nodded. "It's much more than a box. It's a great and terrible mystery."

"It ain't human?"

I understood what she meant was that it was not made by man and was not of this world. I had learned to understand her a long time ago.

"Not by a long shot."

"And now it be where?"

"Doc has it. I asked him to keep it." I sat down with my cup by her feet. "This is how it all began. A few months ago Doc received this book, not in the normal mail, mind you. It just showed up one night on his desk. In the early morning, just after dawn, he called, asking me to come over."

I told Ida all about the book, beginning to end, leaving out no small detail. In the process of my rolling the story out, she forgave me for not already letting her in on something of this great significance. She knew I had been trying to be loyal to Doc and to keep things as quiet as possible. But now things had gotten off course, as Doc put it. Bringing Ida up to snuff, getting her take on things, seemed mighty important. It seemed crucial. I explained about Doc saying he had to find a man and then bringing John Quincy to town and how things really turned upside down from there.

Then I went on to explain about who John Quincy really was, asking her if she remembered Tommy Taylor from across the creek and telling how I found out it was Doc who had patched him up, changed his name, and got him out of town. She didn't seem surprised by any of that, just listened and sometimes asked a question to clarify things. I would slow down and add details about the book itself and what it was like to touch it, open it, and get lost in spaces that were beyond our easy footsteps on this earth.

Finally I got to this very day, with John Quincy at his old place, Doc and me losing ourselves in some kind of blackout, and me snapping out of it as I drove to her house.

"I told you I saw that light," she said.

She tried to describe what she had witnessed. A bright flash of light that scattered out through the trees on the other side of the bank. But from the ground up, not coming down from the sky. It happened when she had walked out to her mailbox.

We talked about me going back into that horrible place, about the unnatural way John's room looked, and about finding him then on the road, his limp somehow gone. I couldn't believe I hadn't noticed until so much later, when we were on the dance floor. Aunt Ida said that was because I'd been noticing other things.

"Well, I was just happy to know he was alive. That we hadn't somehow killed him by opening that book out of place or out of season."

I had told her all about that woman when I came in sobbing. Now I thought about that early-morning phone call. He had called her. The history between them was evident enough. As I thought about it, all of it, I felt I might cry again. Instead I grew quiet. My story had been told. The sorrow had gone into a deeper place. One where tears were kept in silence.

"Sleep now is the best thing for you. You are banged up through and through, inside and out." She stood and led me to my bed, pulled the quilt back, and tucked me in like a child. "Let tomorrow bring a new thing."

Then she returned to her chair instead of going to her own bed so that I fell asleep to the sound of Aunt Ida in her rocker, watching over me. I knew she was contemplating all that I had said and that by tomorrow she'd have something certain worked out in her head.

THIRTY-SIX

John Quincy

I made one phone call to say that the book was within our grasp. That the time for changing things once and for all had almost arrived. But Cilla was all predator, even from a distance. Like something on the prowl. Something insatiable. These were qualities she made no apologies for. She was hungry for power, hungry for money, hungry for whatever pleased her at the moment, but her moments were subject to change and her mood with it.

There are probably many things that a man can have a weakness for. Mine had become her, and it had been such a tiny trick at the time. At first she wasn't demanding; she was alluring but soft. That was in the beginning, when she had filled my deflated ego with a sense of self-esteem that didn't belong to me. She painted pictures of me as the man I wished I was. It was all a lie then—was still a lie now. We were far from the beginning, and now she had been around for so long that it was hard to distinguish what parts of me were left. It was as if she had eaten away what little was left of my soul, starting when she first arrived. Just a bit here and there so at first I never noticed I was doing her bidding. Then it had been as if her desires had become mine. If she hungered, then so did I. And if she was dissatisfied, so was I, and I had to find a way to meet that need. I'd met her in a juke joint in the backwoods of Georgia on a Saturday night. What someone like her was doing there, I still cannot figure out. It was a place that was out of the way. Nothing should have brought someone with her particular tastes to such a place. My tastes were different. They were much more like the place I'd come from.

After I left the boys' home, I wandered. I managed to do nothing more than squander a few years and hustle a few jobs here and there. I kept thinking I'd find a place that called to me, a place where I finally felt at home. That I'd settle down to a simple life. But that wasn't what happened. I just kept moving on. It got to where I'd wake up and go out in the morning in search of a paper to verify where I was. I had become shiftless and shady, and I knew it.

The closest to legitimate I'd ever come was once when I got a job with a newspaper in Macon, Georgia. I worked on the printing press. I was working at a place where people knew my name, where we talked about the headlines like they meant something to us. Naturally, I thought of the old days, that year of working in the back for Doc, but it wasn't much more than a memory of another boy's life. Like it didn't belong to me at all. Something I had just borrowed for a little while.

And always the foot pained me. It plagued me like my nightmares that came as waves, lifting me out of whatever peaceful sleep may have found me. Throwing me into a place where I'd relive that night over and over again. A night where a dark rage trapped inside my father would not be satisfied until it had broken bones and boy.

Yes, I would do anything to take back that night, to get back the life that should have been mine. After finally seeing the book, to know that it was real, to get drawn into those pages of light, and to understand the different paths a life could take, I determined more than ever to have my day. And I realized that the book was capable of so much more than making money. That had been Cilla's idea—to steal the book and then to sell it to the highest bidder on the black market.

Then Mercy was on the stairs as I hung up the phone—her hair in her eyes, barefoot in her robe, and somehow more precious than I'd ever seen her. Where there was darkness in my life, Mercy offered light. My palm itched where I'd held the phone. *"Business,"* I'd told her, although she hadn't asked. A guilty man's pleasure is undue confession.

We'd agreed last night to take the book out of town, to test its limits. But I knew in no uncertain terms what I wanted to test. I wanted to change the limits of time, to flip the past over the bar and begin again. To not go through life with the ugliness of the past, the dreadfulness of that night attached to me so that I thought about it with every step.

So business is what I'd said, but what I wanted to say was so much different. A part of me felt like a puppet, not a man. She was on the stairs as I went back to my room. I wanted to apologize for what I suspected my next actions would reveal. Instead, I reached out and touched her, tried to say thank you with a smile. When I turned around, the smile disappeared. *It's only business,* I told myself. *Nothing personal at all.*

Doc's Journal

Mercy's in trouble. Miss Perry has called me, very concerned. Mercy never came in last night, and she is missing still. On the other hand, she told me Mr. Quincy's return in the wee hours was loud enough to wake the dead.

I never should have brought him here. I don't know what I was expecting. But Mercy was right yesterday; I was only trying to fix my old guilt. I suppose I was trying to fix it for the whole town. Anyone could have done something for him. Opal was the only one who tried.

"We should take him in," she said on more than one occasion. "If he doesn't want that, it's fine, but it's just that we could give him options."

"Take him in," I replied. "Seriously? He's from Bittersweet Creek. He has his own people, his own kind. He wouldn't be comfortable here." These were my words to her. My very words. The audacity! My pride and arrogance—no, the truth. My *prejudice* had left him somewhere in that hole of a life we had visited yesterday, me all the while trying to tell Mercy I couldn't bear it. I could not stand to look deeper into the damage I'd allowed by doing nothing. He was the Bittersweet boy. I was an upstanding citizen, a leader in the community, a man of "honor." How did Opal, that warm and giving soul, stand the sight of me? She inquired about him, asking what I knew of the boy. She hired him at every turn. Once I found them sitting, having lemonade in her garden, and I suspected she was paying him to do nothing more than visit. She said they were taking a much-needed break, that was all. She said it with a bit of a smile and then added, "He is such a bright boy, love. I wish you'd take time out to get to know him." She suggested that I might find work for him at the paper. "A little help in the back for Herman would be nice, don't you think?" It occurred to me that Opal must have her reasons, so I did that much. Then I didn't think much about the Bittersweet boy except to pay him. That is, until they delivered him to my doorstep. Opal rushed out in her nightdress and held the boy's hand as we moved him inside and called the doctor to the house.

She never accused me. Never pointed out how I might have made a difference and how those chances were now lost.

Afterward, years later, she would still say, "Find him, dear. Perhaps he could come for Christmas. No one would have to know." But I would tell her, "No, it's better this way. Let him close the door to his past for good, Opal. Let him make his own way." She silently disagreed.

Now I was the one who had called him back for my own selfish good. The book had opened, and I had seen the pos-

sibilities of fixing what had eaten at me all these years. It
wasn't his salvation I had been seeking—it was my own.
And the more I knew these things, the more I realized that
Mercy must help me keep all the choices locked away. I
slowly concocted a plan to tell the town that I was retiring,
that I needed someone to help fill my desk. I tried to be so
careful, making things look right.

Mercy has already forgiven so much, and still there are
parts she doesn't know.

The determination was made in those hours when I sat
alone with those pages, both terrified and enraptured. It
presented a man's life in such a way that I wondered if it
could be used to alter incidents. Could a slight touch at a
path on a page affect the outcome?

Now I've pushed something into a place where things
have changed, and I don't believe for the better. From the
moment he stepped into the car, I knew even without seeing
him that his limp was gone. I heard it when he came running
up to the window, asking for a ride. That maimed part of
him had become a scar across my soul; its absence was
noticeable to me the moment he moved. But what wasn't
absent was my guilt, the heavy burden that I carried, and I
had stayed silent for the remainder of the drive home. If he
had truly been healed, if his life had taken a turn to such a
remarkable degree, the weight on my chest and in my conscience would have dissipated into thin air. But it was
heavier than ever.

Then there was the matter of Mercy. She knew as well

as I did that something wasn't right there. That house was a dark and brooding place, and then suddenly, a room untouched by time. More than irregular.

Because of my selfishness, now the wrong door has been unlocked.

I must find Mercy and obtain the key. I shudder to think of the consequences unless the path is altered yet again, set back on its natural course. Perhaps the book wasn't for changing things at all. But what, then?

THIRTY-SEVEN

The car had a bent front fender and plenty of scratches, but other than that she had survived. Johnny Cakes pulled it up off that bank with his tractor, and we were able to start it, easy as you please. He checked under the hood and climbed underneath, where he dislodged a few small limbs, then told me with a wink he'd charge me for his trouble later. We'd grown up out here together. That was just our way. One did for the other.

Ida had walked down the road with me, us following him at a turtle's pace as he drove the tractor up to where I figured it ran off the road. Now she got in the front seat and said, "I got my bag packed, so let's pick it up and turn this thing 'round."

I wasn't going to argue with her. I had on her smallest pair of coveralls she could find, and they were swallowing me whole. My dancing dress had been ruined, but it didn't matter. I wouldn't need it anytime soon. My shoes were lost last night somewhere in the creek. Good riddance. They would just be a sad reminder right now of how foolish I had been. But my heart was weary, my body bruised, and I was glad that Ida had purposed to go with me.

"Some battles weren't meant to be fought alone," she said.

I knew what she meant. She had listened to every word I'd told her about the book and Doc, about Tommy Taylor and who he had become. And about the woman who had come to town and danced off with the man named John Quincy. She was right; some battles were too big to handle alone. This thing with the book, whatever it was, was one of those.

We drove the entire way without a word spoken. Guess there was no need. She knew the state of disrepair I was in. We crossed over the bridge looking out onto the expansive horizon, the sun shining on the water in the most beautiful way. All dancing lights, no shadows. Then I thought of dancing and the glittering image of John and that woman, and the tears began again in the silent place, but my eyes stayed dry.

Ida stood in the driveway of Miss Perry's, holding her bag in one hand and looking suspiciously at the house. I was already on the porch waiting for her, but it didn't look like she was budging from her spot. Maybe she had second thoughts and wanted me to take her home. She'd only been here one time in all the years since I'd moved, and that was the visit where Daddy had driven her and Mama over. But here she was, all Ida Mae. All Missouri mud and Bittersweet. There she stood in coveralls and brogan boots, satchel suitcase in one hand, ball cap on her head, the other hand in her pocket, studying the house. She fit in here like a chicken in a lion's cage. She was looking just as leery as the chicken might.

"C'mon, Ida. We might as well get it over with."

"Just remember who you are, Mercy. That'll carry you

through anything." Then she put her head down and started walking toward me.

I opened the front door, and immediately the sound of voices filtered to me from the dining room. I could hear Miss Perry saying something about Bay City and the weather. And there was Sam's gruff growl. He was so difficult he didn't usually eat at the table but instead took his meals to his rooms. Then John's smooth voice added something, but a different voice was mixed in that conversation. That was the one that pierced me through and through. It was the one I heard clearest. All southern charm, like it had walked right off the pages of *Silver Screen* magazine. Oh, it was Little Miss Hello-Tiger-I-Missed-You herself. She was telling a story about something, but all I could hear was the low, sultry rhythm of her voice. I had no doubt she had captivated the audience in the room and all were giving her their full attention, including gruff-bucket Sam.

I pulled the door slightly to, leaning my head against the doorframe. I didn't know if I could do any of this. Why didn't I just get my things out of my room and get back in the car?

As a matter of fact, that was the only thing that needed to happen. I would tell Ida to put her bag back in the car, that she would be going home and I would be going with her. I turned around and came face to face with Aunt Ida, who was standing right behind me, almost stepping on my heels. She looked me in the eye.

"Let's go." I wasn't even going to take the time to explain my getaway plan.

"No, I come to stay a spell with you. We gonna see this thing though till the end, girl." She nudged me. "Open that door. Time's wasting away, and I smell food."

"Then just give me a second, will you?" I sat right down on the top stair and hugged my legs. "Just give me two seconds." I put my forehead on my knees and started humming. Ida turned around and sat down next to me, but she wasn't humming nothing. She just sat, letting me work out whatever I could within myself. I suddenly wanted to talk to Mabel. She would be working today, and maybe I'd walk over, take Ida, and we'd have lunch, and I could catch her up on at least the parts I could mention. I could tell her I had gone to a dance, without elaborating. I could tell her that my car had gotten into a little accident, that Ida had come to visit me, that John Quincy had a strange, beautiful woman in town, and that Doc may have lost his mind. That my heart was broken and yet I was still wearing this stupid key to a book that was supposed to be the keeper of the destinies of everyone—including her.

I couldn't tell her anything. But I missed her wisecracks and talking to her. I missed going to the movies with her and just being a regular girl, trying to choose between red and pink for my nails. Mabel was my person for those things. It seemed I hadn't seen her in a lifetime, as if I might as well have moved away and left without a good-bye.

"Much as I don't want to go in there either, it looks like it's the thing to be done. You've got steps to walk out now. Running back off to Bittersweet ain't what's the answer. You reckon you can take us going to the kitchen now?"

"I can try."

"You're made up of better than try."

I had heard multiple voices, but now the dining room was almost empty. Only Miss Perry sat at the table, but there was the lingering scent of an exotic perfume. It wasn't Miss Perry's; I had no doubt of that. She had the Bay City *Banner* and was reading it over coffee. Breakfast had obviously been served, and there were three dirty plates at the table. She looked up from her paper.

"Certain somebodies have been worried about you." She looked at Ida, then down at her travel bag and took in the full picture. Miss Perry didn't usually allow boarders to have overnight guests. That's when company becomes freeloaders. They check in at the Motor Court. Maybe it was my face or the coveralls or the fact that I'd been missing all night that must have clued her in that what we had here were extenuating circumstances.

"You remember my Aunt Ida?" I asked her.

"Of course. Mercy speaks of you all the time." She began to clear the dishes. "Can I get you some coffee? Have you had breakfast?"

A bedroom door opened upstairs. I could hear the voice of John Quincy at the top of the stairs, then a female voice. Not just any female voice, but the one with the smoke and sequins. Then there was the sound of a door closing and a flurry of footsteps on the stairs, and there she was, all stockings and high heels and lipstick. And that sultry perfume. I had two images then, as if two distinct women were standing side by side. I could see my reflection in Miss Perry's dining room mirror. I stood next to Ida in the coveralls. We must have looked like a pair of country bookends. My hair still had creek mud, my forehead was swollen, and my nails were a ripped-up mess. Scratches ran along my arms, and a long one trailed down the side of my face.

Beside that image was the woman before me, all sugarcoated, polished perfection. John Quincy was standing beside her. She linked her arm in his, leaned over, whispered something in his ear, and laughed a little. She cut her eyes back to me.

They were breathtaking together. Anyone could see that. Then I noticed his shoes and thought about him dancing last night with that foot. I suppose it opened up a whole new world of choices to him. For a flash of a second, I understood everything about Doc's guilt and desperation. I understood John Quincy being willing to do anything to make the past shift on its axis, for time to circumvent the truth. At that moment I might have been willing to open that book and try to make myself into a different kind of woman. But Aunt Ida was at my shoulder, her voice so controlled, so low near my ear that I don't think anyone could have heard her but me. Years later I would even wonder if she had actually spoken the words or willed them to me from her spirit. Sizing up the full extent of the situation. Me wanting so desperately to be something other than who I was. In the blink of an eye, to be able to trade images and lives with the woman before me, standing at his side.

"You were born in a lightning bolt on the banks of the Bittersweet Creek." Aunt Ida echoed Mama's words. "A miracle,

Mercy Land. That's what you are." I'd heard those words all my life. So much so that they had become part of the fabric of my being without me even being aware of them. Mama saying it near 'bout every day of my life from the time I was born. And now Ida speaking them, thinking them, caused my gumption to return. Broken heart or no, I was something to be reckoned with. Not in spite of the coveralls and scratches, those big Land eyes of mine looking back at me, or the mud still sticking to a few strands of that windblown hair. The gold key caught the light where it had fallen out of the coveralls and was resting on that old denim center pocket. I knew exactly who I was. I was Mercy Land of Bay City, a Bittersweet girl through and through, and I had a thing or two to teach folks. I caught Ida's eye and smiled. Smiled in spite of it all. I don't know how many seconds had transpired, but it felt like my world had shifted and cracked open and that I had emerged from the middle of some old, cloudy misperception. I stepped forward and outstretched my scratched-up hand.

"I don't believe we've met. I'm Mercy Land."

"Well, mercy me!" she said. All southern charm, with a thick, sticky accent that I thought a little too contrived. "What a sweet little name. I've heard all about you from John. He tells me you were friends as children. Imagine John ever being a child, big boy that he is now." She winked at him.

"What kind of sweet little name would be belonging to you?" Ida was still standing behind me, reared back with her hands in the pocket of those coveralls.

"Pricilla Payne. My friends just call me Cilla."

"Well, hope you enjoy your visit to Bay City. We're a much

smaller place than I imagine you are accustomed to, but most of us call it home," I said.

I looked at John then and noticed that the wild, over-the-top energy he'd had last night was missing. I pushed it from my mind and concentrated on the moment. I needed to take a bath and get into some clothes of my own and then get over to see Doc as quick as I could. I had a few notions I needed to share with him. And Ida—what would I do with Ida?

"It's good to see you, Mercy. I was concerned about you last night." John had taken a tiny step closer to me. "I was just taking Cilla over to see Doc's special project he's had me working on. She has found some of the events of yesterday quite interesting."

The woman was pretending to powder her nose in front of the mirror. I kept my eyes on John, but I could feel her eyes on me. And I knew Aunt Ida was watching her. It had become a regular three-ring circus.

"Yes." She spoke to the room at large while eyeing her reflection. "Johnny Q. has had the most amazing turn of events."

"Johnny Q.?"

"Everyone calls him that in Atlanta."

She walked past me, smooth as glass, and stood by the door, waiting on John.

"Mercy," he whispered, trying to say something quietly.

"Johnny, let's go, shall we?" She stood at the door, her purse on her arm. Looking cold and perfect. He turned and walked toward her, opened the door, and didn't look back as they left.

Then they were out the door. It closed behind them, and Miss Perry finally put her head around the corner.

"Are they gone?"

"What are you hiding for?" Ida asked her, plain as ever.

"To be perfectly honest, I don't like that woman. There's something about her that gives me goose bumps. I rented her a room anyway."

"Rented her a room?" I cried out. No matter how happy I felt to be in my own skin, I didn't want to live with the woman. I couldn't stomach the thought, much less say the words. Live with her and him both. Down the hall and one room apart?

"Sorry, dear. She's in the room next to you." She shrugged her shoulders and very apologetically said, "I'm getting older, you know. I need the money." Then she changed her expression, looking red-handed, fox-in-the-chicken-house guilty.

"How much?" Ida asked her.

"Double the going rate," she replied, and Ida nodded her head like she understood completely. As if she made business transactions and rented rooms out every day.

Aunt Ida sat on my chair, her hands clasped tight together, looking so out of place in the little room. I slipped my clean dress on and pulled out the most sensible work shoes I owned.

"Aunt Ida, when I heard you downstairs earlier, talking about my name, I just seemed to come to myself. It's like I remembered who I was. Fully, completely, and absolutely remembered me. I want to thank you for that."

"Mercy, you've always been special just the way you are. That woman is all glitter and disguise. You're made up of real stuff, and real stuff makes all the difference. And that's good, because you're gonna need it when you find that book. Doc's gonna need your help."

"He may have made some wrong choices, but for the most part, it was for the right reasons. Or at least he thought it was at the time. I still say that book fell into Doc's hands for a purpose."

I leaned out the windowsill into the magnolias as I twisted my hair up.

"You've really grown up a lot in this place."

"I grew up because of where I came from. You made the growing-up part easy. And all this time I thought I was out here on my own, I was never alone at all, was I?" It was true. I'd never been alone. They'd been watching out for me from near and from far. In prayers and phone calls.

"Let's go see Old Doc, and maybe I can get a look at that book thing before I have to pack it in for Bittersweet. I've got a feeling that time to deal with this thing is running short on you now."

"All right." I got out of the window and slid on those brown shoes. "I am Mercy Land, born in a lightning bolt on the banks of the Bittersweet Creek." I smiled as I picked up my purse and opened the door. "And, Aunt Ida, I will never forget it again." I waited for her to walk through and then locked it. My heart still hurt, there was no denying it, but a much-needed peace ran through the center of my soul.

THIRTY-EIGHT

Doc was already standing at the top of his office stairs when I walked through the *Banner* door. There was no sign of John or the woman. Aunt Ida stepped in just behind me. Doc and I stood and looked at each other. Again, I didn't have to tell him a whole lot of anything. He knew. He had gotten as used to me as I had to him. He could tell I'd been through something tough and miserable. I was cleaned up, but the scratches didn't wash away. I figured the sadness didn't either.

He walked down the steps toward me. It was time for us to finish whatever we had to do with this book. I knew that. Even if it meant we never went back to normal. When he reached the step above me, he nodded to Aunt Ida.

"Did you tell her?"

"Everything," I said, and I had. I hadn't left out a single thing last night in my recounting of the book in all its frightful wonder.

Doc was silent for a little while. He looked over my head at Aunt Ida, and I didn't have to turn around to know she would eye him as long as he looked her way. She wouldn't back down for nothing.

"Good," he said. "Then maybe we can start this thing again. You and Ida come with me. You have the key?"

"I do."

"I've moved the book again. It's not here." He came down the last few steps. "I'm sorry for not telling you everything sooner, Mercy. I just wanted to make things right. To fix them…"

"The way you thought they should be. To do the things you thought you should have done."

"Yes."

Then Aunt Ida spoke up. "Wasn't nothing you could have done different for that boy."

"There was, Ida; at one point there was. But by the time that night came, it was too late."

They were talking like old friends. Old friends who had been in the middle of a long, ongoing conversation about how making one decision could change history or how looking the other way could affect something as well. It became obvious to me that Doc and Aunt Ida had known each other all along and that somehow, someway, they had been discussing the philosophies of personal involvement. I was so floored with this realization that I had to sit down at my desk before I asked them the question.

"How do you know each other?" I asked.

"It was a long time ago now. A whole lifetime of choices ago. Let's be gone, Mercy. We'll talk more about it later. I don't feel right about leaving that book, but something about that boy last night…"

"He's a man," I said.

"Yes, well, I knew when I left you that something was wrong. And that old house of his had been wrong, and I was wrong to open that book." Then he looked back at Aunt Ida. "I've done it again. How can I keep making such critical errors in judgment?"

"You give yourself too much credit for moving the hands of time. You ain't God," Aunt Ida said and opened the door and stepped out into the sunshine.

Still in amazement over their acquaintance, I followed them out the door. We got in Doc's car, Ida in front and me in the back, and drove the short distance to his house. He was constantly looking about him, down the streets, up the alleys. I knew who he was looking for, but maybe it was more than that. Maybe more things had set Doc on edge.

I had forgotten to tell him about how John Quincy had a woman and she wasn't good. About how she was now moving into the boardinghouse in the room next to mine. Ida seemed to keep the same opinion of her, and even Miss Perry didn't like her and had said so.

"Doc, there's a strange woman in town. She's with John Quincy."

"I saw her." He took a right and drove around the block. This wasn't the way to his house, and he kept looking in the rearview mirror. Doc thought we were being followed. I turned around and looked out the rear window. There were a few cars but nothing that looked suspicious. But what would that look like, anyway? Then Doc's words registered with me.

"You saw her? When?"

"I followed you last night. That is, I found you. After I got home, I kept thinking about that room." He paused and asked Ida, "Did she tell you about his room in the old house?"

Aunt Ida nodded. "She did."

He turned left. "I kept thinking about that room, about the way he was acting, and I realized there were a number of possibilities in play, but none of them meant anything good. And I knew I'd let you go off alone with him in that strange condition, changed in a strange way. I didn't know what he was capable of, but I didn't want you hurt. I knew the only place you'd find a band was at the dance club. So I drove there and parked down the street. I came in while the two of you were dancing."

I looked out the window, embarrassed as I could be. Had he also seen me being dropped and forgotten when that woman walked in? I tried not to think about that part. What could a person do sometimes about being so human? About being so vulnerable? Right now I felt like dancing was for fools.

"You never saw me." He turned left again, and we were back on the street that would lead us to his house. "I watched from the corner where it was dark. Then of course I saw her when she came in."

"Who didn't?" I said, remembering that very nonglamorous moment in my life. "I think the whole world saw her, the way she was glittering."

"Not the whole world, Mercy. My eyes were on you. I watched as you left. When I was certain you had left alone, I wasn't interested in what happened to either one of them. I assumed that you were going to the boardinghouse down the street, not driving an hour in the middle of a storm on those muddy back roads. From the looks of you, I wish I'd followed you all night."

"I'm all right." And in many ways I was. I wasn't happy, I was still embarrassed, but I felt a new confidence in my own skin. It came along when I least expected it, with me looking my worst but seeing my best.

"I think you should know that woman is different than she looks, and for another thing, she's not exactly with him," Doc said. "She followed him here. There's a difference."

"I don't know that man. Whatever history we had was between me and somebody else," I said.

"New histories are born every day," Aunt Ida piped in from the front seat.

Doc continued driving while he explained about his moving the book again. It looked like we were headed for the city limits. I finally leaned my head back against the seat and just listened, not worrying any longer about the destination. Doc can tell a good story when he has a mind to.

THIRTY-NINE

Doc Philips

You had driven off with that man who had yet again changed faces right before us. I didn't know what had happened to him when we opened that book, but you saw who got in the backseat of the car. Another version of this same man. I was perplexed by the entire day. Whatever grand schemes I'd had to alleviate my guilt, as you so well put it, Mercy, were in shambles. Nothing at all had gone as I had planned or hoped. Then the final bit was that I had let you ride off with him. I was having serious misgivings about that.

I put the box with the book on my desk and took Harry outside for her walk. I was standing in the corner there at the edge of the fence, turning to come inside, when I noticed two shoes below the bushes of the outside hedge. Then of all people in the world, Whistler stepped forward.

"Got to talk to you, Doc," he said.

Just like that. Now, mind you, I'd already had a full day of things that were beside me and beyond me. I had the box out in the open on the desk, and I was concerned about you, Mercy. I knew that something had overtaken our man there and that he wasn't the same. Not even the same as the man who'd showed up on the train.

"C'mon in, Whistler"—that's all I could tell him. What choice did I have? "But make it quick because, well, just make it quick, will you?" I already had in mind what I was going to do, but Whistler hadn't figured into my plan.

"If it's all right with you, I'd rather stay on this side of the fence."

I looked him up and down, and Harry did too. But she didn't bark at him. She seemed to have decided there was nothing to fear. But I had to admit, even as well as I knew him, Whistler's bad eye in the dark moonlight was enough to give me the feeling that I'd rather be inside. Alone.

"Why, Whistler? My house is safe."

Whistler stepped forward and grabbed the fence post, leaning over to look at me closely. "So you say." He glanced over his shoulder back at the streets, licked his lips. "I've seen some things."

"What have you seen? What things?" I stepped forward and waited for him to tell me things I might already know.

"Been following you, Doc."

"You! It's been you, Whistler, trailing me at night?"

"Just looking out for you." He cast that eye about, a little on the wild side. "Seems to me something else is following you too, but I couldn't say what it is. I guess I've just had a compelling to watch over you if need be. Lately you've seemed a little puny."

Whistler was still whispering. He again refused to come inside the gate. I was relieved that it had been him shadowing me about town, but I still didn't understand. Then he dropped his voice down even lower.

"I know who he is," he said at last, "and it ain't good."

There was no point in asking who he meant. We were both aware there was only one new *he* around this city. "What's wrong with him being here, helping me out some?"

"He's no help to you, Doc. Something tells me he's thinking revenge, and there ain't nobody for him to hit back but us."

"Us?"

"Doc, this whole town looked down and the other way where that boy was concerned. I seen them bruises. Knew he was a kid with a fight on his hands, but I didn't say nothing. But see, here's the thing: he ain't looking for sorry. Like I said, he's looking for payback, and he's not even certain how."

I thought about his words and how some people saw things coming from a long way off. They were the distance thinkers. Right now, I was the one with that incredible book on the desk, but Whistler was the one who was out ahead of me.

"What could he possibly do to an entire town?" I said aloud more to myself than for his benefit.

"Not show up, Doc. Not be where he's supposed to be. Not do something that must be done. Steal from us. Kill somebody. You name it. Look here, he might not even know what it is he's doing, but I'm telling you right now, revenge is the same as murder, and if he could, he'd torch this town to the ground."

"That boy's no killer."

"He ain't no boy no more."

I knelt down and stroked Harry's fur and thought about the night, about who had jumped in that backseat wired like a new man. He was too many people too much of the time. Whistler rocked my resolve into place.

"Care to go for a ride, Whistler? There's somebody I need to check on."

Whistler rubbed his chin and grinned at me through the fence posts. "Why, Doc, I thought you'd never ask."

We drove through the streets of the city as determined as two old men have ever been. What I wonder now is about the sight we must have presented to anyone who saw us passing by. My windows down, Harry hanging her head out the back, Whistler's gray hair blowing in the wind just like mine. Old men weren't usually seen out around town this time of night, but Whistler and I had been keeping odd hours for a long time now. Me stalking the city and Whistler stalking me. All this time he'd been trying to protect me from things he couldn't even name, just based on his uncanny feelings. Well, right now I was thankful for old men with strange leadings, comforted by another soul being in the seat beside me who knew about the past and cared about the future. Our city meant something to us. It was as simple as that. We weren't just a spot on the map that could be erased. We needed each other, and sometimes we failed miserably, but the important thing maybe was to just keep on trying. It had started to rain, and I turned on my wipers as I turned into the club.

"Horns, Whistler. I can hear them from here. They must be

dancing up a storm." I opened the door, but Whistler didn't move. "You coming?" I was starting to get rained on.

"Nah. You go on. I'm gonna cover the door from here."

You were dancing, Mercy, when I walked into the room.

I moved along the inside wall, found myself a seat there in the dark corner where I could watch. I don't know what I was looking for or what I expected to see. All I knew was that the man in the backseat was some kind of apparition of the truth but not the real thing, and that didn't seem like the right thing to leave you to. Not fair of me at all, considering that the entire day had been full of my fault. Repercussions would again fall at my door.

The song ended, and the two of you moved through the crowd out of sight. I stood until I could spot you, and eventually I located you again, standing against the wall. Then I sat down, waiting until a release would allow me to return home again. Instead, that woman walked in.

Age has its advantages. And so does the experience of being a good reporter. Old eyes can test the art of illusion, can see through many things that are not what they appear. And a good reporter knows that what presents itself as the story sometimes is not the story at all. Now, I wasn't moved at that grand entrance the way the rest of the room seemed to be. I recognized the theatrics of it, oh, and a few other things; yes, I noticed those things too. But I had been married for more than fifty years to a woman of grace. I knew what real beauty was, and that knowledge steeled me from being swayed by the ripple that ran through the room. Then my eyes were on you, Mercy, and what I saw was you shrinking farther and farther back against the wall.

Here was the Bay City *Banner* go-to girl disappearing before my eyes. I could see it so clearly: the moxie of you falling away as if nothing was left. And I was glad for a second. It may be wrong to say that, but I felt that any influence he might have had last night, anything that could have happened that wasn't right, fell away. I watched you leave and then waited to give you just enough time to get in your car and pull down the street before I walked outside. The rainstorm was running its full course by then, and it pelted down hard on me as I ran for the car.

Whistler was waiting for me, leaning forward, almost in my face across the seat.

"Did you see her?" he asked, fully agitated.

"Yes, I saw her. Mercy just left. She's going home, looks like just in the nick of time." I tried to shake the water off me as I started the car.

"Not her, Doc! The other one. Did you see the woman who just walked through those doors?"

"Yes, I saw her. Very blond hair, very high heels. Looks like new money and lots of it. Too much, actually. I think I got the picture."

"That's not what I'm talking about." He grabbed my arm so hard I had to fight to keep the car on the road. "She ain't human, I tell you. There was the dark and the rain coming down, and then she walked out of it. Right out of it, you hear me. That's what I'm talking about."

"Out of what, Whistler? You're not making any sense."

"The dark, Doc. That woman walked straight out of the dark.

She wasn't there one minute. Then it was like a door opened in the darkness, and she appeared and walked straight in them doors."

I pulled over on the side of the road, sat there with my foot on the brake, the car idling. I looked at Whistler, and with all his strangeness, his habit of raking his yard in the summer, that weird eye, and his wild hair, my old nose for the news told me Whistler knew what he saw.

"I believe you," I said and steered back onto the road, considering what to do next. "Whistler, I've got something at my house…"

"I don't want to know about it. Don't tell me, and don't show me." He leaned his head out the window for a minute into the pouring rain so that his face was dripping wet when he brought it back in, the water running off his hair and down his back. "Some things a man isn't supposed to know or see. You don't have to tell me nothing. I already saw enough. I knew something was going on. And that him being back here was a part of it. But now that woman—or that thing—done shown up here too, and that ain't good. I don't need to see nothing else." He put his head between his hands. "I'm tired, Doc. Take me home."

FORTY

Doc finished his story and turned and started driving toward the church on the hill. Of all the news I had expected, some story of a woman walking straight out of the dark night was a little more than I had bargained for too. Surely not. Whistler was getting kind of old, and, yes, that thing with the leaf raking could be a clue that he was getting a little unstable. Doc should know better. Then again, what was I thinking when we were on the way to get that book, to look at the very thing that I knew no one would believe existed unless they touched the pages themselves. I knew that Doc had moved the book yet again, but I had assumed that meant it was safely hidden at his house. Had he hidden it in the church? Not a bad idea, I had to say. Not the first place anyone would look. Then something occurred to me.

"Have you figured out who you're hiding the book from exactly?"

"Sometimes I think I'm hiding it from myself. I'm always wanting to open it and never come out. It's like living a thousand lifetimes."

"Those aren't your lives, Doc. You can't just go trailing through other people's wants and want-nots, their could-have-beens and should-have-dones. The book's full of them. But they're not for you to see."

"That's why I trust you with the key, Mercy. Of course, if I'm not to look through them, exactly what am I supposed to do? That's still the question."

Something occurred to me again. A sense that I knew why Doc had received that book. And how that reason was nothing that he had imagined. Doc had been saying something, but I wasn't paying attention. All I knew was that Aunt Ida was agreeing with him, which wasn't common.

"Let's just say she came to town with something on her mind besides love," she was saying.

Doc pulled up in the parking lot of the church and stopped the car. If someone suspected, someone who might want to get their hands on it, they surely would go to his house or the paper, but here? Ida opened her door and got out first. She started walking, but Doc stopped me, saying, "Mercy, if anything happens to me in all this—or let's just say if I'm not around anymore—go see Mr. Balcom."

"What are you talking about?"

Ida was walking into the graveyard instead of the church, and I wanted to yell at her to turn around. I opened my door. When I did, Doc got out and stood next to the door. I started to call out to Aunt Ida, but he stopped me.

"I want you to pay attention to me, Mercy. Time may be short. Mr. Balcom, the director…"

"I know who he is. He's the dead man."

"We don't call him that."

"Yes, we do, and you know it. Everyone in town calls him that." Mr. Balcom owned the funeral home, and he took it upon himself to also help people with things like their last wills and testaments. He wasn't a lawyer, but he had a knack for helping people sort through the messiness of their lives and to bring perfect order and peace to the end of their days. He helped usher people from one place to another as if they were taking a train trip to a faraway country for an extended visit. And he did it all in a very calm, smooth voice.

"All right, all right. But he's a good friend, and he's got the goods. You hear me? He has everything you need in case I'm gone."

It was what I'd been a little nervous about ever since Opal had passed away or on the days Doc didn't seem to have his old pizazz. I liked him full of life and wonder. I liked him cracking wise about the news and making our small town look and feel as important as the big metropolis. He made the people of Bay City feel like we mattered in the scheme of things. Like the giant world might be complicated but the city itself was a crucial part of the complication.

We'd be lost without him.

"C'mon, Aunt Ida's wandering through the tombstones, and you're not dead yet."

As it turned out, the box wasn't in the church. Doc had moved it to Opal's tombstone and then covered it with a large spray of plastic flowers, which he admitted he had borrowed from someone. Then he marched off and put them back where they belonged.

"This is it, Ida."

FORTY-ONE

John Quincy

How many men ever have the chance to play it again? To play it differently? I almost said no. I had walked through the rubble of what remained of that house and the memories there, and there just weren't too many things even worth turning over to keep. It was a place that was born out of death and desperation. Then it was as if Cilla walked in, but I didn't see her anywhere, just a certainty that she was somewhere nearby. But so was Mercy, and her closeness made a difference. So much so that after all my longing for this moment, this chance to change things, I decided that what had been would be. That it wasn't for me to rummage through those dirty waters and try to turn them into something different. I think I was afraid, simply afraid that if I went back, I'd live that night all over again. That nothing would change but that I'd wake up in my bed feeling beaten and crushed. I was ready to turn tail and run.

Then we were back in the car, and Doc said what he did—that I would always wonder—and the next thing I knew, I was agreeing, the book was being opened, and I was back in the house alone. Other people can't travel down that road to your past with you. It belongs to you alone to sift or make do with it as you can. Mercy and Doc weren't a part of my past inside that house. They weren't a part of the secrets or the pain. What Mercy had seen for the most part was Tommy Taylor full of smiles and jokes and summertime. What Doc Philips had seen was the Bittersweet boy hustling for a dime. But that was never the entire truth. That was only a part of it. The darkness was the part that belonged to me alone. And that was the part Cilla understood. "Poor, poor lamb," she would say, so understanding. "Someday you'll make them all pay." With such a softness that making them pay didn't seem like a bad thing at all. It seemed like the exact medicine that I needed for my soul. Pay back an entire town for using me but never really caring about that kid.

Then we opened that book, and I was in the house, lost in a myriad of images of the past that were either real or re-created. In the middle of those images was another road. That was the one that astounded me so. A road where that father of mine had made choices that were right, not ones fueled by whatever demons had ridden him right over the edge of sanity. And in that place, he was there but totally squared away. The house lost that heavy blanket of sickness that seemed to permeate the very walls, and there had been a gentle light, warmth, and for that brief minute I saw what life might have been like given the better circumstance. Given him making different choices. Can you imagine standing where your life might have taken a different turn, where everything was different, where your story would have been written in a different tone?

I walked into the room that had been mine, and there all was well. I walked out again a man who was healed and whistled my way down the road, footloose and carefree. Back to Bay City, I thought. The place of all my dreams. Healed and happy as a lark. I thought that what I saw inside that house had really happened. That the right choices, the ability to make right choices, had been re-created from the beginning.

The first car to pass me and stop was Mercy's. No small co-incidence there, I'm sure. I had never been so full of life. An electric current ran through my veins, and I felt as if I was going to pop at any moment. It drove me like wildfire. I was juiced on this new version of me and went rattling on about this and that. Then the idea of dancing came to me, and I couldn't wait to get my feet, my two whole, matching feet to the dance floor.

That's exactly what I had been doing—dancing and holding Mercy, walking her to the side to rest, standing with my arm about her waist, and considering all the possibilities—when Cilla walked into the room. That's the way she is, finding me when I thought I had forgotten her or slipped past her. Reminding me of so many things. Kissing me right there in front of Mercy, kissing me as a prize and a possession and making her point.

To find that book. To lay her unholy hands on it at all costs. To possess it the way that she has possessed me for so long. I expect that once she gets what she's searching for, I will no longer be a part of the picture. I won't be a necessary link in her plan. She is quite capable of blackmail and extortion without my help. She's very gifted in that way.

And just this morning there we stood, Mercy before me, mud

caked and bruised, looking like a sight for sore eyes. Looking like that tree-climbing Bittersweet girl at ten. I was just about to say, *Mercy, listen to me,* and confess everything to her. But then Cilla called to me. She's as hypnotic as any crawling creature ever hoped to be. She takes what she wants and leaves the rest to rot.

Now we are searching for Doc and the whereabouts of the book. And all the while I am still hoping that something will save me and leave me whole. Perhaps I can get her to leave town. Perhaps if I offer to go with her, to stay with her, she'll forget about it and leave them all be.

But it's too late.

She's found them.

FORTY-TWO

Doc opened the door, and the three of us stepped inside the sanctuary of the church. It was cool and quiet. The stained-glass windows tossed colored prisms down on us as we slowly made our way to the front.

We were carrying something that was more like a piece of a star than anything that belonged in this world. It being in our possession was beyond the bounds of our comprehension. It always had been. I quit trying to figure everything out, because it hurt my mind to think about it. But I did know the box contained the book, and inside that book were the answers to ageless questions. Layers of answers that man would never understand. At least not for a very long time. But here Doc was with it in his hands. Here Doc was with his world full of thoughts of dying, of disappearing, of guilt, when all the while he was the one being trusted to hold the magnificent story of man's journey through this tumultuous life.

Doc walked up to the front by the pulpit. He knelt down and put the box on the floor. My hands began to shake as I pulled the key from around my neck. I looked at Ida and wanted to say, *Get ready,* but I didn't. Because there was no getting ready for this.

There was no way she would understand until she had experienced it. No one could, no matter how hard they might try.

Doc started to put the key in the lock, and then he stopped. He looked at me again and said, "Don't forget, Mercy. The dead man has everything." And before I could protest his foolishness, he placed the key in the lock. I closed my eyes and hoped for the best. I didn't want to get lost somewhere that I'd never return from. It felt very possible that all of us could step into another place that was timeless, like when I had lost track of time at Tommy's house and sort of woken up on the way to Aunt Ida's. Or the way those hours had added up and we'd come to and sat in Doc's office, waiting for real time to find us again. It scared me to think that I could lose track of time and memory. That people could fall away from my life, disappear, and resurface changed in ways that I didn't understand. I reached for Doc's hand as he opened the lid, saying, "Don't go, Doc," but by then it was too late. He picked up the book as the back door of the church was thrown open and she walked in with John Quincy behind her.

I didn't think of him anymore as Tommy Taylor at all. Now I knew better. And if the book had ever altered time in any direction, or perhaps the way that we saw time, it was never more so than at that moment. I thought Doc would open it and find a magic page or passage that would stop the woman from moving toward us. But instead Doc lifted the book from the box and handed it to me. He was passing light, time, lives, memories, and the power of all those stories intertwined. Reaching to touch it wasn't a simple act; it was living and reliving passages of lives.

And one of those revealed to me in a flash as I put out my

hands was the life of one Ida Mae McCabe. I turned to look at her, astonished at what I saw, and I could tell she saw it too. It was her other life, the one she would have had without me clinging to her feet. A good life in Missouri. A place she loved and where even in old age she could have found love again. But Ida Mae McCabe had made a choice the day Mama had me on the Bittersweet. It was a tiny, simple thought that this new life would need her. That it would need an extra hand, a lap, and a laugh. And Ida Mae sat down on the banks of the Bittersweet for twenty-seven years for me. She had sacrificed what might have been, because without Aunt Ida, the path of my life would have been different. I wouldn't have been in Bay City working for Doc at the *Banner*. I wouldn't have been holding this book in my hands. I wanted to say something to her, to acknowledge what she had done, but she had moved quickly to place herself between me and the woman. Then my hands were inside the book itself, disappearing into that light, and Doc was standing up, his chewed-up cigar clamped between his teeth. Then Doc did something he never did. He winked at me and went to stand beside Aunt Ida. They were trying to barricade me. At once I realized why Doc had received the stories, why he'd been allowed this glimpse into those other dimensions, and I knew it was time to give the book back to its rightful owner.

Holding the book, I began backing toward the altar. But Cilla kept coming. Surely there was something that could stop her here. Something inside those pages of breathing gold.

Then I saw John Quincy, and the moment I thought of him, his name rose from the pages. We had tried to will names to the surface to no avail, but as the thought of him passed through my heart, his name rose up like something surfacing from a deep, clear lake. I put my hand deeper into those pages, and the words began to encircle my arm. The letters now moved about me, the golden hue of the ink itself overtaking me, so that somehow the book was covering me head to toe with the knowledge of what it was, and that knowledge came in waves. I knew Tommy Taylor, and I knew John Quincy. And I knew what had happened to him in the course of that missing time at his old house. Nothing. Absolutely nothing. He was as lame now as he had been since he was sixteen. With the twists and turns his soul had taken since then, even more so. Every choice he had made or left unmade had brought him to this moment in this church with this woman who was really not a woman at all, this thing pushing her way past Doc and Ida. They were both struggling with her, trying to hold her back as the words penetrated every nuance of my being. If I had ever thought I would disappear inside the book, this was that moment fulfilled. It seemed as if the book was consuming me.

"It's choices, Doc. It's the stories of choices." I thought I was yelling at his form lying on the floor, but then I realized I wasn't even speaking. I understood now what the book had been trying to tell us all along. That the choices we made did indeed turn the times for ill or for good—for everyone. That one life was attached to the next life and to the next and the next, and those connections went on for generations until I could no longer follow the pattern. And the next minute I didn't have to, as the book was pulled harshly from my hands. The words left me with such an abruptness I felt as though my skin had been peeled back. I took a deep breath and turned, and there he was. But he wasn't smiling his charming smile. He had tears in his eyes and was saying, "I'm so sorry, Mercy, I'm so sorry," as he stepped backward away from me. Then the book opened wide in his hands. He tried to close it, but how do you control something that wasn't created to be controlled? Instead the pages began to fall around his feet, first a few and then in a moment a hundred. The church doors blew open, and a wild-footed wind blew through the sanctuary. Doc and Aunt Ida lay unmoving on the floor. John Quincy had the book and was trying to leave with it, but it was falling apart in his hands. And the woman was so angry as she walked toward him that I could smell smoke.

"Give it to me!" Her words were like razors, and as she spoke, cuts appeared on his hands. And more pages began to fall, faster and faster. The book was falling apart. And the thing named Pricilla began shrieking at him, cutting him with every scream.

This is where time, already so slow I felt a bubble enclosing me, became even slower. Choices were being made breath by breath. And in those pauses between breath and motion, time was stopping, waiting to make the next turn according to choice by everlasting choice.

Then the church fell away from my sight; everything disappeared with the exception of John Quincy. The pages were falling from his hands, blowing around his feet, the deserted, empty street before him. He looked over at me, and it was my dream, except this time instead of the profile of a man, it was the blue-eyed, bleeding face of John Quincy.

Then the woman appeared right there in the empty street. She stepped into that space that I'd been carrying around like a preconception of this moment, and she was still screaming, "Give it to me," as more pages fell out and as his face became cut with the words. Her tongue was a razor full of death. Her beauty was fading now as fast as the pages fell, something shifting inside her so that she could no longer maintain her illusion of perfection.

And Aunt Ida's voice from this morning echoed in my mind, followed by a refrain from Mama. *"Remember who you are, Mercy."*

In my mightiest voice, I stepped forward and said to John, "No, give it to me."

There are times in people's lives that they should take note of; they should freeze those moments for the rest of their lives. Moments of courage without explanation. Moments where they stepped in when there was confusion or pain. When they smoothed the rough edge for a stranger or friend. This was my moment I'd carry forever, me pushing my hand out in front of that thing, and my hand holding her words at bay. She turned toward me and screamed such a sound that I knew it was meant to cause my soul to weep, to crumble.

"Give me the book." I took a step toward him while still holding my hand out like a wall toward her. Somewhere the church bells began to ring. "Do you see this street? Look!" I pointed with my right hand up and down the emptiness. "It's because of you. The people, the town are gone because you always mattered. What happened to you mattered. And what you do now matters."

The woman threw herself to the ground, began to crawl toward him, attempting to slither her way around my outstretched hand. Then she softened around all her edges, stood slowly, full of sensuous seduction, and whispered, "C'mon, tiger. You know what you really want to do. That's for us to share. Imagine how we could be together with that power. King and queen, great and mighty."

On any other given day, I would have withered under her perfect stare. Instead I stepped forward and said, "I was born in a lightning bolt on the banks of the Bittersweet Creek. My name is Mercy Land. And I believe you might be trying to get a few things that belong to me, one being that book falling apart at the seams, and I do say it's got some incredible power. Can certainly see why you'd want to get hold of it, but it wasn't made for the likes of you. Oh, and that man you keep trying to snatch straight to the gates of hell, that'd be my friend John Quincy, and I don't reckon he belongs to you, either. Matter of fact, I just decided: nope, you can't have him." Those pages were still falling like rain between his fingers; now it seemed a thousand pages had fallen and blown down the street. The bells were still ringing out loud and true. "Of course, now, John, you do have a choice in all this. I can't make you give me that book or take one foot out of that fire. But she sure as the stars above can't run over me and take it without your permission."

Aunt Ida was right. Some battles weren't meant to be fought alone. This was one of them. Maybe John Quincy had been fighting battles alone for way too long. Maybe that was part of the problem. All my life I'd had Mama and Daddy like the living rocks that they were. And I'd had Aunt Ida, like a mad banty hen. Who had John Quincy really had in his corner to fight for him except himself? I stepped toward the woman. "My friend says he won't be requiring your services. He's home now, you see. Home," I said again.

The woman leaped toward me like something wild. There was a sound that rattled my rib cage, and with it John Quincy tossed me the book. When I caught it, it was complete again, as if a single page had never fallen, and the woman had disappeared in that violent thunderclap—taking John Quincy with her.

FORTY-THREE

It's been two years since that day. Two years and twenty-one days, to be exact. The moment the woman disappeared with John Quincy, I was standing back inside the church at the altar. The book was in my hands, and I clutched it to my chest until I saw that Doc and Ida were both still lying on the floor.

It took them a little while to wake up, but they did. And after a little extra time to recover, they walked out of there on their own. We spent the day together after that, the three of us. None too eager to leave the others' company. We had just walked through the strangeness of a battle that could not be proven, and our choice now was to be able to look one another in the eye and say, "This is the way it happened, yes?"

It was Miss Perry that fixed us dinner that night, and we shared as much of the news with her as we felt we could. We did let her know that she was down a couple of boarders. We found their rooms already empty. They had known they'd not be back one way or the other.

Doc and I resumed our lives at the *Banner*, but little by little, day by day, he weakened some, and in the process he'd say, "Just handle it, Mercy," whatever it might be. "Just remember," he'd begin. And I would answer, "I know, Doc, I know. I'm bringing it home." And little by little Doc spent less time at the office until he issued a statement that he was making me editor in chief. To make it official, he showed up for coffee with the old men at the lunch counter, sitting there talking politics and trade, weather and funny stories. It seemed he was retiring after all.

Two months later he passed away.

Mama tried to comfort me, telling me that it was his time or that it was the way he would have wanted it. There's a part of me that believes it must have been so or he wouldn't have gone to so much trouble to get ready. The dead man did indeed have Doc's affairs in order.

He had willed ownership of the *Banner* and all its holdings to me. I owned the building outright along with the press and the publication. Daddy thought it was all very interesting, but when was I going to settle down and get married? Mama just smiled and would pat the back of his hand. Aunt Ida stomped her foot under the table and said, "It's 1938, for goodness' sake. The woman doesn't have to get married. Don't you know how important she is? She makes up the headlines!"

I didn't feel important. I felt blessed. I sat at Doc's old desk—my desk now—and leaned down to scratch Harry's ear. She might not make another Christmas, but it sure was good to still have her around. Miss Perry had to relent and let boarders have pets since I had no inclination to move and Harry had been part of my inheritance. The house went to the Bittersweet boy, and that's how Doc had written it: "To John Quincy, the Bittersweet boy, to pro-

vide you with the long overdue home that you have never had."
And so that's the way it was. Until John took possession, keeping
it up fell to me. I could have rented it or moved in, but it has just
stayed there waiting.

Whistler keeps the yard raked and the camellias flowering.

It took me a long while to forgive Daddy all in all. We finally
went for a walk one day, away from Mama, who'd never known a
thing about it.

"His mother had called me, Mercy, right there in the middle
of the night. Your mama thought I was just going out on a min-
istry call to pray for the sick, and in a way I was. It wasn't completely truthful maybe but not a lie either. Forgive me, Mercy, but
sometimes there seems to be no right answer, no perfect way to
solve a situation. That was one of those times."

What was I to do but keep on loving him and realize that he
had probably helped save John Quincy's life a long, long time ago.
Now, once again, the whereabouts of my old friend remains a
mystery.

There's been no sign of John or that woman. Not since that
day. And the funny thing is, the book remains with me, there in
the box, where I last locked it up. Or at least I think it does. Some
things perhaps are strictly imagined, like the evidence we saw of
Tommy's old room. It had never looked that way except in our
own minds. But if we learn our lessons from the stories, if they
change us for the better, then the stories are worth fighting for
and keeping.

I know now why that book found its way to Doc. He thought
it was because he had made a mistake, but we all made mistakes.

Doc couldn't fix the past. And it wasn't about that at all. It was because Doc had spent his entire life loving the living stories that made up Bay City, thinking of them when he first woke up and rolling them over as the last thing before he fell asleep. It just so happened a very special story got away from him. And from me.

Some lonely nights I am tempted to open that box and to search that book out. To think of him in my heart just to see if it will dare show me where he is, but isn't that like cheating? The future is laid out one day at a time for a reason. I think it should stay that way. Somewhere out there John Quincy is still making choices, and I know that one day, if he keeps making the right ones, I'll turn the corner and see him. But in the meantime I have Bay City and the *Banner* to keep me busy.

"Well, Harry, I guess I have you too. What say we check the wires for any late-breaking stories and head for—"

The bell sounds downstairs. "Hello?" I say. I wait for a response, and when there is none, I rise from the desk, saying, "Hello?" again, but now I'm moving to the door with Harry plodding along behind me. At the top of the stairs, I freeze, 'cause there he stands. Right there. A hat in one hand, a cane in the other.

"John?" I start down the stairs. "Is that you?"

He still doesn't answer or move. When I'm standing right in front of him, he chokes out, "I made it."

"Did you?" I ask him, searching his eyes, wondering if he is truly free of the past. Free from his anguish and his anger. He has a few old scars across his face, and they match the ones on his hands. He nods.

"I made it that day, but only to Bittersweet. Right back inside that house where I started. Alone, you understand. But…" He looks off to the side, then he holds out the cane and his arms, brushes a hand toward his face. "Do you see how broken I am? What was I to do but go away again?"

I sit down on the bottom stair. If I ever had any moxie before, Doc throwing all his confidence in my basket for me to run the *Banner*, well, it was enough to bring out the best in me. "Oh, I know more than I'd like to about you, John Quincy. Trust me. Some things a woman really doesn't want to fully realize."

Marie's neon sign flashes on across the street. We realize that words, any words we choose right now, might be the wrong ones. It is easier to just not speak at all.

John leans on his cane, and I hug my knees and watch him. It is just good to see his broken self, scars and all. Maybe they're a good sign of the soul of the man. If he shows up perfectly whole on the outside, there's a fair chance something's ill on the inside.

"Hungry?" I nod across the street. "I hear they make a mean lasagna."

"I am," he says, walking toward me. It's obvious then that the lame foot troubles him worse now. "But there's something I left unfinished that I need to fix." He props his cane against the banister. "May I have this dance?"

It's hard to say no to a man who has your heart. One who's had it for a very long time and been missing in action. I make the last choice that old book's been waiting on; I don't need to open that box to know it will no longer be there. All my questions and all John's news can wait. I put out my hand, and he pulls me into his arms. Slowly, very slowly, we begin to sway to the music of the clicking newswire, the neon light washing over us. This time we bring our story all the way home, one slow step at a time.

A Note to the Reader

Dear Reader,

The Miracle of Mercy Land has carved out a special place in my heart. I love Mercy's "backbone full of worthy." The evolving story illustrates to me how many people let their greatest gifts go unnoticed. How in a culture that has run rampant in judging and awarding people for mirror images, characters such as Mercy Land remind us to consider well who we are and who we were meant to be.

I hope as you turn these pages that you delight in the discovery of what happens on the streets of Bay City and the backwaters of Bittersweet Creek. Also, I hope that you discover new truths stirring in your soul, that you are able to see yourself with a new appreciation for all your created beauty.

This is a story about the choices we make and the love and relationships we encounter and embrace along the course of those unfolding destinies. Ultimately the story shows that we never walk an isolated path but that all our stories are woven into one great tapestry of life. We matter to one another, you and I, in the most amazing ways.

Warmest wishes for your continued journey.

River Jordan

Visit me online at www.riverjordan.us

READERS GUIDE

1. The novel opens with the birth of Mercy Land along the backwaters of Bittersweet Creek, a small, rural outcropping of people where she is raised, but the character later moves to a nearby city. Have you ever found yourself living in a place very different from the one you grew up in? Did you remain there or return "home" again? How did the change of place or the return home affect your life?

2. There is an undercurrent of the influence that Mercy's mother and father had on her life by their steady presence and certain faith. However, another person in Bittersweet Creek also had a lot of input into her upbringing. How was Aunt Ida's influence different from that of Mercy's parents? How might Mercy's life have turned out differently without Aunt Ida? Have you had a similar experience in your life? Were there other family members or friends who contributed to your life experience in a distinct way?

3. Part of Mercy Land's moxie comes from her rural upbringing where she had the freedom to run and romp along the trees and creeks in a fearless kind of way. How was your childhood similar or different? Do you believe having a more sheltered life as a child might cause a person to be more hesitant or fearful of the unknown?

4. One thread running through the novel is Mercy's relationship with Doc. Perhaps in the beginning Doc was a bit
   of a hero, a larger-than-life character to Mercy, who saw
   him and his wife, Opal, as a king and queen of Bay City.
   Throughout the story their relationship changes as he
   becomes her boss, her mentor, and ultimately her friend.
   Have you experienced relationships that have gone through
   stages or seasons of change? How have those changes
   affected the relationships?

5. When Doc's book shows up, at first Mercy is hesitant to
   touch it. Why? Why does she change her mind? Do you
   think she ever really regretted seeing the book and wished
   that Doc had kept the secret to himself?

6. Mercy becomes dedicated to solving the riddle of the book,
   fulfilling that purpose, and it being returned to where it belonged. What characteristics does she possess that allow her
   to tread through such mystical, supernatural waters?

7. John Quincy's appearance in Bay City stirs up conflicting
   emotions and revelations for Mercy. What stands out to
   you as the most prevalent internal conflict? As the story
   progresses, how does Mercy come to terms with these
   things?

8. The story is told through the eyes of three main characters: Mercy, Doc, and John Quincy. Whose voice resonates

most with you? Did you enjoy hearing the story from one
character's point of view more than the others'? If so, why?

9. The novel is set a few years before World War II, in 1938.
   How did this time period affect your experiencing the
   characters, the setting, and the events?

10. The book reveals the paths that people have chosen—and
    the ones that they have left behind. Have you ever consid-
    ered some of the choices you made in life to have been a
    major turning point for you? Do you think that your life
    would have been much different had you taken another
    road or that you would be exactly where you are at this
    point in your life regardless? Is life more a destiny created
    by our choices or an inherent fate that cannot be changed?

11. A strange woman shows up in Bay City in search of John
    Quincy. Ultimately, she knows about the book and wants
    control of it. Who do you think Pricilla really is? If she
    were a symbolic representation for something, what do you
    believe that would be?

12. John Quincy eventually experiences deep changes, but they
    certainly weren't the ones he was hoping for or expecting.
    Do you think he ultimately makes a change for the better?
    When you have experienced changes or events in life that
    have been different than you anticipated, was the outcome
    sometimes better than you expected? Have you learned

things or built relationships through these unexpected turns of events?

13. Mercy comes to believe that the book is primarily a book of stories—one that illustrates clearly how those lives, those stories, interrelate and intersect. Do you believe that our choices affect not only our lives but also the lives of those around us? That even people we don't know are affected by our choices?

14. The daily newspaper in Bay City plays a significant role in the novel. Why is it so important? How does it affect the story's unfolding? Why do Doc and Mercy love the paper so much?

15. When you turn the last page of *The Miracle of Mercy Land,* what is the strongest impression the novel leaves with you? If you were to have one takeaway memory of the novel— something you could apply to your everyday world—what would it be?

ACKNOWLEDGMENTS

This is my fourth novel. Can I tell you a secret? I struggle not to write down again the name of a person I've thanked before. There is no clean beginning and end to the people who sustain and support authors' creative efforts. The circle is wide and never ending. Regardless, there are a few people who have supported me beyond measure but who have never been appropriately thanked.

Carol Proctor, you have spent more hours listening to me lament and celebrate story development on the page and my own in this thing we call real life. My gratitude should take more shape, be more solid and tangible in some way, as in a song or wall painting, but in the end all I have are these words of thanksgiving. I hope you know how much you are loved.

Sonya Caldwell, like a literary muse, you appear at improbable times in my life, offering exactly what this artist needs. Your savvy inspiration helped me and Mercy Land over the finish line.

Ginny Welch, thank you for your constant support beyond the realms of radio and for believing and spreading the word.

Beverly Manders, you are light and love, perhaps the purest soul I've ever known, and I love you.

Brenda Register, you are a better storyteller by far than I am. Now if only I could get you to put the words to page.

Barbara Clemmons, your gracious spirit is everlasting and has blessed me more than you will ever know.

Kathy Patrick, founder of the Pulpwood Queens who leaps tall buildings every day on behalf of writers' words, you inspire me.

Greg Daniel, you have my great appreciation and respect for your continued literary championing as my agent.

Shannon Marchese and the editorial family of WaterBrook, thank you for making me look so much wiser than I am.

The entire team at WaterBrook, thank you for bringing Mercy Land's story to life and putting it into the hands of readers everywhere.

And thanks to you, dear reader, for continuing to discover and embrace the power of story. I applaud you in every way.

Can a lonely elderly woman find a reason to hope again?

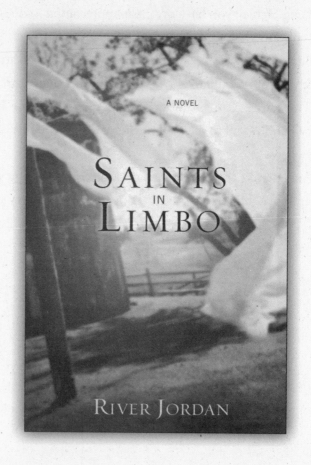

A NOVEL

SAINTS
IN
LIMBO

RIVER JORDAN

Velma True believes her best days are behind her and her life purposes are all "dried up." But when a stranger visits her rural home, he leaves behind a mysterious gift that will alter both Velma's life and those she loves most. Will reliving the past stir up old regrets — or awaken fresh hope for her future?

Available now wherever books are sold.